# THE
# LUMINOUS EGGS
## OF ARYLL-8

BY

DOUGLAS A. DAVY

Library of Congress: 1-4315348561
ISBN: 978-0-9968437-3-7

Requests for information should be addressed to:
A Vegas Publisher, LLC.
www.avegaspublisher.com
avegaspublisher@yahoo.com

First edition: 2017

Cover Design: Elizbeth Mackey

# DEDICATION

To Julia, my best friend for many years. A beacon of inspired research and self- discovery. The best conversationalist I know.

But I still wrote the book.

# THE ARIAN INVASION

Three years before, the Arians had come harshly to Aryll 8. Like uninvited birds of prey themselves, they'd swooped down from the skies. Their explosive blitzkrieg of thermo bombs and firepower set skies ablaze over every large city. Their thrusting introductory entrance upon this world was a devastating show of aggressive military might.

As the dust settled that first day of their invasion, when the sounds of the last bombs echoed to silence, after their spaceships emptied armored hordes onto the streets, there had been no resistance, not one single struggle. When their mad military rage quieted, the Arians removed their battle armors, set up their command posts, and toasted themselves for their great victory. The Arian Empire's military rule became now caught up in the business of being an occupational army. Central areas of this new capital, their Capacity, were cleared by heavy moving equipment. Much of its old former beauty, the soaring towers, the elevated walkways, and the broken pieces of their mysterious, transparent metals; building materials for this entire city of light ended up in refuse dumps like piles of broken glass.

Natives fled to protect their existence. One such woman was Moria.

# THE PURSUIT

Moria clutched a tattered wrapcape about her tall, frail body and darted in and out of the shadows in the back-alley corridor amidst piles of stained glass-like bits of the formerly beautiful transparent buildings. That part of the old capital city of Aryll had not been reconstructed following the surprise invasion years earlier. The Arian military had struck swiftly leaving behind bombed-out buildings and broken spirits as they ravaged and quickly conquered their enemies.

Harsh winds whipped her wrapcape, threatening to expose scars where wings once were; before the Arian government ordered all natives' wings be cropped from their bodies.

Those same winds caused her brown filament feathers to flutter, so similar in appearance to shoulder length hair. Moria attempted to maintain concealment of the child she carried. Overhead, sounds of the two Arian gravity sleds hovered in their continuing, relentless air pursuit. Every so often their brilliant spotlights documented more of her attempts to escape.

Moria ran determined, driven by her purpose not to be captured. She knew she remained one of the few still eluding their barbaric registered confinement of enforced servitude. She'd heard shocking stories of those prison-like conditions, and confinements awaiting any domestic refugee still attempting to escape, but she carried her second child. The barbarians had already stolen one child from her. She couldn't let herself forget the horror when she was dragged onto a surgery table, even though she was heavy with child. The combination of the shock, the brutal wing removal surgery, and the chemicals they injected into her as anesthesia had caused her to go into labor. She had given premature birth to the egg of her son. The Arian medical staff used ultrasound equipment to examine him. In their ignorance of how sensitive this race was to sound frequency, they forced the egg to be born early. This resulted in a plasmic explosion of the amniotic fluids and the immediate death of her son's young body.

They'll not steal this new young life I carry.

The Arian's detection radar zoned in on her location. Two-armed Arian centurion military police landed, dismounted from their gravity sleds, and ran after her in close foot pursuit.

Moria hastened her pace. With bird-like speed, she pushed on until a large piece of concrete caused her to stumble and fall. The Arians descended upon her as she huddled, exhausted in the dust and debris, and clutched her small bundle tight to her chest.

Here was the egg of her still unborn child. After a six-month internal pregnancy, she had birthed this daughter, the next-to-last stage in the cycle, in her membranous egg much the same size as an unborn fetus of the Arian's mammalian genetics. She looked up with a desperate hope in her eyes.

"No," she pleaded, "Please don't take her. I can't lose another child. Please! Let me tend to her birth."

Their stoic faces remained silent. They stood six-foot-tall, muscled and soldier-trained. Their clean-shaven jaws and cropped military hair showed not a hint of sympathy; as if wearing the khaki-colored togas of Arian inspectors made them callous to her pleas. The soldiers roughly pulled and lifted Moria to her feet. Her terror-filled eyes revealed the fear and dread she felt for the egg of her child at their hands.

These centurions were there to enforce domination. Trained to express no emotion, they dutifully wielded devices for inflicting pain or death. Their utility belts encapsulated sciences stolen from a hundred conquered worlds as willing volunteers to be used; service on tap for these sinister warriors.

One of them pulled her backward by her brown filament feather tresses, while the other coldly wrestled away the rude carrier bearing the egg of her cradled offspring. Moria struggled to establish a new grip, but her strength as a native female was no match for their combined aggressions. They tore the carrier with its precious occupant from her arms, brushed off Moria's feeble attempts to resist, and shoved her body down on the alley floor.

"Don't worry, citizen, we'll be back to collect you, later," one soldier warned over his shoulder as they turned to leave. Their short boots crunched into the conquered ground, and they brushed the dust from their uniforms, boarded their waiting gravity sleds with their booty prize, and whisked off.

Moria remained slumped amid the dust and her tears. "I won't forget you," Moria called out. "We were only awaiting your final growth and the critical timings for your external birth. You were so close to being born here with me." Her heart sank as she listened to the increase of whistling sounds from their engines, and watched the military sleds become airborne.

"If only I'd been able to reach the ancient birthing chambers where Orlycia and Yeto reside in the old palace. She knows my royal tribeflock. They would have helped me with the proper ceremonies and conceal my daughter's birth."

Hers was an intuitive species. She felt within her the frequency of her Mother-Bearer planet's connection with her unborn. Her gaze followed the trace in the night's glow of their gravity sled's contrails.

She held a clenched fist and cursed to the sky, "Whatever it takes. However long I have to search. I'll find you. I abandoned my ancestral home to hide you. If these barbarians have their way, I'll never be allowed to know you as you grow. I promise you, my beloved planet Aryll, I shall enact justice upon these Arians. I'll never forgive their cruelty to me and upon all our tribeflock children. My heart burns with the desire to witness their pain. I swear... the time will present itself. I'll find a way to punish their evil Arian race for the lives you've stolen from me, from all of us. My vengeance shall never be tempered nor forgotten!"

Then she added into the winds of their departure, "And as for you, my daughter, your name is Ethra. I shall never forget you. Not ever!"

# BIRTHING BEFORE THE ARIAN INVASION

There had been a time before when the children of Aryll had been born free. When Aryll's skies were filled with the flight of happy voices and the birthing of new children was natural according to their traditional old ways.

Aryll, the beautiful azure planet of joy and light, had been kind to her avian races. Her blue skies and mild climates expressed themselves in warm oceans and verdant plains. There were mountains young and old in her development, and volcanic activity continued in part. Dense forests covered vast areas of the lands. Zolag trees were the dominant tree species. In the more tropical areas, fruit trees, nut trees, and citrus thrived. The children of Aryll had risen to become sentient beings in an evolutionary form similar to the ways mammals evolved. Bipedal like the species of other planets, they stood upright and walked on two legs, but here upon Aryll, they also had a set of wings which grew upward from their shoulder blades, and they flew like angels. Children were born true in genetic patterns reminiscent of their tribeflock's bird-like origins. In their most ancient tales, giant condor-like primitive human forms, known as Thunderbirds, had slowly climbed the evolutionary path to intelligence and perceptions. And as part of their species development, family trees had grown from birds of different natures, and plumage colors, diet, migratory or not, to become a rich

6

mixing of tribeflocks living in harmony with their world.

A female became with a child from the physical intercourse and mixing of genetic material from the father. A female could also hold male genetic material within for years before she became fertile in harmony with an unseen energy signal from her planet. Some tribeflocks chose only one life mate, while in different planetary regions, other tribeflocks mixed and had relations more freely with several partners.

The birthing of the young for any of them was similar in its cycles. A pregnant female developed the fetus internally like mammalian strains throughout the universe, but instead of the mother going through protracted labor pains to deliver a live infant, on Aryll the birth occurred in two phases. The pregnant Mother-Bearer delivered the unborn fetus into the outside world after six months contained in an egg similar size and fashion to a human mammalian birth. The three remaining months of her last trimester the child would mature outside her body enclosed within its membranous egg. The new life completed its growth and birth cycles independent of the mother's body for very special reasons.

The egg was encouraged to complete its cycle by sound frequency. Special birthing chambers had been dug into the natural stone and crystal formations deep beneath each of the world's forty cities. These chambers were carefully designed to resonate acoustically pure notes. They were lined with transparent metals and lit up by natural piezo-electrics from crystals in the chamber's walls.

All natural births had been relegated to these special chambers. Sensitivity and attention to the song and musical sound were the basis for language and communication on Aryll. These chambers were acoustically tuned by their understanding of the sciences of sound.

When the times were correct for the birth, as notated by the songs emerging from the fetus inside the egg, it would be brought to the chamber. Special cantor singers served as an external choir, and with the help of their planetary Mother-Bearer, matched the songs of the life force within the unborn egg in harmonic resonance. This ceremony assisted the birth to stay in balance.

Sonoluminescence, the compressing action of sound frequency upon the amniotic birth fluids contained inside the egg's membrane, would bubble until it triggered the unborn's final harmonic birth response in song. In the final phases completing the birthing process, the egg would burst apart like an explosion of sound and song reverberated off the chamber walls with its cadence described as a soft wind, an ocean's roar, the crackle of a warm fire, or the gentle hiss of light rain. The birthing fluids would evaporate amidst sequins of a brilliant white opalescent light, and the newborn would stretch its wings and join the outside world.

Within the birthing chambers, immersed in the choral chanting of the ancient ceremonies, the process provided safety for each new tribeflock member to emerge; victorious and healthy into the physical world of flight. These special acoustical chambers were designed to focus and facilitate the young ones. Each of them was birthed in an atmosphere focused on the harmony and love of their specific tribeflock members – from Doveal, Owlface, Peeptweet, and Raptor— and from their Planet Mother, Aryll. All young lives of Aryll could instantly recognize their own Mother-Bearer and began making their first fluttering efforts in flight toward them within minutes of emergence into their physical world.

# THE STATE INCUBATOR

A large prefab fold-building originally meant to be a warehouse, housed the state incubator. Other modular pieces allowed the rapid military assembly of practical, dependable buildings for a variety of utilitarian functions.

After the first attack waves of the conquest, all native unborn eggs were confiscated, gathered, and placed there. Purportedly supervised by the best professionals of the Arian scientific and medical staff, the eggs containing all the unborn children were tended to upon artificial nesting tables.

The trained medical staffers assigned there were accustomed to working in Arian cloning and nurturing centers. The staffer's experiences ranged from various human species across a wide range of planets. The state plans were designed so each of these new Arian citizens would have its own cautiously handled, proper Arian-supervised birth, and then be channeled from the incubator into state homes and state mind programming, and onto educational facilities for their Arian culture education.

That was their plan.

# INSIDE THE INCUBATOR

Rushing their short flight, the two gravity sleds hovered onto the landing pad marked Official State Incubation Facility. The military police inspectors dismounted and quickly pushed through the emergency entrance with their recently confiscated bundle. Once inside the cavernous institutional-gray building, they saluted the receiving official.

The older inspector spoke first. "Dracus 12, team leader, here's another egg for you. Took quite a struggle to get it, too. Why can't these native females of Aryll 8 just accept the inevitable?"

Another mid-aged centurion, Marcus 342, looked up and sighed from behind his post, he returned a remark in a bored tone from doing little all day. He accepted the quiet egg.

"It's been almost three years since our arrival. There are so few of these native offspring left to be born. You'd think they'd accept proper Arian procedures by now, and just get on as new member citizens of the empire. The will of the state knows better than the voice of any one of its citizen-subjects."

This nodule of repetitively programmed truth had saturated their minds from birth from their earliest memories of sleep in their teach-beds. They all shared a silent nod and resumed their duties. Marcus 342's tired eyes widened as he listened to the muffled, musical tones coming from inside the egg.

"Wait! This egg's nearly gone full term. Listen to it. We've got to process this egg STAT!" Marcus 342 slammed a button activating the emergency scramble signal, sending its screeching scream echoing down the long corridors.

Two lab techs burst through an adjoining door and rushed to his aid. The rag-wrapped egg was delicately placed on a soft-lined roll cart and zoomed through the door marked INCUBATION CHAMBER- PREPARATION; the first procedural step within this protected, factory-laboratory. The lead tech on duty, Regus 234, barked commands to his assistant as they raced the cart from receiving.

"The sounds emanating from this egg are nearing hatching frequencies. This process can't be allowed to happen! It must be suppressed now. Prepare the maximum strength Gene 10 and AR-15 injections upon arrival into the prep lab."

His partner, Nero 42, acknowledged, "Right away, sir."

Inside the Intensive Care Prep Lab, they gingerly unwrapped the blanket to reveal the cradled glowing egg. Inside the leathery outer membrane, luminescent fluids of golds and greens shimmered, holding within a growing fetus about to be accelerated into its external birth appearance. The unborn fledgling, in the human-like shape and design of natives of planet Aryll, stirred to reveal the bud development nodes of its small maturing wings.

One of the senior staff, Doctor Zarius 88, rushed in to examine this newest arrival. The medical technician, Regus 234, spoke. "I've asked my assistant to ready the maximum Gene 10 and AR-15 injections, Doctor."

"We must inject the chemicals. Vaccinate this amniotic fluid." The doctor glanced at the instrument readings. "Sonic resonance and luminosity levels are getting dangerously close to full term with this one. We haven't faced this dangerous a situation in months, and I don't want to fight that again. This egg might explode in our faces. We've lost two staff members in the last year by their lack of attention."

Two large syringes were delivered to the prep table. Doctor Zarius 88 grabbed one and, with difficulty, shoved it through the exterior membrane.

The brown, murky AR-15 vaccination swirled inside; attacking the amniotic fluids like muddy water mixing into a crystal spring.

"Quick. Hand me the other syringe."

"Yes, Doctor."

He again forced its needle, also with difficulty, through the strong outer membrane of the egg despite the fluid's resistance.

These injected vaccination liquids flowed inside to attack and mutate the body of the fetus. Their combination began to cause noticeable cloudiness and dimming of its shining radiation as the chemicals attacked its living glow from within. The Gene 10 was attacking and killing the living tissue on the wing nodes so the wings would be destroyed.

The cherub-like unborn child within the egg sounded its liquid-muffled screams through the membrane and squirmed in pain. Slowly, as the resonance of sounds diminished from within, the appearance of the egg began to take on the expected appearance; a flat, dull sheen.

"Good work, men." Doctor Zarius 88 breathed easier. "I think we got it in time."

Two backup attending team members from the nurturing staff joined them and stood close at attention. They had been summoned here in response to the STAT call. The doctor motioned them toward the egg.

"Here's another one for your nurture team. From the looks and sounds of it, or I should say her, this one had almost gone full term."

"See how the wing nodes on the back and shoulders were beginning to sprout? These latest batches of AR-15 will take care of the luminosity, and with the Gene 10, our proven chemical treatments will dissolve and suppress all continued growth in those wing node tissue areas."

The two female nurture staff workers rolled the egg carrier into the larger incubator facility.

Philis 56 whispered, "It does seem a shame they have to chemically treat these little ones."

"I know. They won't develop functional wings." Boni 6 responded. "But it has to be better than those mass surgery camps."

"That state decision came down from the highest levels. Orders from Prime Director One himself, they say. He was emphatic. Clip the wings from the remaining population. Keep them in check."

"I witnessed that first wing-cropping ceremony. It was a terrible mess. The medical staff tried to use an anesthesia that didn't work on this species, the former royal female panicked, one of the Arian soldiers broke rank to the embarrassment of the new Prime Director 87. The ceremony was shut down. We still had to crop off all the wings later, but with no more ceremonies. It was tedious work to enforce that surgery order upon the entire remaining winged, native race."

"Well, they did evolve from birds. How else could they be confined and controlled from flying off?"

"I saw some old picture images from right after this planet's takeover," Philis 56 responded. "The young fledgling native children looked like a bunch of little chickens. The natives used to talk about being born from luminous eggs. You'd never be able to keep those little devils in their teach-beds."

They giggled nervously together for a moment before the doors opened to reveal dozens of dull eggs stored, warmed, and being incubated on sterile hospital-like racks. Once assigned, this new arrival would also be recorded and placed in a specimen identified crib.

Boni 6 examined the bundle. "Look. It already has a name, in their script, written upon the rags wrapped around this unborn egg."

"How do you know it's a name?" Philis 56 challenged.

"Well if it isn't a name, I'm recording it, anyway. We'll call this one Ethra."

As the egg's internal shine and sounds continued to wane, the small unborn female life within struggled, kicked, and finally became docile. The birthing process would move slower now. After one last, brighter flare of luminosity, the fledgling inside succumbed to the dulling effect of the chemical vaccination treatments.

The egg's appearance dimmed to assume the same dull sheen as all the others in the Arian Empire's care. This state-run incubator would be the only welcoming platform it would receive as a newly conditioned and subjugated member of Arian society; a member now meant to join the other dull eggs of Aryll.

# PRIME DIRECTOR ONE

Back on the planet Ariana, the home ruling world for the entire Arian Empire, Prime Director One relaxed upon his divan. Balmy breezes filtered around the stone columns outside his villa. Casual toga robes, made of the softest silken fabric woven from cocoons of the rare spider worms on Wexel 9, loosely wrapped around his ancient body, and radiated the vibrant yellows only he, and those of the highest of ranks, could wear. He spoke to his closest adviser, Horacious.

"We must speed up the success of occupation forces on Aryll 8. You are part of my highest Inner Circle of Aeneus. You and the others share with me the rejuvenation secrets of the crystal baths. I value your thoughts."

"My Prime Director One, I, feel in accord with you. The Arian Senate and I remain true to our purposes. Because we rule by royal blood, we acknowledge you as the embodiment of our temporal power across the empire. You control the military by your commands. You lead as our true High Priest. You dominate the frequency of our thoughts as true Arian children of the gods by your arts of quantum entanglement."

"I have lived many centuries, Horacious. I have been this empire's leader, commander, and high priest. I accepted this role not long after we departed old Earth in the last of the God's space arks. Our race has journeyed far since the fall of Rome."

"You have led us well, Prime Director. Your steadfast inspiration steers our steady course forward into space and time. You have never swayed from the injunction given us by the gods to go forth and multiply."

Prime Director One waved his hand for wine. A slave woman stepped quietly forward to respond to his command. "Ursula. How long have you served me and my needs?"

She bowed slightly before she answered. Her lithe form and scanty attire did nothing to conceal the beauty she'd inherited from her native race on Exile 6. Her brown skin and perfect body confirmed her as an obvious choice for the first concubine. She pushed back her long black hair and let him see her dark eyes and smiled.

"I've served all your needs for nearly five years now, Prime Director One." She poured the wine before asking, "Are you displeased with me? Have your crystal baths been the wrong blend or temperature? Have you been dissatisfied with my performance satisfying your body's sexual needs? Have I spoken out of place?"

"No, Ursula. I remain very satisfied with your services. I do, however, need to confide facts to Horacious which must never leave these chambers. You do understand that injunction, do you not? If any hint of this discussion were to be leaked out, I would have to put you to death. You give me great pleasure with your life. I would miss having you here, especially after you have weathered all the proper training."

"You need not be concerned my Prime Director; I would certainly warrant death if I were to abuse your confidentiality." Ursula showed her deference with a small bow.

Horacious approved. "You have done well, Ursula. I know

16

members of the Arian Senate who could not have answered so clearly."

"Come to me, child." Prime Director One motioned her closer. "Give me your wrist." Ursula extended her arm so that he might touch her wrist. The Prime Director picked up a sharp knife from the table before him. With one swift slice, he cut her wrist. The garnet blood flowed. He grabbed a napkin and wrapped it tight. "Hold this to the cut, run down the hall to the attending Medi-corps officer. He will dress it for you. Now go!"

Ursula had been stunned by the swiftness of the cut, the shock of the pain, and the blood. "As you wish, Prime Director." She mumbled as she hurried from the room, barely hiding her hurt at his actions.

Horacious gave the Prime Director a quizzical look but said nothing.

"I needed to be certain she was not within earshot of what I will now reveal to you. It is better to inflict a slight wound than to have to terminate a good slave."

"What can be of such a serious nature to inflict this injury just for privacy?"

"I need for you to understand why the conquest of Aryll 8 is so vitally important, and why it must succeed."

"Is it not just another part of our empire's planetary expansions?"

"No, Horacious, it is most certainly not. You express the publicly allowed views of this. These actions are not the real cause. As you well know, I ordered a second, advanced team of archeologists to be part of the occupation forces."

"As conquerors, we have always looked to benefit from the races we plunder. Have they come upon a startling discovery

17

that needs absolute security concealment?"

"Horacious, let me remind you of our core motives for expanding into the vast regions of space. I have led and held this empire together since almost before the times our fleets conquered this home world of Ariana."

"And you are a legend, Prime Director One."

"Recently, before my ordered decision was sent out for the invasion, I'd become privy to some documents. These records spoke of times from our earliest Arian Empire's pre-history long before the victorious campaigns taught of in the empire's standard knowledge programs. We speak little now of the treasures and gifts the Gods bestowed upon us as we left Earth for the vastness of space."

"I thought those were the stuff of myth and legend."

"And so do the majority of our Arian citizens. I will now reveal to you; the legends of the Cave of the Arians and the God's gifts contained within are more than just legends."

Horacious leaned back into his chair to hold back his incredulity.

"Those secret archives herald from the earliest days of Arian military campaigns in space. Aryll 8 was the first planet to be attacked. Before I speak further, I can also assure you of something else. All unworthy persons tainted by knowledge of this volatile discovery have been forever silenced."

"How is it this history has never been revealed?"

"Because, during the first Arian attack upon Aryll 8, we were resoundingly defeated! The victorious native races confis-cated our blessed gifts from the Gods and sent our attacking Arian fleet into retreat. It seems the commander of that assault lost communications with his scout ship carrying the archives' location. This knowledge had faded into legend. Until this discovery, it was thought no records remained of their existence. Recovering these writings proves they exist and give accurate information from those who had witnessed the site."

"Why must all this be kept in secrecy?"

"Our current traditional view of Arian history praises the first major victories in the Drestic star systems and celebrates our eventual conquest of this home world of Ariana. As this became the center of Arian power throughout the passing centuries, it became our focus for the beginning and successful expansion of the Arian Empire."

"So why is now the time to redirect command upon Aryll 8? By all reports, the last three years have been less than eventful. You moved us to approve the removal of Aryll 8's first Prime Director 87. He's being replaced by Prime Director 32 for failure in his disciplines, is he not? Have your two archeological groups found something?"

"Horacious, the normal Arian battle plan for a planetary conquest is like the capture of a pigeon. A great bird of prey flies high above the unsuspecting pigeon until suddenly he folds his wings tight to his body and drops into free fall. The pigeon never detects the bird of prey high above him until it is stunned by the impact. The raptor's talons slashing into its back and ripping it from the skies comes as a complete surprise. The raptor lands to leisurely to use its beak and talons to tear the prey to bits and consume it live on the spot.

"Other birds, drawn by the screams and cries of the dying pigeon, land in the trees around the feasting raptor. They cry and caw and curse the predator for his actions from the safe distance of the surrounding forests. The trees echo with the cacophony of their cries until the bird of prey finishes his meal, leaves the scraps, and flies away. Those who have given such protest quickly dissipate to safety."

"I'm aware how our Arian forces utilized such procedures in their attacks but the campaign was successful, wasn't it?"

"Just as our Arian landing craft dropped their eagle-like formation in for the attack much of the planet's population went missing; disappeared even before our para-soldiers put boots on the ground. After almost three years, these mysterious disappearances have yet to be solved. Fractious 5, Prime Director 87 for Aryll 8, has not only failed to solve that mystery, but it appears his Arian mind programming also weakens. He's given far too much allowance to the remaining native population members. Under his watch, our Arian archeologists have not yet been able to locate the Cave of the Arians."

"What then will you do now, Prime Director?"

"We stand at a crucial turning point in the history of this Arian Empire. Until now, I've been able to mentally control the entire empire from here. However, the science and technology I've used show signs of weakening erosion, even into dissipation. I have grave concerns about successfully maintaining our mind programming. I'm reaching the limits of my control using the technology of entanglement techniques.

"It should come as no surprise to you, Horacious. My absolute rule of the Arian Empire depends on a composite application of quantum entanglement. Like the capacity for one atom to mirror and cause actions upon another atom at great distances, so do I rule across the stars. I am reliant upon the effectiveness of our mind programming implanted within the very minds of our citizens as a direct and effective system of governing across the vastness of Arian space."

"How does this relate to frustrations concerning recent happenings upon Aryll 8?"

"Serious evidence of programming erosion in the mind of a military trained and trusted director is a crucial warning sign. It displays a signal. Other serious cracks are fermenting and are about to appear. Unfortunately, it must be rejuvenated. I am positive those ancient gifts from our Gods have the ability to refresh the potency of spirit in minds across the empire. I must have them if the empire is to survive."

"What if the archaeology team can't locate them?"

"I have larger plans in motion taking that into account. I shall replace Prime Director 87 with one who will guarantee me that he will instigate the necessity for me to choose Aryll 8 as the first candidate for Stericyclation."

"Those terraforming plans call for instantaneous and total sterilization of all planetary life! Is such a drastic project necessary?"

"I shall order the withdrawal of our forces into middle space, and then sterilize all organic life upon that planet. Aryll 8 will be dead! From that platform, and without the mask of any organic energy frequency interference, I am certain our most sensitive technologies will be able to detect and measure the radiation and location of the God's treasures I seek.

"The planet will become a compliant and successful greenhouse for chosen restock and replanting. This will be shining example of a cooperative world; a most wondrous win-win situation for my empire.

"The treasures of the Gods will be MINE! Once discovered these treasures would be employed, knowledge of them can be made public; there need be no more erosion of minds. Citizens across the empire will be renewed in spirit. I shall use their energy and technology to revitalize my control of our collective future."

# THE CAPACITY

The new Arian Capacity on Aryll 8, as the invaders now called it, had a name of its own that Arians couldn't speak in the native tongue. It would have translated roughly to something like Regulis, Raptor Clan City. Their cities were gathering places for descendants of various avian species for their specific tribeflocks.

There had been great beauty and song in each city. Each one uniquely caught the emergent dawn of the twin suns in the stained-glass-like brilliance of its transparent buildings. Cities that captured the glow of each new sunrise day translated its joys. Its sound and radiation permeated the air and floated along with the slightest breeze. Their constant mild weather fostered the fragrant blossoms of the Zolag trees and many other semi-tropical flowers.

Now, with the Arian occupation, harsh sounds of construction clogged the Capacity. Sounds of the marching Arian military, gravity sleds, and the barking of commands filled the plazas and squares. The city longed for a return to its original peace and natural harmony.

In most designs, their structures reflected a group-dominated way of life. Square, barracks-like architecture was their motive in design with no feeling given to taste or beauty. Their mind-controlled education cared not for aesthetics. Dull colors reigned, like the gray and brown tones of their stark and somber lives. Buildings were meant to be living storehouses for guards or soldiers or equipment and included prison-like dwellings for the remaining native population of Aryll 8, all of whom they'd mustered into indentured servitude in some capacity.

Arians, motivated by history and mind programming, designed to duplicate some of the glories of ancient Rome in both style and magnitude. They believed themselves as chosen descendants from a soldier race who'd left earth long ago. They praised the gods who graced and inspired them with technology to carve out and conquer new worlds in space for their empire. The Arians saw true wealth as gained by plundering others.

One abiding myth they hold is the Cave of The Arians, a mythical cave holding artifacts given to them by their Gods. They believed these gifts confirmed them as chosen people.

On most of their colony worlds, some small token of sovereignty was allowed. Seemingly tolerant acceptance of local customs, religions, and governments was manipulated only as a public relations concession against any revolts, and as long as the tribute kept pouring in to fill their coffers.

# MORIA AT THE OFFICERS' CLUB

The formerly bedraggled refugee Moria and her contact Sumira had little trouble getting through traffic to the Arian officer's selective place of evening entertainment where she would meet Harcos 86, Communications Secretary. Sumira helped Moria transition through the serious Arian-like body changes needed to become accepted into this military's establishment and pretend she'd never given birth. Sumira supplied Harcos 86 with native females willing to go through makeovers to increase their appeal, and in return, as club manager, he let her prosper from the kickbacks.

Moria allowed her auburn feather tresses to be piled high on her head in the latest local style. A colored scarf accented the yellow-green of her eyes and flattered the ecru dress with its side slits and fashionable plunging cleavage exposure.

Sumira had her makeup staff cover the natural ruddiness color of her skin tanned by Aryll's two different suns during her long years in the Zolag forests. She made a striking contrast to most of the other females, Arian or native, inside the club's quiet interior. Sumira measured her first impressions of this place and tried to keep her informed.

*The Club's appearance is still reflective of Arian bland-ness. However, it is supposed to be the best they offer their officers. In the end, it's just a dimly lit bar and service lounge like ones they've seen on their many other worlds. They tell the girls all officers' clubs seem to smell the same.* This, Moria reflected in her mind as she wrinkled her nose.

A video screen image of some alien musicians played their form of soft jazz in the background. A liberal number of better-dressed native females fancied up the appearance of the club with their glitz and glamour. Sumira ran most of these girls, so she nodded to them as they passed.

The native Doveal hostesses were dressed colorfully in various styles of evening dress to match shades of their filament feathers. These females were allowed into the club because they'd subjected themselves to surgical duplication of the mammalian curves of Arian women. Moria wondered if her new profile looked as odd to them as theirs did to her. These females sported breasts, various amounts of cleavage, and fixed their feathers in styles that mimicked real hairdos as she had done. They, too, accented their mouths to play up their thin lips. These females played their roles as any other off-world geisha. They worked the clubs and were paid gratuities based upon services rendered for the occupational forces.

Peeptweet tribeflock members handled the more menial wait-staff tasks; cleaning off tables and delivering orders. They worked in white uniform wrapcapes that covered the scars and remnants of their original smaller wings. They were all slightly shorter in height, and none had been through the body-altering surgeries the Doveal hostesses had endured.

The acrid smoky smell from the burning of many varieties of herbs used, such as orlac, was not pleasant for Moria.

Orlac was useful as a battle stimulant and pain suppressant.

In times of truce and temporary suspension of fighting, its lure could so easily become addictive. Here on Aryll 8, in the boredom and long time spans of occupation, alcohol and orlac were becoming dangerously appealing illusions as a remedy for malaise.

No native of Aryll would ever smoke except in some of the highest ceremonies, and the alcohols which appeared behind the bar offered her little appeal. Sumira had trained her well. Moria did not need to read the minds of this crowd to register just how many of these officers showed the signs of excessive orlac use.

# PRIME DIRECTOR ONE PROCEEDS

Prime Director One ordered Aries 45, an ambitious middle-rank military officer, to report to his private offices.

"I shall waste no time speaking with you in trivialities, Aries 45. I have enough information concerning your profile to know you are a hungry one. By all reports, you obviously strive to prove yourself to me and to rise in rank and status levels of this empire. Have I misjudged you and your intent?"

Aries 45 did not hesitate a moment before responding in kind. "Prime Director One, you have assessed me correctly. I offer you my complete loyalty in whatever proposition you might offer me."

"Then my readings have been correct. I have an assignment. Fail me? You'll lose all chance for any career advancement. Make our private agreements known to any other person; I'll see you dead. Are we clear in this matter?"

"I have placed myself in harm's way in battles for the empire before. I have no qualms offering the same conviction obeying your commands in any other matters."

"Then I will trust the voices of your ambition. I have a vital need for leadership of the occupational forces on Aryll 8. At present, my confidence in Prime Director 87 wanes. I would like you to assume leadership over that planet. Your position will be approved through the administrative channels

I control. Do I have your word and your bond to obey my absolute commands in these matters under penalty of death?"

"Your wish is my command. What must I do to present you with a victory?"

"You will assume the title of Prime Director 32. You will be sent to re-orchestrate Aryll 8 under the premise of increasing agricultural productivity and strengthening discipline upon the native population. You will use the reason of native rebellion and the attempted assassination attack upon Prime Director 87 to achieve my actual goal in this. You must find undeniable reasons to request the complete Stericyclation of Aryll 8."

"I fully accept your proposition. But I had not been made aware there had been any attempts upon the life of Prime Director 87."

"That action has been a long time in the planning and training phases, my new Prime Director 32. You need not know its source, its course, or its direction. Simply play your part in this, but rest assured you need to hurry your plans. You are about to receive relocation assignment orders."

"I always remain a humble servant of the Arian Empire, sir."

# A PLOT TO KILL

Fractious 5, also known as Prime Director 87, often worked long hours trying to coordinate the business of running the planet. He wearily entered his living chambers, and before his hand could activate the light switch a blur of motion thrust out at him from the dark, and the painful blow of a heavy object slammed into his head. Fractious 5 instinctively raised his arm to partially block the attack, but it knocked him to the floor steadfast.

Whoever the assailant was, he was quick in moving to take advantage of the surprise attack. Fractious 5's hand found the office notebook he'd been carrying, and he raised it to prevent whatever assault could come. The quiet pain to his body defined the next weapon a knife, and his body came alive to counter its stab with a leg sweep and dropped the attacker to the floor. Fractious 5 rolled to straddle the dark figure and pounded his head with precision blows until there was no more fight. The dark figure lay motionless on the floor while he made sure the knife and his opponent were far separate as he stood to switch on the lights. He bent to remove the black hood and revealed the attacker's face.

Fractious 5, calming his adrenalin from the intensity of the attack, started to feel the bruises on his throbbing forearm. He was puzzled as he stood above the body. He didn't recognize the person, but the attacker's uniform was worn only in black ops training.

He sent out a message to Maximus. "Bring two trusted men to my inner quarters. I have some serious cleanup for you to perform."

Maximus snapped out of his late-night mode. "Serious cleanup? I'll gather a detail and report at once, sir. Do you need a medical staffer?"

"No. Once a survivor, always a survivor, my old friend. I'll be waiting."

Maximus and two para-soldiers, whose faces Fractious 5 knew well, arrived quickly.

"You have a large bruise and a cut on your arm Prime Director." He spoke as the other two bagged the body. "This uniform is the empire's native youth militia. They are being trained to replace more battle hardened Arian troops on Aryll 8." Maximus examined the weapon. "He tried to take you out with a knife? If he had used a gun, he might have succeeded."

"It would have been more easily explained if this young native was able to pull it off, but a knife kill demands the greatest focus by the assassin."

"Why now? There's no rebellion going on here. What would your death gain for high command?"

"Maximus, only Prime Director One could have ordered such an assassination. I'll tread ever so cautiously from here on in. He obviously has an agenda in mind that does not include me. You'd best watch your back as well. I will find out what's at the root of all this, but for now, make sure you dispose of the body, so we don't have to speak of it again. And men, I know you from our long service together. Speak nothing of this incident to anyone. If you do, it may also endanger your lives. Is that clear?"

The two soldiers prepared to leave. They nodded in accord. One spoke. "We understand, sir. We've served with you too long to lose you this way."

"Then you are dismissed with my thanks."

The late evening clean-up detail vanished into the night.

# A CALL FROM PRIME DIRECTOR ONE

It was little surprise when Fractious 5 received an early call from high command next morning as he was having his first cup of tea. Citizens across the empire knew the wizened face of Prime Director One. Everyone was also aware he would stop at nothing to have his demands obeyed. He gave Fractious 5 a long serious look at the view screen. Not surprisingly, Prime Director One's practiced face gave no indication of his treachery or involvement in the previous evening's recent assassination attempt.

The Prime Director spoke to measure his appointee's reactions to the voice of command he'd practiced and perfected. "Fractious, nearly three years ago, your leadership in the conquest of Aryll 8 was successful. Under your able military command, another new planet was added to the myriad of glittering worlds already dominated by the iron grip of my rule.

"I've decided it's time for you to take another step forward in your career. I've learned from my years of experience maintaining this empire that it's better to have a single strong, wise man dictate the conduct of our citizens, decide upon uniform types of clothes for all to wear, and the best kinds of foods for us all to eat. I work all waking cycles to coordinate everything. My mind is always about orchestrating everyone's well-being according to the teachings of our Gods."

Fractious 5 smiled and nodded. Being well-versed in filtering through this kind of military rhetoric, he detected a slight undertone of disappointment in the voice.

"You know what vital importance it is to achieve obedient consensus from a newly conquered population like Aryll 8. It's the first call for any Prime Director. I've charged you in this. To accomplish this important task, a population must be made to desire and accept our rule.

"Fractious 5, the population of a new planet must not just consent to become Arian citizens. They must be made to appreciate the value complete cultural reorganization leadership provides for them. An occupational military leader must engineer their minds to accept whatever propaganda is necessary.

"Are you receiving me clearly? You've been in control of this planet for almost three years. The results of your occupation have been very lackluster indeed. Reports I've received cause me serious doubts as to whether I should continue to address you as Prime Director 87. I've even heard rumors of a rising underground anti-Arian rebellion.

"In light of this and other vitally serious considerations, I've reached a final decision. You will assume another planetary assignment." The withered face of Prime Director One stared out from the view screen of his high command, measuring the face response of his former battle commander.

Fractious 5 remained guarded in his expressions and response. The very recent attempt on his life had awakened his battle instincts to the ways of this leader; a leader who was tenacious in maintaining his position and willing to use any treachery to maintain his grip on power, rank, and dictatorial control.

"I have been called many things, Prime Director One, and been given a wide variety of assignments and titles. You are my commander. Any changes you deem fit would in no way affect my commitment to be of service. As ever, I am under your complete authority, sir."

It had always been easier for Fractious 5 to be wary, and to understate his part in any of these military-political affairs. He'd survived too many combat campaigns not to be overly cautious about the one supposedly in total support of his actions. The machinations of his last evening's conflict had reminded him of that.

"I readily accept whatever title or assignment you deem fitting. Especially now since this planetary prize has been secured for you."

"Yes, I've been watching you, Fractious 5. It's always the quiet ones I monitor the most. You don't need to be modest for my benefit. I've seen your reports. My eyes and ears across the empire report back to me about everything that goes on everywhere. This planet has not presented you with an easy task for you to rule, so I now deem it advisable to move you on.

"The Office of Arian Thought Monitoring will confirm your new position with no concerns. Aryll 8 has offered little resistance. Most of your troops will remain to secure the continued peace of our occupation."

"You are well informed."

The dictator seemed pleased enough with his assessment of the situation. "You have now been informed of my final decision. Rest assured, even after your new assignment orders come through, the Arian flag will continue flying over our new Capacity.

"I feel our mission can be more successful by appointing Aries 45, who seems to have the right motivations to carry on there as my new Prime Director 32."

"I'll be prepared to acknowledge your wishes when your chosen replacement arrives to accept that title."

"Very well. Then you stand so ordered."

The viewscreen went dark.

Fractious 5 threw his cup across the room and stared at the screen with incredulity. "Aries 45? Prime Director 32? I've dealt with that man before. Do you know what you're about to inflict upon this gentle world, Prime Director? A man who is the epitome of ambition and deceit? You force me to want to wash my hands of this whole affair and of the evil plots you two must be planning.

"Despite the power you hold, losing this title concerning the life of this planet will not stain my record, and you shall not crush my spirit. I will continue to assist this world in any way I can from wherever you send me until I'm no longer able to draw breath."

# BACK ON ARIANA

Prime Director One reclined onto the pillows before his next sleep cycle. Ursula, his personal slave, and consort, curled up next to him after satisfying his sexual needs. In a tender voice, he touched the scar he'd placed upon her wrist. "I regret I needed to cut your wrist, but it resolved any doubt of your confidence. It forced you to be absent."

Ursula sighed in her drowsiness. "I believe I understand your actions, sir. It was better to inflict just a little pain to guarantee my life."

"You are wise beyond your years, Ursula. That pleases me. These are times when I must be even more driven by our God's purpose. I am not immortal. I will eventually have to set this body down and move on. In the meantime, I pursue the best path for leading this empire into its grand new future. I have a calling. Even our Gods recognized I had the strength to rule. I stand dedicated to order any action I feel necessary. I'll crush any opponent who would resist, and I'll strike a final blow upon any plot which would attempt to constrain its total supremacy. I am dedicated to performing any action; anything and everything I deem fit to see it hold together as an empire."

"You are strong, sir. You take care of me, and I take care of you."

"Yes, you do, my child, now rest."

# PRIME DIRECTOR 87 AND HIS RULE

Fractious 5 faced a brilliant crimson sky as scarlet swirls of clouds buffeted him. He marched with other Arians shoulder-to-shoulder. They pressed and squeezed against him, stifling his ability to move. He longed to break free of them. The image of Prime Director One loomed down from above them all. Other faces strained in grim detail as they laughed and murdered the races before them. He felt the terror of the victims stomped beneath their booted feet. Fractious 5 screamed to make it all stop.

Without warning, the scene changed for him. He was floating from clear azure blue space to the surface of Aryll 8. Warmth and peace greeted him from this soothing world. He felt free, at home on Aryll 8 where the people of this world welcomed him. He wished never to leave this state of allowance it offered him.

A call woke him from the nightmare as if he quivered on the edge of some unknown larger than he could ever have imagined. He was shaken to the core by the certainty of his feelings as he thought of his former Arian life, a life so easily discarded by its leadership; a life so disposable that an overt, threatening attempt had nearly killed him. Having thwarted the attack, he was now politically being manipulated into a new assignment. High command had ordered him off Aryll 8.

After the call, Maximus asked. "Are you all right, sir?"

"I sense vital forces are at play here, and it's certainly more than high command will reveal to me. I've dealt with performance pressures before, and this is not just about my duties here. This is not just Prime Director One, and the Council of Planetary Directors trying to force my hand. Their warrior mode of conquering and dominating has moved our race across the stars for centuries. This is something new; something much deeper in its cause."

"How's your arm, sir?"

"Sore, but better than my attacker's."

Maximus paused a moment. "We disposed of that annoyance. It won't bother anyone else."

"Thank you. Stay alert. Is Harcos 86 on duty today?"

"No. I think he claimed to be sick."

"Very well. I need to think. No appointments today."

"I've discreetly posted guards at your quarters and your office. Get some rest."

"Thank you, I'll check with you later." He spoke aloud to himself after Maximus left him. "I expected struggles when changing battle strategies. Establishing a static occupation army has never been without tension; especially keeping all my troops on ready alert. I've survived surprise attacks before, but here no one has found any trace of the missing population in all these years. And another thing to ponder; why have there been two archeological teams scouring this planet for treasures and not once reporting back to me?

"There is one area where Prime Director One is correct. I am having deeper humanistic patterns of doubt in my heart about our truths. Something within me is new. I've been changed by being here on this planet. I've carried the weight of command on other worlds, but this is something more personal. The overt civilian torture, the abusive questioning treatments by the inquisitors, the cropping of wings, the stealing of their young, all of which, forced by my position, I ordered. It's causing me deep personal feelings of guilt and regret. I'm having nightmares and soulful reflections about these Arian methods. I've developed uncertainty as to whether any real value has come from ordering such policy decisions upon a peaceful, non-combatant cultural world. I'm no longer so callous, and I regret it if I ever was."

He sat on the edge of his bed. "Hell, can I even trust my personal staff? I've long suspected them of sending duplicate reports of all my activities directly back to command. Harcos 86 has the ambition to do that."

Fractious 5 recalled how, after the final Arian conquest, he'd sought guidance for every strategy change with Prime Director One. "I remember how definite he was about the questioning and cropping of wings. He ordered all their wings clipped. And I passed that policy order to all troops under my command.

"I once believed that would facilitate rejuvenation and reclamation of Aryll 8 into a prosperous Arian economy. I believed this planet could rebuild to occupy its newly acquired status as a rising success for this glorious empire. What did I do wrong?"

# MORIA WITH PRIME DIRECTOR 87

Sumira's friends socialized with the Prime Director 87 so she convinced Harcos 86 and his office staff that Moria should meet with him. After bargaining, an appointment was scheduled. Moria couldn't pass up this possibility if it could help her locate her daughter.

Fractious 5/PD 87 waved Harcos 86 away. "I'll speak to this native woman alone. I can handle this better in private."

"Are you certain, sir? Shouldn't I stay as a witness?"

"She's only one native woman. You've already scanned her for weapons, I'm certain. Leave us."

Moria spoke boldly and held no strain of political correctness. "So, you're the main leader responsible for these policies of occupation? How could I ever repay you after your glorious arrival bestowed upon my tribe and me so many notable memories?"

"I do believe we've met before, Moria, but I hardly recognized you with this new look. Is this why you wish to speak with me? To further chide my reasons for being assigned here? You know I've been a military man all my life. In service to this empire, I've never been encouraged to feel emotion or remorse for any of my actions." He looked into her face and felt the need to explain himself to her. "I remember your incident with the wing clipping; I would never have wished that upon anyone. You still carried your child inside you. They should never have injected you with those drugs, and when your child was prematurely born, they should never have turned the ultrasound on him. I gave the orders that it would never happen again. I seem to be losing the aggressive Arian edge of my previous training. Something you said to me is about to occur. I'm being re-assigned off this planet."

"Does that increase your feelings of being lost and out of your league, Prime Director? What do you want from me? Do you expect me to give you more insight of your future? I don't want you to agree with me about your rude assault upon my world and my body. I have come here for intelligence. Direct me. You've probably not been informed. I've recently given birth to another child -a daughter. She was torn from my arms by your unfeeling centurions. I only wish you to locate her for me so that I might get to know her. This is my only request of you. As you see, I'm your captive audience. What price must I offer for this information?"

"Stop it." He sensed the deep pain he'd caused her. "I didn't let you come in here so I could gloat about my supposed rank and power over this world, or over your life. I recognize you have this vital reason to be here. I will not ask favors you have no obligations to pay me. Even though we come from different worlds, my honor as a man would never permit me such behavior."

"Then you are the man I thought you to be, sir. I thank you for that. I only want to ask you to return knowledge of my child."

"Moria, I want to communicate with you, to this planet, to the others of your kind. I don't understand. How can this world be causing these deep changes in me?"

Moria stopped to reflect upon this man. "Even though much time has passed since we last met, I could never recite to you the patterns of your losses. Suffice it to say you are immersed in this planet's Changeover. I can sense this is happening to you, but I do not know what the result will be. I do know you and your kind serve an intrinsic importance to this experience, but I can't offer more specifics. You see?"

Moria gave up her edginess. Her words softened. "Fractious 5, I can read your mind. I can feel your internal conflict. There is nothing permanent about anything in this universe."

"I vividly recall what happened to the first young life you were forced to birth upon the surgery table."

Moria replied, "That event you witnessed, in all its cruelty and sorrow, was a shock that you and your species needed to witness. It should have taught you to handle creation and universal processes more carefully. The life-spark that occupied my body for a short time span will be aware of its mission success. It chose to serve as that example to awaken you."

"If that's true, then what lesson should I learn if I assist you to locate this new daughter you speak of? I believe I get a sense why your feelings can't handle the loss of another young life's potential."

"How are your young Arian lives handled? My daughter will never be given life choices based upon deeper knowings. She will never be taught how her life will develop and be part of the universe's purpose. Is your race prospering in its purpose by orchestrating simple bio-mechanical births? Are you a body and soul, or only a programmed, unwitting, moving part for your insidious Arian Empire's war and conquest machine?"

Fractious 5 sighed. "I'm becoming increasingly aware; speaking these same words and teachings leaves a vile taste with me." He sat back in his chair with a weary look. "Nothing about my coming to your planet has played out as I expected it to. Help me to learn, and I will help you find your daughter."

"You are not here upon Aryll to satisfy your empire, Fractious 5. I can read it in you. You carry a spark of greatness. You may not grasp it now, but your race was attracted here for a much larger purpose. You will be sent away from this planet before these changes happen. Your destiny is to realize more of your true self. You will learn more about how to obtain your goal before you leave here. That is all I may tell you now."

Fractious 5, alarmed by the truth in Moria's words, asked, "How did you know I've been reassigned? What am I to do then? I was designated Planetary Director and should be stronger in the leadership of my Arian people. I sense your knowings and truth more intensely even than any prior battle experience."

The cracks in his Arian programming were allowing perceptions of an unknown to cause him some fear. She looked deeply into his core inner being. He stood and gestured to the door. "Moria, I have faced many challenges, but your perceptions cause me great imbalance. I must ask you to leave me. Other duties demand my actions. I will alert my staff to check about your inquiry. You must not attempt to visit with me again before I get reassigned off this planet."

"There is one source which may help you, Fractious 5," Moria added. "I suggest you pay one last visit to Orlycia and Yeto. Make it an official visit before you leave. It will give you more support than you could realize. How else might you get to understand this race you were expected to rule? Don't leave our world with only bad memories."

# BAD MEMORIES

Fractious 5 shuddered as he remembered the nightmare of the feather merchants. Those vile salesmen had been granted a concession to collect surgery carnage from the mass clipping of wings. Those money grubbing, hyena-like scavengers were allowed here; buying those native wings to sell their feathers as curiosities across the rest of the Arian Empire.

Fractious 5 remained haunted by the memories of that cropping ceremony and its results. He finished his glass of brandy while his body unwound from the interview with Moria. He knew he had to release concern about reasons for this and his re-assignment if he was to get any rest at all. His reign as Prime Director 87 was over, judged and seen as weak, ineffective, and unable to win the admiration of either his fellow Arians or the natives to Aryll 8.

The alcohol worked as his mind slowed down, but facts still floated in his brain. Sedio grains not blossoming into harvests as expected, Arian occupational military still patrolling on full alert, no results locating unknown, missing members of the population. Doctor Rotz 27 unsuccessful with increasing reproduction of native members. Gene 10 and Ar-15 vaccinations not working as planned. The survival rate of newborn natives was so very low there were few natives to produce crops and provide labor. Barely enough laborers to work the fields, and he never once requested a need to import labor.

His body faded to exhaustion, and he slept.

# OFFICIAL VISITS

When Fractious 5 returned to his office duties, he was met by Harcos 86. "Did your visit with the native female prove interesting, sir?"

"It provided me with much food for thought. She pointed out how I might win more tacit support from the natives."

"And how would that be, Prime Director?"

"She suggested I make an official visit to the former leadership. After the disastrous spectacle produced during the initial cropping ceremony, she said I might learn more of the native species I was assigned here to rule."

"Was she protesting our Arian methods of proceeding? Did she give voice to any rebellious spirit and demand justice for her people? Arians usually blustered with insecurity at any resistance or questioning concerning the righteousness of Arian ways."

"No, I didn't feel resentment about any of the events which have occurred. She was straightforward. She is trying to locate a daughter taken from her. Follow up and get me that information. This whole conquest scenario holds larger mysteries than our Intel has so far revealed. She put the question directly to me. Why hadn't I already made an official Arian Prime Director visit to Orlycia, the recognized former ruler? It has been an Arian policy on other worlds and what if, with this small concession, I could allow this Orlycia to feel support in her isolated life?"

"I can see how this has some appeal." Harcos 86 gave him reflection. "Reports have it Orlycia has recovered from her problematic wing cropping. She is still captive in that old palace as a political prisoner. You might make some token efforts to encourage acceptance of our occupation in exchange for more personal freedom. She can't fly away. She's too high profile to hide. She might be of some political value."

"This action seems right to me. Make the arrangements. I will pay her an official visit. It can be seen as my recognition of her native rank; an Arian gesture to seek harmony with our newest citizens. Politically, it will cost me nothing and the empire has everything to gain by peaceful co-existence with these natives. Perhaps she may give me clues as to the location of the remaining population members."

"That might be unlikely with just one visit, but it might pave the way for better negotiations." He liked the feeling of ordering actions.

# THE ORLYCIA VISIT

Fractious 5 flew with two attending soldiers to speak with Orlycia. His pretext was official, but he wished for more of a personal visit. An older native, Yeto, Orlycia's staff of one, met the party at the door. The old man's head was covered in the short, gray, hair-like filament feathers of the planet's elders. The man's angular and lean face, with a sharp, slightly bent nose, clearly identified him from the Owlaface tribeflock. Yeto ushered Fractious 5 and his bodyguards into Orlycia's presence. Queen Orlycia's gossamer down covered her head in brilliant white colors that hung above the feathers and flowed to her shoulders.

When all gathered together, Fractious 5 spoke first. "It is not as a conqueror I come to you. I have been a man of honor. One who's fought many years for the glory and expansion of the Arian Empire."

"You were sent to our world to continue your commission doing this glory and expansion activity, Prime Director 87. That is the reputation by which you are known is it not?" Orlycia, the true queen of this world, embodied and spoke from the hopes and fears of her population as the burden of her function. "I have little to say to you, Prime Director. I have been forced to endure your humiliations and torture before my people. You and your savages have killed and mutilated our bodies. I can read your mind. You were made to believe you had come here in full control of your destiny. Recent events have filled you with leadership doubts, and your performance has given high command doubt enough to order your reassignment, has it not?"

Fractious 5 tried to mask his surprise at her knowing. He motioned to the two members of his attending staff to depart the hall. "The two of you should wait outside. Yeto, I believe that is your name? Could you please escort these two officers to the gravity sleds outside? I need a few more moments alone with your queen.

"Orlycia," Fractious 5 addressed her after the others had left the room. "You have given me cause to ponder, your planet and race have presented me with the most puzzling of situations I've ever encountered. You easily read and perceive parts of me which I have been forced to hide from others of my race.

"My conditioning works diligently to filter out and suppress those deeper perceptions. In the empire I've occupied, anyone who might even begin to harbor doubts as to the correctness of Arian thought is quickly brought under control. And yet you see right through my most effective shields and look through my thoughts and behaviors as if I stood naked to your gaze."

"Fractious 5, you think your apparent victories here are historic, but these campaigns of yours should be more likened to dust in the wind. You seek to control and seek to gain status only by actions. You and your race have waged such destruction upon so many worlds that you've lost your compassion seeking this illusion of control.

"I tell you now, Prime Director, or whatever you wish to

call yourself, although you appear to hold the destiny of my life and the entire population of this world under your command, I assure you the grasp you believe you have upon its citizens is weakening. Your savage ways and your domination by violent control will be short-lived upon all your planets.

"Your high command may inflict itself upon us temporarily. It may try to eliminate you and exchange your ruler for another, but your radiation and mental patterns are not valid here. Your self-styled image of serving yourselves at a cost to all other lives in the universe will no longer be tolerated upon my world or any other."

Orlycia paused to peer directly into his heart. "For you, this is not a visit of political appeasement. You have no idea of how easily my race can look into your heart to read what truly lies there. Fractious 5, you have performed a lifetime of honorable service for your race. You have obeyed your superiors. Now, the Universal Law of Attraction has drawn your life and your consciousness here."

He stood in silence.

"You came here to grant me the generous political favors of allowing me to keep my residence as my own, and to be able to use my private incubator should I become with child. You think if I am allowed to remain in my home with Yeto, my only supporting staff, this action might justify the violence and abuse your leadership and your race has inflicted upon all of us; the true children of Aryll.

"You have been counseled by another of my tribe. I can read the frequency of Moria in you. What moves in you is deeper than those thoughts you would not like your superiors to know. After almost three years of planetary directorship, you are beginning to experience erosion and doubts about your state education and programming. You begin to perceive how the violence of your invasion thrust upon my world gives little satisfaction for your spirit. Your mind control and conditioning programs are developing cracks."

Orlycia spoke with the gentle firmness of her function. "You best be careful, Fractious 5. Aryll is a powerful planet. Her intelligence was responsible for sending the unspoken signal into the universe that your crude conquering race responded to. You were invited here only to serve as a catalyst for her great Changeover. There is not a simplistic way to explain these things to you, but it is a foundation of true reasons why you are feeling the deep doubts and personally tortured conflicts from your inner being self."

Orlycia laughed. "It has been said that if you were to utter the word SECRET in a room full of clairvoyants, they would all break out in laughter. You have arrived upon a world full of sensitives."

Fractious 5 wrinkled his face into a partial smile himself. "I think I begin to understand. And this is why we have met. What purpose can be served that I, who serve the Arian Empire, can be so easily humbled by someone, not of my race? Someone I am expected to rule and to govern, and to control by the all-powerful, fear and trembling image, I should represent to you and your race?"

"When a soul is confronted with a real unknown, its first reaction will be of fear. Your natural fear, Prime Director 87, should naturally be heightened. You've been drawn to Aryll as part of a larger unknown than you've ever encountered before. Your mind may react quickly enough to rationalize these fears away, but I believe your inner being has brought you here to face the fear of this unknown in another way."

"You suggest I might serve a greater purpose here?"

"This planet is ancient. This planet is maternal. She possesses an intelligence that your race has yet to understand. The fact you are here at all, the fact you have come here to communicate with me in person, tells me you are more than just the sum of your training, mind controlled education and military and political accomplishments. There are no accidents in the universe. Questions will continue to grow within you as much as you are open to them. Are you ready to experience this awakening? Stay here and you will feel the experience. Or will the weight of your dark history hold your spirit in its bondage?

"Fractious 5, you think you've only brought disaster and pain by your conquest, as I previously said. You will soon leave us for a posting upon yet another distant star, never knowing the joy you have secured for us here."

"How can you speak of joy, Orlycia? I've represented all that's been destructive upon your world."

"No, Fractious 5, you are part of a much larger picture here, far beyond all that. Forces are at play you could never have learned about from your Arian programming. We all stand upon the leading edge of an even greater journey than you can imagine. This reference is personal, about your life journey, not the ride inside a spaceship your body will be forced to make."

Startled by the force and directness of Orlycia's delivery, he said, "Few words can express how you've touched me with your revelations and forthcomings. I need time to digest this information. Please be assured, I will justify to my superiors that no more interference shall disturb you here."

"Allow our sympathetic thought vibrations into yourself

that they may assist the acceleration of your inner journey. This acceleration is possible because it is of your will to raise your consciousness. The destiny of Aryll's Changeover was foretold to us long ago. Yeto and I chose to remain here to be in service to this great affair. We were aware of the hardships we would physically endure. Please sit and rest. I 'm now willing to reveal something to you on trust. My body has recently confirmed to me I am with child."

He nodded at this new information and did as instructed.

"You, in your desire to treat me fairly, have issued orders that will guarantee my rights to keep my child here in my private incubator. You have no idea what a boon you have granted by that action. Yeto and I are dedicated to serving our planet by nurturing and training this male offspring. With your heartfelt granting of that permission, nothing in your Arian Empire's presence will be able to change that."

He had little difficulty hiding his surprise. "Orlycia, it seems more than I thought was possible. I am very pleased. Something I've done may provide easement from the unfortunate cruelties my orders forced you both to withstand."

"There is more to reveal to you. Something that will inspire you. Something which you will carry within as your life's journey takes you off this world. I'll explain to you a myth core of your culture. As your race moved to conquer the universe, your race was driven by the myth of the Cave of the Arians."

He registered surprise on his face. "How do you know of this? I've heard this legend from my earliest days, but I thought it was a tale to inspire soldiers with a sense of history and pride. Like a marching song to move us into battle."

"It is not a tale. The cave does exist, and not just in your myths. True stories like this are often repeated to teach simplistically. Your warrior-based culture has drawn its strength from an ancient Roman culture started by the legend of Aeneas. This figure still inspires Arian expansion into space. As the legend goes, he had both divine and royal parents."

"You've read my mind for this knowledge?"

"It is at this point I should remind you, if a legend has been at play long enough, its believers will speak of Gods. That should be a God with a small 'g.' For any real understanding, you should substitute the word 'visitor.' The Laws of the Universe, when demonstrated in technologies or abilities unknown to a primitive culture, usually get translated thusly.

"Your gods were beings with more freedom to travel, and by your legends and many other stories relating their behaviors, there certainly was no guarantee of their honorable behavior with the local population. Accounts of such visitors rarely fail to include affairs and mating with the local women."

A blissful, relaxed state had settled upon the mind of Fractious 5, but his perceptions were focused and acute. Orlycia continued. "Aeneas is said to have been given a crystal of great power that he lodged inside a golden statue. He was told as long as he had this statue and the crystal in his possession it could reveal and inspire his followers to greatness. Even now, this history justifies the proud expansions the Empire has laid claim to. They have always asserted they were destined to rule the stars."

"These are only stories to saturate the minds of Arians in their sleepbeds."

"Not so. You must remember these were given as gifts from any Gods. These are real, physical technology-producing objects. Your high priests of the Temple of Aeneas still read passages from those ancient works, do they not? There remains a curiosity to locate the Cave of the Arians where this statue and its crystal of power are said to reside. Am I correct?"

"Yes."

"And in that legend, within that Cave of the Arians, that golden statue still anchors the power and focus for your Arian culture. It and other artifacts were carried off the world by your old gods to draw their descendants, by inspiration, to leave Earth and conquer new planets far out into space."

"Yes, Orlycia, but how is it you speak of our greatest teachings in such detail?"

"Has anyone ever gone back to Earth to regain possession of this mythical cave with its gifts and its golden prize?"

"I have heard of attempts being made, but so far I know of no success in this."

"Then I will clarify this whole affair. The Arian Cave is located here on Aryll."

"That's not possible."

"Yes, it is. Centuries ago your early ancestors traveled here after they acquired the interspace technology to leave Earth. They were even harsh and war-like then, and they attempted to conquer our planet.

"The natural technologies of my people were far too advanced for them to do so. We had developed both weapons and defense systems to protect ourselves. Your ancestors were easily defeated in their attempts to conquer us. We saw no point in violent retribution upon your ancient forefathers. We offered them a chance to retreat from our world in exchange for one concession."

"And what was that?"

"We kept the golden statue and other relics your gods had

given your race. We lodged them deep within our mountains in a cave they would never find. To this day, the cave remains here, sealed from all detection by cloaking. It is here in our starlight dimension."

"But what good would come of that action? Was it for punishment or a tribute?"

"Neither. Fractious 5, our council of elders is very wise. They did not use that power of influence. They understood our race could not change the path of conquest your ancients were set upon. In their long view, however, using their acutely developed cosmic perceptions, they observed something else. One day the savage traits of your Arian race would be of vital importance for OUR future."

"You're telling me the vile Arian conquest I led has a value? This action was fulfilling prophecies concerning your Changeover?" Fractious 5 was flooded with relief in the realization he'd not caused all this arbitrary pain and suffering in vain. "Why this is important now? We came to invade and to conquer your world with Arian aggression."

"Because, my dear Prime Director, Aryll can transmute your aggressive actions into the exact, volatile, catalytic force trigger she needs to facilitate her planetary changes. She needed the fire of your energy to be returned here to spark her great Changeover."

"Your Prime Director One is aware of the increasing energy needs of your race. He knows if he is to retain his weakening mind control, if he is going to continue to alter Arian life under his domination, he MUST possess these artifacts of power. Obviously, he's not revealed the true reasons he is so desperate to find these treasures."

"Is that why Prime Director One planned have me killed?

To get me out of his ambitious way?"

"Be at peace. You are a young race. Your leaders do not work well together. You will eventually give up these immature behaviors. He embodies the worst of your empire's leaders."

Moved with new purpose, he blurted out, "I must leave you now. Orlycia, Yeto. You have given me so much to ponder. I'll take this knowledge with me, and work toward these higher understandings until I die."

"There is no such thing as death, Fractious. When you leave the body you now inhabit, think again upon Aryll. That frequency can return here to learn, to be nourished, and to grow in deeper understandings in another less temporal form. Be well in your travels, Fractious 5. We'll meet again if you so choose."

"Orlycia, even if they send me light years away, I'll not forget you, but I have something vital to do before I leave."

As he exited the palace and entered his craft, his thoughts were dominated by that new future, He was determined. He'd carve it out for himself and for all other Arians s. *I'll not leave here, now. If I overlook my orders and set a new course for the highest mountains, I could be the one to finally stand within the Cave of the Arians. I could rekindle the gifts of our gods for the good of my race. Even if I fail Orlycia, I'll not forget these revelations. Even if they may kill me, my memories shall never surrender this experience.*

# PRIME DIRECTOR 32

Slight pomp and ceremony were afforded the newly appointed Planetary Director 32 as he arrived on Aryll 8's Spaceport Landing Facility. Harcos 86, acting Planetary Communications Command, and former colleague, met him.

"We have a situation, sir. This has been coming on for some time, Aries 45."

"We've been assigned together before, but now you will address me using my proper planetary rank and official title. We both know this will benefit our careers more favorably if we work together to shape this new assignment, from that more progressive platform."

"Of course, Prime Director 32. It won't happen again."

"We both served under Fractious 5's military command, but we're not the same wild young men who entertained thoughts of greatness on Regulis 3. There will be times to exchange stories once my new administration gets established."

"I understand you fully, sir. To continue my report, former Planetary Director 87 has pirated an airship and is attempting to elude our capture. His last message to Arian Air Command contained some ravings about pursuing the legendary Cave of the Arians. He has declared his intent to rediscover the true spirit of Arian greatness."

"Send this out as my first order, Harcos 86.

To all Arian Occupational Forces: Capture former Prime Director 87 or shoot him down. This reassigned official has obviously gone insane or lost all sense of Arian honor and service to duty. As combat-trained professionals, we have all witnessed this kind of programming breakdown before.

With Fractious 5, even a man of his experience and training can become stressed beyond his final breaking point when driven too heavily by the pressures of his office."

Prime Director 32 added, "Dispatch our best pilots to track him down and bring him in. Use emergency override controls if necessary to redirect that ship. Whatever he thinks he's doing with this madness will not be tolerated under my command. We must find him and either eliminate him or reroute him safely to his reassignment upon Zon 14."

"Right away, sir."

# FRACTIOUS 5 APPREHENDED

By use of a master override upon his flight controls, the former Prime Director 87 was captured in flight and brought back to the Capacity to stand before his replacement.

"Aries 45, I know you've been sent here to replace me. I understand what you've been charged to do here. Your desire to evoke your vile stericyclation plans will end in failure."

Prime Director 32 made a great show of addressing him as a public example of power. "Fractious 5, you will submit to the orders of our most high Prime Director One. You have been ordered to a reassignment upon Zon 14. These two soldiers, and your second in command, Maximus, will accompany you in the fulfillment of that command."

"I am prepared to leave you to this world, Aries 45, but I ask you to allow me to change this uniform and wash my hands of any responsibilities for leadership decisions you may execute upon this planet after I'm gone. I love this planet. She will honor my desire to disconnect from any trace of your forthcoming tainted rule."

Prime Director 32 waved approval and a clean uniform, and portable washstand was provided. "Fractious 5, you have been absolved of all responsibility for any future decisions. After accepting reassignment upon Zon 14, no one will link you to this planet, ever again."

He stood on the launching pad of his future. "Prime Director 32, I'd like to make one last address before I depart."

Aries 45 nodded for him to continue.

"I want to address this planet, its tribeflocks, and all true Arians within reach of this pronouncement. I, Fractious 5, make a vow to this Mother-Bearer planet, and to all her children. I shall never cease to support the elevation you will soon experience into your next phase of universal development. I commend you as you move into that glorious future. I hope one day to return and bear witness to your glory.

"And to all true Arians, I promise you I shall never cease in my attempts to free the true hidden treasures held within our mutual spirit. May we all truly discover the highest calling the gods have charged us with."

Prime Director 32 signaled the two standing guards to escort him and Maximus as they boarded the departing spacecraft. The hatches locked behind them, and the craft departed leaving Fractious 5 with a clear mind concerning his future.

# TERI 38, INCUBATOR INSPECTOR

The oldest inspector, Teri 38, reached his destination and he had a job to do. Before him, perched naturally upon this high point of the land, sat the former royal palace. It had not suffered damage from the assault, so its yellow transparent metals gleamed in the fading sunlight.

He removed his helmet to wipe his balding head and smoothed the wiry gray hairs that had twisted under the headband. He was already thinking of the meal and the shower-wash he'd get after he went off duty, and maybe a glass or two of cold froe beer. He had a few friends, but food and drink were always dependable and steady companions.

He replaced his helmet, gathered up his folder of forms, straightened his uniform, and approached the door of the old building. He found the cadence of a marching step helped remind his aging body of his official task, but he didn't continue it for long. Today is only another day; he reminded himself. Just finish this inspection, and another shift would be complete.

He'd walked this beat for years now, and he'd never once been called upon to meet or deal with its residents that he knew as former Queen Orlycia and Yeto. The building showed no signs of war. A natural feeling of grace and peace lingered.

Teri 38 tucked in his uniform up front where his growing stomach was fighting to ease over his utility belt. He even touched the hand plate, a respected local custom of this planet, to give an audio signal before he entered the structure. An older quiet-faced native man wearing a dark cape appeared in the open doorway.

"I am Yeto," was all he said.

"I've come for the private incubator inspection." Teri 38 tried to sound official as he received a gesture to proceed. Entering to follow Yeto's lead, he couldn't help but notice the slow dignity of the native's walk. Its grace was definite, even though this old native appeared to be only a servant, part of the original staff.

Teri 38 observed the burn marks on Yeto's neck and remembered he saw when the man's wings were removed years earlier. He was the first to experience loss of his wings. His was the first, and then all others followed during those terrible days of the mass surgery camps.

Teri 38 had seen many domination techniques used upon races of other newly conquered planets over the years. What he witnessed in the actions ordered by Prime Director 87 was somehow different.

He was never unduly cruel in his reign, for an Arian; he never seemed inspired about doing his job. No wonder they had long since demoted and transferred him down in rank to a mere inspector.

Teri 38 understood some things. This continuing leniency would cost the newly appointed replacement, Prime Director 32, nothing in political popularity ratings.

Besides, Orlycia's presence was easily explained to superior officials as a hostage. The fact she was about to produce an offspring only strengthened the empire's ability to maintain a stranglehold on her life.

As they crossed the great hall, the servant pivoted his face almost completely around on his neck with a look from his piercing eyes. Teri 38 shuddered a little as he remembered his tribeflock had such flexible abilities. Yeto touched an interior doorplate and opened a door into a set of private living suites.

These quiet rooms remained as possibly the last refuge of a serenity long gone from this world.

# INSPECTION TIME

Orlycia stood with her back to Teri 38 and Yeto looking out the tall windows. She could easily read the thoughts of this intruding Arian. It stirred her memories back to Prime Director 87 and the reasons she was still allowed to live here in the palace.

These minor Arian recognitions now afforded to her seemed meager indeed. She'd been allowed to live in her museum, and to have one member of her staff, but was also considered a prisoner under house arrest.

Teri 38 wondered if Orlycia would recognize him, forgetting that her mind heard all that.

An illuminated, life-sized Pictart of the former male ruler hung in the great hall. A startling vitality, calm, and determination shone in the king's face. Here pictured was a man of strength flying through the clouds. His sleek, regal wrapcape billowed between the wide spread of his wings. Teri 38 was still thinking about it there, high upon the wall. So much so that he failed to realize Orlycia had long since turned and now watched him and heard his thoughts.

"That is a Pictart of my king and my life mate," she spoke quietly.

"I've never seen anything like it." The inspector managed to reply. He had always been shy around women, and he was a bit tongue-tied at the beauty of this benevolent creature. She had recovered from when he'd first seen her during the wing clipping. She seemed filled with power and mystery. He felt drawn into her gaze.

He shook himself out of her spell, and in his best official voice he said, "I'm Inspector Fourth Class Teri 38, here in an official capacity to register and inspect your private grow nest, survey number 10050078."

"I know you, Teri 38," she sighed, "You are the first Arian who ever showed me any civilized behavior. You were there at the first wing cropping; ordered to stand only as a witness. You were only meant to observe the actions of that ceremony. You, however, were flooded by realizations your heart could not abide.

"You broke rank, jumped onto the stage, and expressed all the healing care for me you could muster. Your response to that situation did draw in the healing energies I needed at that moment. You unconsciously demonstrated to me your race does carry seeds of evolutionary greatness within them, even though much of those qualities remain suppressed in your race by the entanglement-mind control of your leadership. Yes, Teri 38, I remember your kindness from so long ago."

Orlycia spoke as she turned. "The nest is this way."

# THE OFFICIAL INSPECTION

Yeto drew back a curtain to reveal the small incubator area. The soft glow of lights whirled and ebbed in multicolor radiance from top and bottom of the nest. Its arched cover caught small reflections of that light. Steady, clear sounds of its background tones which flowed together like music filled the air around them. There in the center, nestled in soft feather-like down, was Orlycia's unborn offspring.

He busied himself recording the temperature, atmosphere, amniotic nutrient values, and size of her unborn child's membranous egg. All these features were noted and logged. "What doses of Gene 10 and Ar-15 does the egg receive?" Teri 38 asked, as his bureaucratic registration questions wore on.

There was a silent moment before Orlycia in a flat and controlled voice replied. "For these last days before birthing, I have enough doses on hand for the administration of the required 100 units per day."

Yeto stiffened his posture, standing guard, poised and ready in the corner of the room closest to the back of the Arian inspector. Yeto's right hand moved under his cape to touch the handle of the ornate dagger he held in readiness should he need to defend this unborn child.

Teri 38, insensitive to any tensions in the room, moved to the last of the questions on his inspection form. "Are there any noticeable luminescence or bright light shining from within the egg? Are there any signs of noticeable wing development?"

Arian Science has mutated these genetic developments of this native race for its continued harmony. Those confident thoughts, those official dictums rang in Teri 38's ears. Those questions seemed so brief and so simple on the state registration forms.

The brightness and the atmosphere of the lights altered Teri 38's focus from that temporal moment. The incubator lights triggered Teri 38's mind back to the pains and disorientation of his past, and their failed efforts to control his mind. He still had vivid recall of that static hiss from the audio-sleep programming, the shorting wire connections of his teach-bed; always shocking him with stinging pains as he tried to sleep. Now his brain responded to those memory shocks by having a small seizure shutdown.

For a moment, his mind thought he could see brightness within the egg, or perhaps even the slight flutter of tiny wings, but then he was carried again back to clouded memories.

Yeto stood poised and registered Teri 38's mental distraction. He waited, deadly attentive, hand on his dagger, ready to strike. Orlycia, tense to protect her infant, started to hum a song to ease her tensions. She hummed to calm herself, to calm her unborn son, and it unexpectedly started to calm Teri 38 as well.

Teri 38 felt the natural love Orlycia radiated to her unborn. Emotion flooded over him that he'd never experienced before. He'd been genetically born in a tank without parents.

He moved closer, both to cover his nervousness, and to complete his official look at the egg's translucent shell as it reclined within the nest. Cautiously, Orlycia moved her shadow to dim and shield even the lights of the ceiling unit. Her heart pounded as Teri 38 logged his findings. He recorded a negative check mark onto the slate:

NO luminosity.

The comment, "You'll not find any wings, either," nervously slipped from Orlycia in the tensioned silence.

Teri 38 could smell her. She was very close to him now. He momentarily became distracted by her mysterious, inviting smells; sweet, and light, and airy. He struggled with the distraction.

"But we both know I have to check." He sighed, meeting her gaze. He was melted by the unspoken concern in her soft eyes. Even though he'd never known a mother's touch or a mother's love, he could feel hers.

"Those are my orders, ma'am." He managed to fake his best clear and official tone. He moved to get a closer better look.

Orlycia returned to humming a soft lullaby for her unborn son. His egg nestled into the soft down of her family's traditional birthing nest. The down of this incubator had been placed there, feather by feather, by generations of her ancestors. She hummed now for her unborn to stay calm, not to stir lest his tiny wings move into view, and not to reveal his true nature.

Teri 38 found her lullaby soothing to his mind as well. He'd never had massive seizures, but he would slip into an open-eyed stare sometimes. He'd gotten the reputation for being dull, half-witted, and lazy. Now he felt his mind slipping into another seizure-stare.

He tried to fake his condition as one of intense focus, but Yeto and Orlycia were clairvoyant. Their minds read his quiet withdrawal. They held their responses; waiting for his body's actions to re-animate in his duties. Yeto's hand poised steadfast upon his dagger. Orlycia continued her song.

Teri 38 finally clicked back to conscious awareness. He jerked slightly and knocked over a small stand next to the incubator. His embarrassment accelerated his personal involvement. His mind screamed.

*They saw your mind falter. Get away from them. Just finish up and go! No one can be allowed to see your weakness. You will be culled as a diseased one!*

He blinked to appear efficient and behaved casually to cover his momentary blackout. He gave another quick, perfunctory glance, then scribbled on his forms. For the last question, "Any noticeable wing development?"

Teri 38 checked Negative.

# DRING PASSES INSPECTION

With tensions broken, Teri 38 stood away from the nest, put on the appearance of efficiency, and gathered his forms and test results. Orlycia turned her eyes to Yeto and covered her sigh of relief. Yeto maintained his alertness, but slowly withdrew his hand from the knife handle under his wrapcape.

"Notify the state incubator officials promptly after the time of its birth. There will likely be one inspection after the birth and another before he begins his training and work assignments. I'm aware your species matures more rapidly than ours. You will be allowed to keep him here with you only through his early season of growth. The State will then assume direction of your offspring's education and work out performance ratings for his training and employment. They'll decide what to do with him."

As the inspector turned to leave, he found Yeto close enough at his elbow to reach out and touch him. Somewhat startled, Teri 38 turned back to Orlycia.

"It is a male. Isn't it?"

"Yes." A small smile caught the corners of her mouth, "It is a male. I shall call him Dring."

Yeto was relieved to swing and secure the great door behind the inspector. "I am thankful I was not called to perform a deadly duty this day."

Inside the nest, Dring's young royal life stirred. The luminosity from his egg shimmered in the light, and within it, he stretched his wings.

Orlycia found herself flooded with new resolve. "Thank you, Mother-Bearer. Your steadfastness helped spare my unborn offspring. My oath to you is strengthened. Yeto and I will train him to fulfill his destiny."

# STATE INCUBATOR

Philis 56 questioned her more senior partner on the consulting staff. "I don't understand. The normal vaccination doses of Gene 10 don't seem to be causing a response on this new arrival. The extra 50 mg solution dose has not only failed to produce the proper dulling effect; the luminosity seems almost more persistent in its attempt to reoccur. Also, the term-life birth of egg 34 is long overdue. Shall I consult the doctor?"

Her more seasoned staff supervisor, Boni 6, took it all in stride. "No. Just double the doses of Gene 10; that usually does it."

"You've done this before?"

"Tell anyone else and I'll deny it, but yes, several times when I got bored, and when it takes too long to fill out extra request reports. These native egg-things are tough. I'll tell you, one of them had to be injected with over 420 mg of Gene 10 just to stunt his wings, and then the outside membrane had to be surgically removed when he was trying to be born."

Philis 56 gulped out, "Cut off him?"

Her more senior companion nodded. "Affirm fact! Usually, they pop out, but filling him full of that much Gene 10 thickened up the inside of the membrane. It felt like leather boot material, but that little guy was still singing. He never lost that slight glow they get inside."

"Does the staff have any answers for that?"

"No, they've been trying to figure this out the entire time we've been occupying this miserable planet." Boni 89 was definite. "Even just since you've been assigned here. I've seen standard doses increased three times in the last three months."

"What happens if the medicine stops working on them?"

"Maybe they'll just be eliminated. Maybe those rumors for that stericyclation procedure are correct. A word to the wise. Don't ask sensitive questions like that in front of the wrong people. Our success here is being watched closely. Rumor has it Prime Director 32 was newly promoted to take up a planetary leader position on some inside track from Prime Director One. His career in the Arian body politic is rising, and they say he means to make a success of this world."

Philis 56 caught the tone. "Right, just follow orders and stay out of the way, correct fact?"

"Wear the shielding thick on your posterior, as some might say."

"Right!"

# AFTER THE INSPECTION

Yeto breathed a sigh of joy and relief as the door was closed and locked behind the Arian.

Beyond all probability, the egg passed Arian inspection! This day would be celebrated throughout all the histories of Aryll. He thought *Dring will never taste their chemical poisons and our young prince will be born with wings.*

Back in her innermost chambers, Orlycia rose from her rest and looked out over the changing profiles of the city that had once been her domain. Raised to be royalty and trained from an early age in the ancient songs, she would be ready for the Changeover. That chosen honor was hers alone, and she found herself willingly in service to this great female principle. Aryll regulated her populations by unseen signals.

Answering her prayers for fertilization, her body finally responded to just such a signal before this birthing. She had almost given up hope. Ages ago she'd experienced physical love with her absent life mate Ospra. Within the three-year span since the invasion, she had nearly reached the time limits for any possible gestation period. But Ospra stayed true to his promise. Even now, focusing upon her life mate's image on the Pictart, she was aware of his presence. His mind spoke to hers, again.

*These years have been long for you, my love.* Her King's mental voice registered in her mind with inflections of great tenderness, *Soon the time will appear when those of you who stayed behind will be elevated and return here to safety.*

*Our son is destined to be catalytic within all this. His frequency alone can trigger the Changeover. He will be a crucial, activating, integral part of Aryll's final and complete transformation.*

The king's thoughts were oft with her. The Arians knew nothing of this, of course, because they weren't attuned to the unseen dimensions of this or any other planet's deeper life.

The technology of the Pictart was created by essence art. Its living holographic image was in total sympathetic resonance to any life it depicted. In this case, to the king now dwelling in an unseen, living dimension of this world with most of its population.

Orlycia peered into the nest. "There is much you will need to learn very quickly, Dring."

The outer membrane that had once been a tough and rubbery shell was now becoming very thin and transparent.

Her unborn, fledgling within was calm. His eyes looked up to her through the shell, and he smiled. He was completely attuned to her and their Planet-Mother, Aryll, at that moment. And, it was rapidly growing time for her son's arrival. Orlycia felt it.

She could tell that as she registered his life radiations beginning to increase within the egg. With insistent regularity, his singing tones and harmonic songs were beginning to increase. Their energy surges which started slow moved now on louder waves of sound. These tones would soon be strong and clear enough to engage the universal sonoluminescent forces of this cold fusion process.

As inevitable as the tides which move the great seas, his birthing time neared.

# TO THE AGRI-CAMPS

"Well, Teri 38, I think we've finally found a place to make use best of your individual talents." Dracus 128 spoke from behind his desk.

"And where would that be, sir?" Teri 38 recognized this tone of voice. He'd heard words like this his entire military career whenever he was about to be fired from a position. Some officer was always trying to make it sound like re-assignment would be good for him, but it was usually a duty station no one else wanted.

"Yes, soldier, we're going to assign you an area of responsibility more suited to your talents. There won't be any upgrade in rank at this time, you understand, but if this assignment works out, well, let's just say it would be demonstrative of your great value to the empire. Recognition for your accomplishments is bound to follow."

"Might I then ask again just what this new assignment would be, sir?"

"Certainly, soldier." He handed Teri 38 an envelope. "Your orders and your shuttle travel info are in this new duty packet. You're taking over supervision of one of our Agri-Field locations. You'll be shipping out immediately. Is that clear, soldier?"

Teri 38 accepted the folder. "Yes sir, perfectly clear, sir.

Do I get any orientation training for this new assignment?"

"You received all the training you'll need previously. It's all explained in your new duty packet. Dismissed."

He managed to give Dracus 128 a parting salute before the officer's door slammed shut behind him.

Returning to his quarters, Teri 38 packed his meager bag of uniform-issued-possessions. Living in state camps and military school training, he had never felt any real roots. He was always a little different, always on the outer edges of programmed activities. He was barely able to force his mind to create a convincing act, even during rallies or public assemblies. Other soldiers sensed no enthusiasm in his repeated responses, so they made fun of him or enjoyed letting him be the butt of their bad humor.

"Maybe my life will all work itself out eventually. Maybe I'll find a friend. Maybe I'll be recognized for something good. Maybe my next commanding officer will write up an official compliment report on me. Maybe there's room to take a walk out there. I'm in good shape for that from my street duty. And maybe tomorrow will be better than today."

# TERI 38 LEAVES THE CAPACITY

Teri 38 rode the moving walkway toward the air shuttle depot. Observing the passing incoming traffic, he was drawn to a fresh face. It was a woman officer arriving from some off-world duty.

Philomystic rank bars covered her upper arm. Those special class officers were trained to extract, exploit, and secrete native technologies from each of its conquered worlds.

They passed each other, progressing opposite directions on the moving walkway.

A weary Cest 21, the Philomystic First Class, looked up from her orientation packet. She'd arrived on Aryll 8 from Zon 14 by a regular troop carrier. Even after hitching rides on dozens of carriers over the years, she always found it to be a learning experience. But now she felt eyes on her from the outward-bound lane. An odd feeling rushed through her. Their eyes connected for a moment. It drew her to focus more intensely on Teri 38.

Something else caught her about this old outbound trooper. Something unusual shone out from that lost look in his eyes. She turned it over in her mind. He appeared to be shipping out to the frontier somewhere.

Then the moving walkway carried them in opposite directions. The transitional moment was gone; they passed with only that one, brief exchange of a look. For Cest 21, it was her job to observe. She'd observed that haunting look before. Why did she find it so compelling now?

It was late in the day. Assigned to a transient traveler's room in the shuttle bay, she could report officially for her new assignment tomorrow.

# THE BIRTHING TIME

Deep in meditation within his private quarters, Yeto found his past lingering there only as a distant dream. Memories of his youth from the Owlaface tribeflock and his apprenticeship days becoming an adept in the starlight arts of Prana-Bindu filled his mind. Then Orlycia beamed him an urgent mental signal that cut directly through Yeto's reverie.

*Yeto, come at once! My son is about to appear. His birth is upon us!*

The birthing song began: Deep within the birthing chamber, in the Caverns of Amenti,

Lies the threshold; appearance portal.

Placing egg newly upon it. Thus, the birthing can continue.

Fulfill the ancient prophecy. And let the Changes ring!

---

Orlycia carried her son's egg in a soft cloth; the membrane rapidly becoming thinner and more transparent. Inside it, the soft hum of his songs and the inner glow of its energy process radiated bright enough to beam light up through the fabric. Yeto guided their way through the great hall to the back of the inner chapel.

"We must hurry, Yeto." Orlycia was insistent. "He's

moving quickly into the last phases of his song before his emergence."

Yeto, pressing his palm over a concealed hand plate, and heard it respond in a resonant harmonic note. A portion of the wall opened to reveal the downward proceeding corridors behind. Cool air moved over them as they rapidly entered to continue their journey. The wall closed and sealed itself behind as they passed.

The natural caverns beneath the palace held the acoustically designed birthing chamber. Cool stones clicked under their feet, and dim lights twinkled from the walls as they descended. Yeto watched over Orlycia closely that she not slip or stumble as she hurriedly carried her precious cargo.

The corridor lessened in size as they descended in a narrowing spiral. Each level focused them on to tighter landings.

Orlycia said, "We must take our positions and start the chanting immediately. The sounds of pure sonic tone levels coming from him are increasing in volume."

Soft lights shimmered and glowed greens and yellows from the walls. This huge natural chamber had been carved out and lined with polished transparent metal. Overhead the cathedral-like ceiling soared thirty feet upward into a perfect dome and a single golden pedestal font graced its center.

"We must hurry, Yeto. Help me place him in position." Her voice echo-amplified to fill this entire interior space with its sound. Designed with exacting auditory sciences, lights powered by the piezoelectrics from the massive, compression weight of stone pressing down upon the crystalline walls, this space was engineered to amplify every sound frequency with complete acoustical accuracy.

In their evolution, the children of Aryll refined bird-singing-languages not only communicated ideas. Discovering how emotion-driven songs could directly affect their physical, material universe, their ancient races developed understandings of sound wave application until it became one of their highest arts.

They practiced the use of sound waves for levitation and sustained flight. They became sensitive how to refine and anchor special sound resonances within living creation evolutionary processes. They found out how to accelerate the lucency of their birth Sonoluminescence and to facilitate this process itself.

Yeto assisted Orlycia in unwrapping the egg and helped to align it vertically within the deep, bowl-like top of the golden font. "He is now prepared. Let me escort you to your position."

She gave her son one more glance as Yeto steered her to her protected seat against one of the curved walls. Yeto then rapidly crossed the hall to a similar seat awaiting him directly across the chamber from her own.

Yeto began the birth chant. His voice increased in volume to activate this ceremony's special, resonant, harmonic echo of sound and frequency within this acoustical chamber. Orlycia joined his drone-like chant in her octave. Soon their two voices rose as one; building a precise, harmonic, unimpaired frequency match.

Responding in kind, the chamber joined its own sympathetic response to resonate, amplify, and return their sound's harmonic echo. Oscillating his song from within the font, Dring became totally attuned to the frequencies of the harmonies they chanted.

With increasing intensity, this sound was also intensified

by tribeflock members in the starlight dimensions. Feelings of love and support from millions of unseen witnesses poured in from their place in the universe.

Three lives' combined voices soared with triadic accord. Their music palpated throughout the surrounding structure. Their chanting tones resonated off the walls, the lights, and the pedestal font. Its sound waves accelerated the egg to vibrate in a rhythm sympathetic to the tone of their unified voices.

Their plangent acoustical waves activated mechanisms within the font. The securely held egg slowly became immersed in levels of warm electrolyte fluids. Yeto and Orlycia increased the fervor of their chant toward its crescendo, and the chorus frequency of voices continued to radiate in kind from their unseen world.

Imperceptibly at first, but then more urgently, the surface of the egg began to quiver. The electrolyte fluids, responding to this sonic alchemy, glowed more brightly as the urgency of cavitation increased. Soon the liquids pulsed wildly upon its surface. Then a total synchronicity; energy pulses from the egg, the resonance from the chanting, and the wavelengths of all energy vibrations filled the chamber in a harmonic.

Within the egg, Dring's unborn body became even more restless and animated. His arms, legs, and tiny wings were reflexing almost in a ballet as the sound, light, frequency and fluid movements converged. Bubbles formed within the egg's amniotic fluids as internal temperatures pushed close to the nuclear plasma range.

Finally, the egg's outer membrane succumbed and burst into a vibrant, fiery ball of light. Fluids erupted from the font and sprayed out into the chamber like the burning sequins of a skyrocket and instantly evaporated. The chamber totally glowed in resonance to this climactic miracle. Even the ground shook and echoed beneath their feet.

As the last echoes faded, Yeto and Orlycia paused in their chanting. In the afterglow of this ecstasy, Prince Dring, newborn heir to the Raptor tribeflock throne of Aryll, sat up in the font with a laugh and a gurgle to wiggle his wings.

Orlycia sank back exhausted into her protected seat. She held back momentarily to observe the last of Dring's birth fluids evaporate, to form a hazy pink fog around her son, then dissipate before he outstretched his arms and wings and demanded to be picked up.

# ARYLL SINGS HIS BIRTH

Across the planet, Arians and natives alike were curious about the trembling of the soils beneath their feet. Alarms screamed out from vibration sensors. The tremors and sounds of howling traveled for miles and through the walls of every structure.

"It was ghoulish." some said.

One Arian claimed, "It sounded like the shrieking whale-fish of Popol 54."

"I've never heard anything like it on any planet." said another battle-weary veteran. "I've experienced some bizarre occurrences, but nothing disturbed me like this."

The trembling slowed but continued for almost an hour. The government scrambled patrols of gravity sleds to review the slight damage and attempt to identify the source of the disturbances. Their investigations proved nothing, causing those alerts to be soon recalled.

In his private chambers, a cold chill ran down Prime Director 32's spine. "I will find the source of all this," he muttered into his glass of brandy. "This is MY planet now, and I am in control here!"

# EVENTS WITHIN THE STATE INCUBATOR

The ground movement startled the state incubator's evening shift. Moreover, the dull sheen of the egg's amniotic fluids began a transformational change in their nests. Every egg held in incubation began to increase in lucency. Despite attempts at doubling injection doses of their poisons, one by one, every native egg switched from their insidious dull status to one of increasing light.

Alarms caused Regus 234 and Nero 42 to rush to each egg and check settings on temperature and their fetus motion detectors. From inside every egg membrane, internal light blazed blindingly bright. Temperature ranges kept rising within nearly three hundred eggs. Every egg in the building became luminous in response to a deafening sonic scream which echoed everywhere throughout the structure.

Philis 56 grabbed Boni 89. "Get some earplugs and follow me."

Doctor Zarius 88 said, "Stay calm, everyone. You have your emergency procedures. Follow them, and don't panic."

From within the eggs, the unborn began to voice themselves in song. Their combined chorus rang out from their membranes to match the harmonies and outside frequencies of the unknown screams surrounding them.

Marcus 342 recognized their songs and shouted at the

top of his lungs over the singing and the background sounds. "These eggs are moving toward a simultaneous birthing event. Protect yourselves when they start to explode!"

Each of these tiny lives were being moved by something far beyond the medical staff's understanding and control. The volume of their individual songs kept increasing as their planet rumbled beneath them.

"My god, those are birthing songs!" Regus 234 cried out. "Take cover!"

Nero 42 was lost in his aggravation. "It's coming from every damn one of them. What shall we do?"

Philis 56 grabbed Nero 42's shoulder to calm him down. "There's nothing we can do. These eggs are about to explode and be born."

Alarm bells screamed, staffers and doctors tried desperately to handle what appeared to be a mass birthing. The increasing volume of sounds and a brilliant radiance of diamond-clear light beamed out from every egg as their chorus of song was blending and growing in volume.

"My ears can't take much more of this." Boni 89 shouted as she covered her ears with her hands.

The crescendo of song from all three hundred eggs was piercing as every one of them reached its critical point. Staff members ducked and ran for cover as the eggs began to pop. One by one, membranes exploded into light, spraying their tainted fluids into the air, and onto the shelves and walls around them.

The wing nodes on their young bodies had been deformed by their poisons, but still, each fledgling vigorously burst from its membranous prison. The building reverberated to the melodious symphony of combined songs, flashing explosions of birthing, and with the clarity of a brilliant crystal light that blazed throughout the facility.

As the songs began to subside, and the light of these luminous births began to dim, one by one, the staff revealed themselves from their hiding places. While the egg holders remained, they were awash with putrid, tainted amniotic fluid.

All the babies were alive and gathering strength. Despite the scars and traces of deformed wing nubs and inability to fly, these young fledglings of Aryll's tribeflock were kicking and ready to grow. The cacophony of screams and cries were as deafening to the staff as their births had been.

Doctor Zarius 88 screamed over the din. "Call for all doctors and staff in the Capacity. We need all hands on call down here. Stat!"

# BACK AT CLUB ENLIST

Regus 234 entered the club and spotted Dracus 12 and Francus 534 at a side booth.

"You are never going to guess what happened. It started with the ground trembling and all those weird sounds. That was bad enough, but whatever happened certainly isn't going to be able to explain the light show and the fireworks I escaped. ALL the eggs birthed at the same time."

"All that happened from the noise and trembling?" Dracus laughed. "If they all birthed, you're going to be out of a job."

"It was right before I was supposed to get off my shift. Everything about this planet is bizarre! I stayed late and helped clean up the mess. Nobody ever expected all the eggs to burst simultaneously like that. I need a drink."

"I agree." Dracus waved his hand for service. "Everything about this place... bizarre...you can say that for sure."

Francus 534 was a little drunk but joined in.

Regus 234 added, "The doctors and scientists are still puzzling on how it happened. Scalar energy? Quantum leap? Good old-fashioned alchemy? The eggs just tuned themselves to those trembles. It must have been the right sounds, because all the eggs sucked up those tunes, and went nova!"

# ORLYCIA'S NEW OFFSPRING

Yeto helped Orlycia gather up her new son to return them to her private quarters. Dring fulfilled his first primary obligation of being a new winged male.

After their trek to the surface, they re-entered the great hall. Orlycia adjourned into her private chambers to tend to Dring, her new son. Yeto, now left alone, looked up to the Pictart of his King Ospra.

"I'm left here with your life mate, Orlycia. My oath to you and the council is firm. I will protect them until the Change-over and beyond. Dring's education must now take precedent over everything. He will grow and mature quickly. We both stand ready to help him."

Yeto's Owlaface tribeflock was more prone to the scholarly arts; the Doveal tribeflock tended toward domestic arts, creative expression, and well-being; and the Peeptweet tribeflocks happily embodied activity and service. Only the Raptors embodied leadership practices extending over the greater populations. Yeto knew all these skills.

"I will never fail you in Dring's training. I will emulate every confidence to him, and I will never allow him to doubt his ability to complete the monumental tasks his birthing lays before him.

"Will Dring accept this? Will he be able to weather the

accelerated training? Will he develop the skills and rise to the stature needed in these short time spans before the grand Changeover occurs? Will he willingly rise to this great opportunity for planetary service to guarantee all of our futures?"

"Never doubt me. I will honor your charge. He shall be ready." Yeto's heart soared at this promise.

# IN THE CAPACITY

Cest 21, Philomystic First Class, awakened to the trembling and noises in her temporary quarters grabbed her executive orders and jumped on the moving walkway toward the main headquarters.

She had developed her skills to near telepathic ability over the years, and used these journeys for practicing her personal sensitivities. A promotion? A change of location? A demotion? Perhaps chastisement for some rules infraction? She would read these things in the looks upon the faces of her travel companions; in the expressions of personnel, she traveled with. Originally, these skills were developed to be only an intrinsic part of her assignment duties.

Her official work always hinged upon research of newly conquered alien cultures. Cest 21's rank allowed her to keep living out assignments on planets forming the empire's outer perimeter edge. It allowed her more independence and freedom of choice. To recently vanquished races, she often represented their first contact with anything other than a hostile intruder, the Arian conqueror, and the victor appearing now only to gather spoils of war.

To that end, she learned native languages, studied psychologies, and questioned motives. Cest 21 had little use or need for the gadgetry of thought-sound-translation devices. She dedicated herself to learn and master native tongues whenever possible.

This understood, she now wasn't quite certain what was happening within her. Echoes of memorized Arian texts sounded more than just a little flat and hollow of life Even though she'd trained hard and achieved a top security clearance, moments of doubt often caused her focused mind to wander. Immersion in so many other world cultures, and mixing closely with lives so different to her own had become abrasive to her Arian conditioning and worn down her programming. Mental cracks appeared in their subtle control over her.

She brushed back her long auburn hair and sighed as she entered headquarters. She was tall for an Arian female; her rank also allowed her the privileges of more casual travel attires than her other military companions. Hard years under a variety of Suns etched more color and lines on her face than her thirty-five regular years might have done.

But the deepest cracks were in her Arian programming. They'd occurred in her last assignment deep out in the Great Green Sand Desert on Zon 14.

Her wise friend, a Puka on Zon 14, had told her, "My child, what you feel and experience is real. The essence-spark seed of its living knowledge will stay and grow within you whenever you are open in your quiet moments. Allow it in the right way. Continue to ask, continue to struggle. It will respond. Struggle on. Your future holds much more for you." The iridescent purple eyes of the old Puka flashed just the smallest enigmatic smile in her mind's eye.

Now she had been reassigned. But what was its real purpose? Despite her security training, that reassignment information was blocked from her.

# MONITORING MINDS

Cest 21's choice of lonely assignments over the years had been noticed. The Ranks of Accreditation and Monitoring began to register a drift from strict Arian Empire dogma in her reports. They'd seen this before. It was described as collateral damage for fringe personnel.

Philomystic researchers were prone to becoming distracted, going native, and slipping from Arian-sanctioned ways of field research. It was for just this reason this office monitored all reports for their regularity, their length, their views. They read all the journals and between the lines of all the journals. They scrutinized all platforms of communication, measuring their content for any drift away from Arian loyalty.

They had come to a decision about Cest 21. There was no doubt; they detected clear evidence of program erosion. Reassignment, retraining, and memory purging were ordered. Their simple recommendations included specific orders. This was to be her last independent assignment. Such strong independence of thought as she was demonstrating, could not swelter or be left too long. Not with a mind like hers. No telling what she might do.

This would already have been ordered except for the special duty order from Aryll 8's new Prime Director 32.

# CEST 21 AND PRIME DIRECTOR 32

Cest 21 was directed into a staff meeting already in progress in the Capacity Command Building. Prime Director 32, newly appointed planetary leader, addressed the representatives. Mottled, heraldry-colored attires of about fifty various military officials, scientists, doctors, and others filled the room. An image of Aryll 8 was upon the background screen.

Prime Director 32 spoke, "Some of you I have known and served with. Some of you have also been recently assigned here. Since I am also new to this command position, a full status review is in order from each of your respective areas. Anyone in attendance may stop this meeting to question for points of clarity." He smoothed his decorative toga.

"I'll make my statements clear and concise. This planet is very remote from our core, and the central star systems. By accepting this appointment, I've risen to the status and position of Planetary Director. This came as recognition for my years of loyal Arian service. I've been charged to reorganize this planet's occupation quickly, successfully, and profitably for the empire."

He pompously continued. "This has been a planet with a checkered past. Since the empire's conquest nearly three years ago, my predecessor Prime Director 87 supposedly did everything by the book, but with little results. He failed to discover anything to increase his success or recognition, or be effective. No startling scientific facts or technologies have appeared. After the initial invasion, he won no more battles to bolster his military valor, and he wasn't even decedent enough to win reputation disobeying orders as a tyrant.

"Now I'm stationed here. I have greater ambitions. This assignment offers me only another stepping stone in my career. With success on Aryll 8, I'll be in an advantage position to move on to a better world. Any of you who assist my rise to power will earn the right to be advanced in your careers with me." He took a dramatic stance, looking past the view screen's image of the planet's photo to the stars beyond it.

"The state's programs of Centralized Growth-Nurture Facilities have been a painfully slow implementing success here. Poor administration excuses were extended as to why this was so. Former leadership suggested unusual and mysterious events characterized this planet's initial conquest, and these same features continue to hamper successful planetary rehabilitation.

"The Arian Empire is built upon successful expansion and growth of its domains, not by bureaucratic rhetoric and excuses. The empire grows by the fruit of its branches."

Many audience members nodded in agreement. Scientists and officials puffed their chests a little and looked at each other seeking a united accord. The military ranks slightly stiffened their backs to attention. Long years of individual mind programming switched on automatic stimulus-word response from each.

"The empire does continue to grow and prosper at home and in its other branches. I have received personal dictums from our illustrious Prime Director One. His messages coming from Ariana have been very clear. Re-Education. Repetition Enforcement. Repeated Disciplines. These are his three R's for any long and bountiful rule."

After another dramatic pause, he gripped both sides of the podium and continued, "We've learned never to lose momentum as our great expansion moves forward. It has proven its truths and shown us to be bold, to be aggressive, and to show no mercy. Our glorious history has unfolded itself in victory after victory throughout this galaxy and in many others."

Fervor of applause broke into a roar from the assembly.

"Where native inhabitants are concerned, we've developed proven methods. Elimination by genocide of the adult majority successfully purges old cultural patterns. It lessens resistance and converts entire worldly populations quickly. It leaves the empire with an easily re-educated population mass. The young and adolescent are more easily and successfully programmed to establish dependence and accept dominance. Given this grand new citizenship opportunity, these younger members learn and thrive in the ways of their new Arian government."

He raised his fist to the sky. "The good of the state and permanent bonding to the empire is virtually guaranteed."

The audience cheered and applauded.

"Some members of our Central Senate have questioned these direct methods, but less stringent and less disciplined ways have always led to a history of trouble and insurrections later. I will not have this planet serving as mute testimony to that.

"My way of imminent leadership is to be loved and feared. I've studied all your files. I've hand-picked many of you to assist my great plans. If you are here to carve out your more successful future, then abide by my commands. Assist me with your insights. With your help, I shall turn this planet into a production success for all of us and for the empire."

The crowd again acknowledged his provocation with light applause.

Cest 21 listened from the back of the hall with her arms folded upon her chest. She was not so easily moved by this crowd's hollow applause. As a young Philomystic, she had long since learned to read this man. They'd even had a brief affair during cadet training. She had been young and naïve. He'd only been known as Aries 45 then. She knew to tread very carefully around his greater ambitions. He'd moved on because of her lesser ones.

He still retained that lean and hungry look, but now his eyes reminded her of the wolf-kind warriors of Mmiog 86. As strongly as those savage, animalistic beings seized their prey, this man strived for power, control, recognition, and he would stop at nothing to get it.

Cest 21 was more mature now. She'd learned much from her years of off-world experiences. One of her biggest lessons was to know when to keep quiet.

# HE LOOKED DOWN UPON THEM ALL

Prime Director 32 gestured broadly as he played to the crowd. "You know the history of our assault and conquer. Our intelligence reports monitored population numbers before the attack. The native and indigenous populations offered no resistance. Here in the Capacity, flags of the Arian Empire flew the very first day. However, when the smoke cleared, instead of millions of new subjects to conquer, sort, and reorder, we ended up with only a handful of natives."

Prime Director 32 faced them all down. "Important questions remain. Where have the others gone? How did they disappear so quickly? Are they waiting for a surprise attack upon our forces? This uncertainty has kept a full garrison of crack guards on alert and ready for nearly three years. We cannot put this picture together. Eventually, Prime Director 87 crumbled under its strain. It disrupted his retraining; he lost his disciples, and he allowed boredom and insubordination in his troops."

Satisfied to end his address on that note, he closed with, "My new staff members, confirm facts about quarters, assignments, and duties with my centurions. Everyone will be scheduled to report to me back here within one day. I will expect full reports and recommendations for each of your specified assignment areas."

He slowed the pace. "Remain here in attendance until you are dismissed. I will call upon many of you within this remaining day period. Others of you will be recalled privately after that time."

The assembled crowd stood to attention and applauded as he left the stage. After his exit, the crowd quieted and milled together, moved at clearing their assignments, and waited.

Cest 21 settled in to digest her readings concerning this meeting. She hoped she might be called soon. She was eager to decipher her part in this Prime Director's obvious bid for power.

# PRIME DIRECTOR ONE

Prime Director 32 returned to his offices when his private communicator erupted with a signal of an incoming call.

"Are you able to receive communications from Prime Director One?" A crisp voice appeared from the seasoned face of a high-ranking attaché.

"Yes, of course. I am in my private quarters alone. Proceed with the communications."

The wizened face appeared upon the screen. "So, my newest prime director just finished his first staff meeting. Have you any solutions to the problematical mess there as of yet?"

"Prime Director One, I greet you."

"Oh, cut out all the protocol, 32. I have my spies everywhere. I already got the upshot. You stirred them up with a rally speech about the Arian party line. You haven't had boots on the ground long enough to know your new staff or to give me any real report. I know all that, too."

"Yes, Prime Director."

"I just wanted to make sure you and I both remember our agreements concerning your appointment to Aryll 8. You haven't suffered any lapse of memory about what you've promised me, have you?" Prime Director One's eyes glared through his image upon the screen; his voice carried its insistent pitch and timbre. Prime Director 32 felt that voice resonate throughout his whole body.

"No, sir. I'm very clear about my role. I'm to speak of bringing about a total reform of the conditions here. Blame everything on my recent predecessor, and remind everyone he failed in enforcing proper Arian ways."

Prime Director One stopped him. "Yes, but... answer my question. Why did I jump over the natural chain of promotion and command to appoint you a Prime Director, 32?"

"I managed to catch your attention with my promises."

"And what did you promise me 32?" PD One waited.

"I convinced you I'd cause a major increase in tribute return for the investment of time and finance put into the conquering of this planet. I staked my entire career upon these promises. You saw fit to allow me this opportunity."

"Stop hiding behind this groveling manner. Be bold."

"I promised I'd create large drama about turning around the levels of Aryll 8's small agricultural production, and to find a working solution to increasing native reproduction."

"And most importantly, what else did you promise me, my new little director?" He waited to hear his new appointee's convictions.

"I promised to you personally I would facilitate your plans that Aryll 8 should be the first planet for the use of stericycla-tion technology. I've promised to prepare the ways for you to initiate that great, personal-political victory for the Arian Empire and for yourself."

"Good. That's correct." The enigmatic image and voice of Prime Director One begin to fade, but its message held on to haunt him. "Remember me, 32. My eyes and ears are all around you. Get me results. Prove to me just how clever you can be in your drive to succeed."

# PRIVATE MEETINGS

Armed with new resolve, Prime Director 32 ordered a small glass of brandy to help him relax. A young soldier was admitted, and began with an official salute.

"At ease, soldier. No one else is looking on. Karos 9, isn't it?" The Prime Director was aware of the white braid of rank hanging from Karos 9's right shoulder. "What is the total status count of the natives? Report fact!"

Karos 9, a man quick to feel and read the tone of response necessary, replied. "Sir, reporting numbers at last reading of the wrist-homer signals are 3,456 and 353 newly born young in the incubator facility waiting for census processing.

"Initial investigations of all forty cities turned up only a handful of survivors remaining in each, no trace of others has ever been reported. These natives have all been cropped and had wrist-homers attached; the newborns will soon be ready to receive theirs. Our history here is constant. Even from our most persistent and rigorous questioning, up to and including the use of inquisitor techniques, nothing has ever yielded any satisfactory explanation for these small numbers of the population."

The young officer finished. "In the opinion of this office, the remaining population lacks the ability to hide information of this importance; they appear to suffer either a certain lack of knowledge about all this or they suffer amnesia as to its cause."

"It probably looks good on paper, soldier, but it doesn't find me any new answers, does it? Dismissed. Keep looking. Call in the medical representative on your way out."

Karos 9 passed Doctor Rotz 27 in the hall.

"Doctor Rotz 27 reporting, sir."

"I've requested you for assignment here because of your extensive successes in handling alien species, Doctor Rotz 27. I'm hoping for great things from you." Prime Director 32 sat back in his chair. "As medical director, will you review the reproduction status of these natives for me?"

"As I'm certain you are aware, the reproduction methods of this planet far differ from those of our master race, or from any other species race we have encountered anywhere across our empire.

"We have advanced in our progress here with scientific control of native births to a point where we can firstly, dull inherent luminosity and secondly, genetically mutate wing development with chemical controlled vaccinations before they're born.

"One ongoing research we've failed to grasp is this Avian-bird-like race's mastery of sound frequencies. Our research continues on how these sonic potentials might be used for betterment in genetic enhancement, for military weaponry applications, or possibly even for crowd controls."

"I've read most of this in your briefing files, Doctor. Tell me something more about the leading edge in your research. I desire a scientific breakthrough of these mysteries. It would further both of our careers to work together in close co-operation in these areas."

"I heartily agree, Prime Director. If larger financial disbursements were channeled into this research, I know of several other genetic specialists who might become great assets to the successes of my staff." He smiled as Prime Director 32 nodded in accord.

"Each female we've surgically opened for examination has carried only four of these unfertilized eggs within her. Fertilization of an egg appears to happen only at special times, and apparently through an unconscious, external, planetary force signal. However, it has so far eluded our research just how this fertilization gets triggered. It also appears a female can hold potent male reproductive genetic material for quite a long time, possibly up to the full three years since our conquest."

"That's a vital question, Doctor. Can you be more specific? I need to know how long a female of this species can hold genetic material or delay fertilization. What can you do to produce more discoveries about this mysterious process you describe? Can you discover the signal which triggers a native pregnancy to begin? I have patience up to a point, but inspire me with new possibilities. I expect to see some great breakthroughs from you.

"Your primary goal after this meeting is simple. How quickly can you increase the native rate of reproduction?"

"It shall be my principal focus, Prime Director 32. The state imposed genetic mutation, and alteration has already been perfected. It's fortunate this birthing process allows us to continue research where the life and health of the Mother-Bearer are totally separate."

"I'm here to remind you, Doctor; there are no problems; only opportunities for growth. I shall offer you every support here. This mandate comes directly from Prime Director One himself. Solve these mysteries with all due haste.

"As a side incentive, I hope I don't need to remind you Planet 4 of the Fegilus System is prime for conquest. Rank, position upgrades, and funding for new research facilities could appear very quickly based on one's research and success on Aryll 8. You are dismissed, Doctor Rotz 27. I will expect to hear great results from you very quickly."

Then he paused, "Send in the Philomystic Cest 21."

# CEST 21 AND HER PACT

"So here you are." Prime Director 32 smiled.

"Cest 21, Philomystic First Class for the great Arian Empire reporting, sir." She stood at her best imitation of attention. The smaller man, Prime Director 32, let her hold that posture for a beat or two to look her over. He liked the subtle fire in her eyes. It was stronger now even than when he had previously known her. He'd sorted through her more recent files carefully.

"Oh, do relax, my little Philomystic First Class. I'm not about to bite you." He smiled in a calculating way. "Could I offer you a small brandy? I never travel anywhere in the empire without some little touch of luxury. It's one of the small advantages to rank, now isn't it?" He poured her a glass before she approved, and extended it to her. "Please sit here, and we'll just have a little chat and catch up." She sat on the chair across from his and eased forward to accept his offer.

"Another raw world for you, Cest 21?" He raised his glass in a small toast. "Or will this one be different?" She met his gaze, acknowledged his toast and took a sip. "I've followed your career with interest. I found your file very interesting as you moved up in rank. When our relationship ended years ago, I wondered if we'd meet again. I see from your service records that you've continued in the same thrust for answers that has always driven you forward. That's why I called in some markers and requested you for this new duty assignment."

"May I speak frankly with you Prime Director?" She set her glass on a side table.

Prime Director 32 let out a small laugh. "I'd be very much surprised if you hadn't asked that. I rose through the ranks too, as well you know. Pardon me if I've misread you, but you've been shunning urban planets and city assignments for years. Using your rank and reputation to stay on the fringe of the empire's conquered worlds for a reason?"

She admitted it with a slight nod.

"You're a researcher always looking for new possibilities. You're driven to discover the mystery behind each new face; within each new race. You can't hide that fire within you. Not from me. You're only mildly interested in new technologies. You have that enigmatic smile; just the right kind of look in those green eyes I'm seeking for.

"You've been out there walking a razor's edge with your career, my darling. You must have assumed the Office of Internal Monitoring has noticed those subtle changes in the attitude of your reports lately."

Cest 21 felt her heart stop for a moment. *If he's right, this may be the last assignment for me.*

He didn't make her wait long. "Very powerful people run the Internal Monitoring structure. They do know how to erase memories. They do have their certain style in methods for patching over cracks in the training of Arian minds. Unfortunately, I doubt your independent mental style could live through all that."

"All right, Aries 45...Prime Director 32. If you feel this is an accurate assessment of me, why am I here? What do you want now? You can't still be dwelling on space dreams we shared as cadets. Whatever carnal knowledge we had was only the stuff of fantasy. To further your career, you gave away the things you loved, and one of them was me and our relationship. What do you want of me now?"

"I'm going to make a success of this position. I meant what I said out there. This planet needs to be tamed and turned into a productive asset for the empire. That's my assignment; I don't wish to extend my stay here any longer than is necessary. In setting the course of my career, I would never consider this is as my work's destination. I need your skills. This is the frontier. I don't mind the maverick in you. I need someone with your predisposition. I need solutions fast, and I don't care if you obtain research results for me outside the state norms."

"That sounds like a test of my loyalty."

"You've developed excellent skills in your ability to communicate with the native races. You let yourself get personally involved. I need that skill set. No one else can seem to get through their Arian programming to seriously perceive what's going on here."

He looked into her green eyes. "Cest 21, I only want you to do your job. I won't interfere if you bring me results. My offer has to be better than allowing the Office of Internal Monitoring to immerse you into a recycling bin for your Arian mind, isn't it?"

She stayed focused. "When you put it that way, I'm persuaded to agree. Where would you suggest I begin?"

"Good girl." He smiled. "First, you will interview the former queen Orlycia. She's been allowed to keep her last independent incubator active for an approaching newborn. You are to speak with her and her old servant, Yeto. Learn all you can of their lives and beliefs. Any information you can gather could help unlock the mysteries of this strange world. You'll have a free hand under cover of my command. You will report only to me."

Then he took a moment to practice his dramatic pause. "I expect this independence I offer you to bear great fruit, my little Philomystic First Class." They exchanged a look of understanding.

"Now go. This has been a long day for both of us. Report directly to me alone and only to me in person. I don't want any other channels reading your reports. Remember. Nothing written. Is that clear?"

She nodded in agreement.

"Now get settled in your new quarters. Meet me tomorrow night at 0800 in the officer's club. We'll talk more about this over dinner. Also, remember this planet has only a twenty-hour day. Reset your chronometer for this local time."

Cest 21 nodded as she rose and left the room. *You're right about one thing. I'll certainly never deal with this Orlycia and Yeto like any ordinary Arian.*

# DRING'S LEARNING SESSION

Orlycia knew the high stakes of Dring's education. She smiled at young Dring as he became immersed in their teaching-learning experience. The three of them, Orlycia, Yeto, and Dring, sat in comfortable chairs, like three points of a triangle. She and Yeto were actively think-projecting directly into Dring's subconscious by the holographic energy in their minds. They used the natural law of "two can pull a third."

Dring now sat in a state of total calm and trust after his earlier exercise walking and flying within the great hall. He smiled as their minds transmitted and printed holographic images. His stock of learning and references expanded exponentially. By masterful application of these ancient arts, the young children of Aryll's tribeflocks not only could absorb vast amounts of knowledge unhampered by the need for vocal speech, but it also strengthened their abilities in non-verbal communication.

Yeto, as the positive output terminal, selected the territory, speed, and the level of instruction. Orlycia functioned as the negative input and as the grounding reservoir for energy.

This vast body of accumulated, imprinted knowledge would remain dormant within Dring until he needed to activate it; until he called it up consciously or unconsciously. It was analogous to the influences of astrology; the stars indicate; they don't impel.

Life would always be a new proposition for Dring. He would find each discovery an increasing wonder. Experiencing life within his reality, he would always feel the "sense of the first time." Also, he could also access truths drawn directly from ancient wisdom before making it a positive act.

What a difference from the Arian methods that force memories, conditioning, thoughts filled them with politics, and hackneyed repetitions flavored with Arian judgment pressed upon them while they slept. Dring learned, in sympathetic resonance, the ways of life itself; all that was positive and progressive for the genetic line of his tribe.

Orlycia thought. *Dring is nearly full up for today. He will need to take nourishment and to get some exercise to make this session positive for his body.*

*You have confirmed my readings.* Yeto smiled. *If he were older, these sessions could go on much longer, but he is young.*

"Dring, it is now time for play and feeding."

He blinked his eyelids, smiled, and jumped into the air to spread his wings and flew. "Yeto," he burst out." Will there be time for more flying lessons after feeding? Mother, are there any more of those trillia seeds left?"

# MORIA MEETS CEST 21

Cest 21 had little trouble getting directions to the officer's club. The Spartan-like barracks of her meager rooms were lodged directly across the parade grounds. She chose to keep her attire close to official, but her feminine curves were still tastefully displayed in a light khaki skirt and jacket.

She made some concession to being social by allowing her auburn tresses to flow down to her shoulders. Around her neck, a colored scarf accented the green of her eyes. She had little use for makeup to cover the natural color of her freckles and the ruddiness of skin tanned by a dozen different suns on as many planets. She made a striking contrast to most of the other females, Arian and native, inside the club's quiet interior.

A Claxus 8 group playing their form of soft jazz filled a video screen. A liberal number of better-dressed escorted and unescorted native females showed some attempt to enhance the appearance of this club as slightly more upscale.

Cest 21 never spent much time in those places. The acrid smoke from a variety of burning herbs such as orlac irritated her eyes and alcohol offered her little appeal, other than a cordially offered small dose every so often.

After making inquiry of a young centurion monitoring the door, she was directed to a private back room. Upon entering, she joined Prime Director 32 and another officer. They were accompanied by a strikingly attractive native hostess.

"So here you are." The Prime Director greeted her. "Please sit here next to me. This is Harcos 86, my close consultant, and a friend. And this is Moria."

After brief pleasantries, the two men rose and excused themselves. Cest 21 had never been one for small talk, but this was her assignment. "You look very attractive, Moria. How long have you worked here?"

"This is the first chance I've had to speak with a native female of your species, and of your tribeflock as well." Moria's tone was polite but succinct.

Cest 21 caught the crispness in this voice and now took her own time reading Moria. *You are telepathic. Those were my very own thoughts you spoke back to me. I'm new to this world, but I've dealt with this before.* Cest 21 didn't sense an attack from this female, but responded cautiously, reminding herself to send her thoughts out clear and precise.

"Philomystic First Class? What does that mean to you?" Moria continued to speak as if she hadn't read Cest 21's thoughts. "I can gather the facts and history of your rank's formal principles from your manuals, but you don't feel or think like any female soldier I've met so far." Moria remained enigmatic in her expressions.

Cest 21's mind contemplated her next thoughtful move like a chess master. "My choice for duty assignments has kept me to tours on many outer rim planets on the edges of the Arian Empire. I've spent most of my military career immersed in the cultures and the learning of all those worlds."

Moria spoke again but dispensed with the small talk. "And have you found your Self yet?" Moria addressed what she was reading in Cest 21's mind. "You don't radiate the party line's thought patterns. Are there many other females like you?"

She laughed at this frank questioning. "No, Moria. I could never say I was representative of the Arian ideal for its military women, but I'm usually better at concealing it. But what of you? You've made over your body and taken on much of the profile and appearance of the Arian race. It would appear that you, as well, would not be representative of your tribe-flock. Would I be correct in saying it that way?

"If my readings are accurate, why would someone with your talents and sensitivities make these radical changes in body appearance? My senses tell me you hold an intelligence and sophistication far beyond any need to work in a place like this."

Moria was pleased to have a real conversation. "You are correct in your terms. You've picked up a bit of mind-speak on your own. Good. You're correct in much of what you say. I was born into what you might call a noble class within my Raptor tribeflock. The fact of my physical makeover or my purposes in being here will be my little secret until I decide whether I trust you or not."

"I realize trust must be earned. Use the full extent of your sensitivities, Moria. Probe my mind. Read me as deeply as you like. As you've already demonstrated, I'm not as sensitive as you are. I'm not hiding any secrets you couldn't read."

After a time, Moria relaxed in her chair and smiled. "You have no idea what you are about to meet here. These are the times when our mother planet is about to manifest her triumphant Changeover. She has already begun the movements of her planetary body and voice her songs. If you were more sensitive, you'd know what she sings about."

"Is this something only to be felt by the females of your species?" Cest 21 struggled to find a reference from within her study of myths.

"No, my Arian companion, this will personally affect all of us more than you could ever imagine. It would appear your quest for self has brought you here."

"Can you tell me more of this?"

"I've read some of your immediate future. He plans to send you to meet Orlycia and Yeto. I sense you'll find more of your purpose here by mixing with them. She has recently given birth to a male heir for her line. Study hard upon how she speaks of him." Then Moria spoke directly into her heart. "Don't attempt to be anything but honest with either of them. In their presence, if you try to use the word 'secret' it will only make them laugh."

"I truly appreciate that council. What of you, Moria? Haven't you, too, recently given birth to an heir for this planet's future?"

Moria's mood snapped into focus like a gunshot. "How did you know that?"

"I don't know; we were talking, and the thought came to my mind."

"You've already become sensitive to my frequency of thought. Our mother planet is gracing you. I've probed your mind as deeply as I could and have found no seeds of deception in your intent, so I will reveal a little of my story."

After sharing her story of love and loss, she added, "I will stop at nothing to find my daughter. No price is too great. I endured this makeover for that reason. She knows I'm looking for her. I'll find her if I have to entertain every officer here to get that information." She stopped herself. "I reveal too much.

We've just met. You might place me in a vulnerable position."

Cest 21 was quick to speak. "I assure you, I will honor your confidence in me. These matters need to stay between us. If I can help you in any way, I will. I may have access to records. I may be able to research this. Read my thoughts on this. What was the name you had chosen for her?"

"I was to call her Ethra."

The door opened as Prime Director 32 and his aide, Harcos 86, re-entered the room. They smelled faintly of orlac smoke.

"Did you two find something to chat about?" The Prime Director asked.

The women exchanged a knowing glance. Cest 21 spoke first. "Yes, thank you, Prime Director, we found our conversation time most enlightening."

"Good, then let's order up some repast. And after that Harcos 86 will escort you back to your quarters."

"We'll have our function meeting tomorrow, Cest 21. Report to me around mid-day. Moria and I had started a conversation before you arrived. I'm sure you'll understand, won't you?"

"Yes, of course."

Moria's enigmatic smile spoke volumes about the special duty assignment the Prime Director had in mind for her.

# DRING'S TRAINING

Precision flying came easy for Orlycia's young Dring. Yeto spent every moment possible training him on such things like proper breathing. Aryll's were mammals but breathed differently than the Arians who worked hard to inhale then allowed it to dissipate. Tribeflock members allowed the air and its energy push into them. They exerted more labor to blow their breath out. With no need to gulp at the air as they flew, they were constantly being connected and charged with its energy and force.

Dring's body matured quickly. Already as tall as Orlycia's shoulder, he demonstrated great curiosity, even in thought, but he could occasionally be overly stubborn and self-centered.

His accelerated training had to be completed before the Arians took Dring away for education and assignment in the workforce. They could force Dring to be assigned to the Agri-fields, a servile city labor camp, or some even lower form of labor. Until he grew mature enough to be assigned, Yeto pushed to keep him focused on his destiny.

She instructed his mind and soul in songs to accelerate its maturing. Yeto handled training Dring in disciplines, and practical physical Prana-Bindu exercises crucial for him to learn if he was to conceal his wings.

Dring needed to posture and fold his wings tightly enough

to conceal them under his cape for extended periods of time without being detected. He also learned his three eyelids worked; how to blink from bottom up, from top lid down, or how to move his third, clear eyelids sideways to cover his eyes when he flew.

For his protection, he also learned how to control and mask thoughts from the other native workers. Many of those still retained varying telepathic abilities despite their pre-birth chemical poisonings.

Dring knowingly held the genetic keys in himself to facilitate the planet's advancement. He could selfishly choose to avoid her pleas for his help. And while he had doubts about his ability to achieve all that was expected of him, Dring knew he held the future success of his people and his planet in his grasp.

# DRING AND THE FUTURE

Orlycia received a courier message. A new Arian, a Philomystic First Class staff member named Cest 21, would soon pay them a visit. The reasons given supposedly explained away as, "For the further continuing, peaceful native population integration of Aryll 8. For their acceptance and orientation of their place as citizens of the Arian Empire."

*I must be well-practiced in my responses to this new inspector,* Orlycia told herself.

*It's crucial Yeto, and I keep our senses sharp and focused. And Dring...he flies around the palace so much. My main fear was that in the sudden assault of a surprise inspection, I might not have enough time to get Dring's cape tightened enough to conceal his wings.*

*Dring must rise to those challenges and discipline himself to play the part of a downtrodden native for a while. He must hide his talents and abilities. Being out in their world will test his ego, his character, and his development to the core. His choices and his independent acts will certainly provide pressured challenges, and test him to see if he would ever deny his true self.*

*If only they would allow us a little time more for his training,* she thought. *He will be full grown and mentally prepared if time grants us even a few more months.*

# YOUNG DRING GETS HIS ASSIGNMENT

Dring, the rightful heir to the throne of Aryll, was running out of time. His body reached its full height, and his muscles grew; responding to their accelerated training and his nightly covert flying missions.

The transfer of Teri 38 from this old sector of the Capacity, fortunately, had also caused a resultant time lag in assigning a new Arian patrol monitor. None had begun any regular appearance.

This precious delay allowed Orlycia and Yeto a small but vital window of time free of the iron fist of his obligatory duty-assignment.

Finally, Orlycia received Dring's official notification. His orders were clear. At the end of that month, he would be visited by a review examiner. Then, upon successfully completing his exam, he would immediately begin his assignment as a worker in the agri-fields.

In some ways, Orlycia was much relieved. Tensions from raising Dring so secretly had been wearing heavily upon her. Stature demanded she embody her concealed fears in mental silence. The fields were isolated from the Capacity's closer scrutiny. Orlycia could fervently believe Dring possessed the strength to survive the challenges he must face.

Old Yeto's loyalty and support remained strong. Orlycia

also drew strength from the elders, and other members of her tribe, and especially Ospra's remote presence in the unseen starlight worlds through his Pictart. She still desperately missed the embrace of her life mate's wings.

# CEST 21'S ASSIGNMENT: FIRST MEETING

Because of its style and design, the former palace was easy to locate from the air. It was an even more beautiful close-up. Cest 21 admired the Suns' glow radiating through portions of its yellow transparent structure. She landed her gravity sled softly and shut it down. She'd chosen a level piece of ground next to the closest Zolag tree facing the grand arches in front of the palace entrance, removed her helmet, hung it on the handlebars, and shook out her trusses.

Before her stood the ancient, former royal palace. She prepared her mind as she had been trained. As with any first contact, Cest 21 was never certain what to expect from a native species' former planetary rulers. Within the empire, former independent cultures were normally ruled over by fear, political manipulation, extortion, or by clear threats of military intervention.

Despite the fact this was not her way, far too many times it left her at a disadvantage in her wish for real communication. She's been given little information about this assignment. She hoped Moria's instincts were correct about her personal destiny.

Cest 21 stood tall and composed herself, making ready to enter the palace. She'd done her research on this Raptor Hall, home of the Eagle tribe. She sighed as she moved toward the main entrance. She took a deep breath and let it out slow.

She admired the architecture of these bird-like people. If form did indeed follow function, the tall carved doors, rounded at the top, fully opened, would have allowed the wingspan of any adult citizen to fly through.

*I need to think like a native;* she reminded herself. *I desperately want to be at my best for this meeting. As Moria taught me, a race this sensitive telepathically needs me to be very careful. I would never wish to alienate these people.* She kept turning over mental reminders to herself as she approached the big doors.

She studied in sacred architectures and in the ability to read subtle expressions of energy where its flow was directed by mass, structures, and the arrangement of objects. She could feel herself responding to the regal nature of the palace. She became engrossed by the feelings, the smells, and of its atmosphere. It began to respond to her life frequency and to assist her feelings of relief. Her heart felt lighter and in her mind, she could almost hear singing in the air. She felt a new lightness in her step.

Cest 21 respected the local custom to touch the hand-plate to give an audio signal of her arrival. She had studied images of the staff member, Yeto, and the former queen.

After a short wait, Yeto appeared in the doorway. Very angular and lean, his sharp, slightly bent nose rose above his cape. He gazed upon her with the same soft, penetrating eyes she'd experienced from the old Puka on her last assignment.

"I am Philomystic First Class, Cest 21. I've been newly assigned to follow up with a visit after the initial incubator inspection."

He gestured for her to follow him, which silenced her nervous chatter. "I am Yeto. We've been expecting you."

126

# CEST 21 MEETS ORLYCIA

Aware he was an Owlface, Cest 21 couldn't help but notice the dignity and grace in his walk.

As they crossed the great hall, the height of the ceilings and the huge open beams which soared over her head fascinated her. *I wonder if members of this race would use those beams upon which to perch. I don't see many chairs or benches here,* she thought.

The old servant Yeto, in owl-like fashion, turned his head almost completely around and slowed her with a look from his piercing eyes. "You are correct. As an avian race, we enjoyed the freedoms of flight. Heights and places to perch upon were very natural to us."

Cest 21 tried not to overreact as he spun his head and returned his gaze forward. *Remember your training*, she told herself. *Be shocked or surprised at nothing.* She was rendered speechless by his body movements and amazed at the accuracy with which he'd read her thoughts.

As they reached an interior door, Yeto touched the interior doorplate opening the doors to a private living suite.

When Orlycia approached her, Cest 21 was struck by her grace and slender beauty. Orlycia's white, custom fitted cape billowed slightly as she walked, and her soft white feathers flowed to her shoulders in gentle curves much like Cest 21's hair. Her eyes were dark and penetrating, and there appeared to be few wrinkles on her face. Her lips were small and tight. A young male walked beside Orlycia.

"I am Cest 21, Philomystic First Class. I must apologize if my visit is disturbing you. I'm not aware if there's any form of royal greeting or ceremony which I should offer at our first meeting."

After a moment of quiet assessment, the former queen spoke. "Yeto will stay with us. I am Orlycia, this is my son, Dring, and admittedly I've had little contact with females of your race. My initial readings of you make me curious. You present an entirely different radiation than others of your species. Are you unusual for your gender and your race, or is this difference in frequency part of your official assignment? From my experience, the idea of anyone of your species extending anything remotely resembling courtesy seems out of place."

"As a Philomystic, I've chosen to remain cordial and to peacefully greet contacts and to welcome cultural exchanges with new species on planets across the galaxy. My ways of dealing with other beings of intelligence have been seasoned by experiences with many cultures.

"I've moved away from hard Arian training methods I endured in my youth. Experience has taught me a few simple truths. I've found it more likely any true knowledge of others must start with knowing myself."

A small smile moved Orlycia's lips. "I can read these things from your thoughts. Whatever training you once followed has grown thin by the abrasion of reality."

Cest 21 breathed a sigh of relief. "I welcome your reflections. It is my wish to learn from you and your world."

Orlycia hesitated before she spoke, but then revealed some of her true thoughts. "How ugly are your factories, barracks, and fold-buildings of your designs? They represent your discordant attempts to dominate the natural, harmonious lands upon which they squat. With as much sorrow the intrusion of your species has inflicted, how much more pain must my world endure, or her children labor through to face its future?"

Cest 21 kept silent, feeling her emotions stirring in sympathy. She was ashamed to be associated with these deeper truths Orlycia was speaking. It revealed to both Yeto and Orlycia how much her mind control training could no longer mask.

Orlycia read her sympathy and continued more strongly from her convictions. "Deep within me the truth and the promise of my planet's freedom wells up. My young offspring represents the last unique member of our old former race. The living legacy of this great house is not yet fully depleted.

"Your new director has sent me his official dictatorial decree. My son will soon be stolen. He's officially been assigned; transferred to an agricultural facility." Her words spat out her disdain.

"My tacit support accommodating this action will be served up as if it shows 'native political acceptance' and 'support for your invasion.' It carries a bad taste, not unlike the tainted grains your glorious empire forces our tribeflocks to raise as food. Clearly, it wants only a servant race here. It is unaware we are all in the throes of imminent planetary changes. What this planet has in store for all of us will extend beyond anything your race could possibly comprehend."

Both Orlycia and Yeto held their unblinking gaze upon her; probing her reactions with their minds.

An overwhelmed Cest 21 was caught in the tangled web

of language and the functions of her job. She had never dealt with any race this perceptive. Moria had counseled her to speak her mind honestly and with no deception, and she accepted that advice with sincerity. "I admit it, in the past, my function as a researcher has been employed to further the empire's purposes. After my last assignment on Zon 14, something within me has been profoundly changing. Please, allow me to appeal to you both. I've been made aware you both could detect any falsehood in my statements, so I beg of you. Can you help me on my quest for deeper awareness and knowledge of my higher self?

"I feel my life is at a crossroads. Whatever path my life had been on before has become invalid. I've lost my grasp as to how to proceed. I feel the passion in what you say as much as I long to kindle my inner purpose.

"My superiors suspect this functional erosion exists. They have concerns, about my overall mental programming, particularly regarding my loyalty to the empire. Finessing me into this assignment for his selfish reasons, Prime Director 32 may have unconsciously presented me this one last opportunity. Other superiors would have ordered a full assessment of my career, registered my mental differences from their classical Arian philosophy, and erased my mind by trying to reprogram it. I would never survive trying to act Arian like all the rest of their entangled ranks."

Cest 21 furthered the conversation by adding, "As it happens, you are not the first contact I've had with a member of your tribeflock. I feel fortunate to have had time to converse with someone you know. Her name is Moria. She and I spoke with limited mental dialogue. She seeks information about a daughter the state has stolen from her. She, too, carries a determination of will I'd never witnessed before. I've promised to help her in any way I can."

Orlycia continued to let her mind probe Cest 21. "I sensed something within your being had been touched, and now you wish to help Moria? Be at peace. We are gentle beings with those we trust. I do perceive those new, bright sparks growing within you that were ignited far from here. This is your destiny. Moria must have sensed this in you as well, or she would never have told you any of these things. And she must have masked her frequencies well. I was not aware she was in your Capacity. She has changed her thought radiations. How does she fare?"

Cest 21 felt unusually calm. She had only just met these beings, and yet she felt completely at ease. "Moria has altered her body to be accepted into high military, political, and social circles. She will stop at nothing to locate her child. I assured her I'd help her in any way possible. She asked that I pay close attention to the both of you."

"So she read my frequency in your thoughts. Moria and I have known each other since long before the coming of your race. She does carry a fire of intensity which will not be stopped. You may believe her. If Moria tells you she will stop at nothing to satisfy her intent, you had better stand true to your promise."

Orlycia and Yeto exchanged a silent nod in mental agreement. "You may call me, Orlycia. Yeto and I will assist you. We're both trained in the ways of the green emerald. If you have truly made this call to the higher forces of the universe, we will serve as your representatives. We're both honor-bound to respond to any genuine spiritual request, and to offer you only our best guidance and council in your next steps toward a real self-development."

# DRING GETS JEALOUS

"I would like to help as well. I had better learn how to deal with these barbarians."

Orlycia smiled at Dring. "You will play a major role in her later development. For now, your training needs to occupy all your time. As it now stands, we have precious little of that time left with us." She added her shielded thoughts only to him. *Dring, you must not become prematurely active with this one. Yeto and I must deal with her first to see who she is inside.*

Dring's thoughts couldn't hide his petulance. *You never let me get involved, my Mother-Bearer. You both make all the decisions around here. I'm no longer a fledgling!* He sulked as he left the room.

Cest 21 broke the tension. "What did you mean when you told Dring, 'You have little time left with us?"

Yeto joined into the discussion. "Your Prime Director has sent us a notice. Dring is to be taken from this home at any time. This message carries with it the stench of his struggle to rise quickly by political manipulation and his quest for power."

Cest 21 responded in kind. "Certainly, those attributes are foremost in the mind of Prime Director 32. However, if I use the slight flexibility he's allowing my new position to delay this transfer for... observational studies, that should buy you at least a little more time together. Besides, if I convince him I'll learn more for my selfish reasons in the bargain, it should be an easy deception for him to approve."

"I feel the harmony of your actions." Orlycia took Cest 21's hand. "If you truly wish to journey on this path, we may all see this through to an amazing future."

"I must go now. I'll attempt to set all this in motion with my first personal report to the Director. May I return after I meet with him?"

Orlycia smiled. "I'm relieved you are moved to try."

"I shall look forward to more time together." She gave a slight bow and moved toward the exit.

"We have now registered your frequency, Cest 21," Orlycia called after to assure her. "We will always be able to know of your location anywhere on this planet."

"I have only been able to study the idea of family from outside. My race has worked so hard to control and dominate those connections. You have now stirred some of my deepest, hidden feelings. You've given me the first sense of coming home I've ever felt. I vow I shall never betray that."

"We read that in you, my dear, but you must go now to set this plan in motion."

Cest 21 held tightly to her bag as she exited the palace. Her mind was flooded with plans of how to assist herself and this race to join the empire as productive and beneficial.

She looked out over the Capacity past the old structures, and toward the lights of the Arian complexes. *There is an order in their race. Maybe there could be a real peace between us all now. Perhaps I might help leadership understand.* She felt a new lightness of heart. *I might also get the deeper answers I need for my journey.* Plotting her next step, she heard a low, pleasant, slightly musical hum in the quiet background noise around her as she mounted her gravity sled. *Odd, I don't recall hearing that noise before.*

# CEST 21 REPORTS

"Send her in." Prime Director responded.

Cest 21 smoothed her uniform and entered his office.

"Well, let's hear some good news. What's your reading of these natives? Report fact."

She responded in top diplomatic form. "We got on surprisingly well. I've dealt with much more hostile first-time responses in the past. The natives of Moringa 34 nearly poked their spears into me before they finally became willing to communicate. With these natives from Aryll 8, I feel certain I'll be able to win their confidence with ease."

"Are you beginning to suggest something here? Giving me some assurance I wasn't wrong in your appointment? I wish to be encouraged by your readings. I've been doing some of my research. I've found Moria to be quite an excellent conversationalist. You do remember meeting her the other evening, don't you?"

"Why yes, of course, sir. We had an excellent chat. Might I ask what you've decided from your dealings with this native female?"

"Despite our racial-species differences, Moria seems quite clever and has an excellent understanding of our empire. She could easily quote many of our leader's directives verbatim, and she can see where our progress might be of great benefit to undeveloped worlds."

"I do have one request."

"There usually is. What now?"

"One of their concerns comes from notification their young male offspring is about to be assigned."

"Why should that concern them or you or me?"

"Since I've only had the one meeting, it would be prudent to add more data to my research. If only I could observe them interacting for a little more time. Your orders to me seemed most emphatic. You wished me to scrutinize a family grouping of this species in depth. If I might be allowed to witness these adults dealing with their younger member a little longer, I'm certain I can win their deeper confidence. When they begin to let their guard down around me, when they accept and trust me more, I'll have gathered additional Intel, and I'll be able to contribute my findings by reporting with a more accurate assessment.

"I feel certain a more complete research case file will contribute greatly to your success here as a planetary leader, Prime Director. And to earn your confidence, I'll still confirm any new observations immediately, and only with you, sir, as we agreed."

"I love to keep this staff on their toes, Cest 21. I can tell by my readings, my choice of you for this job was correct. Remember, it is difficult to fool me. I can see through this. Your curiosity drives you to achieve success, and your hope is to clear away the suspicions which some important groups have voiced about your loyalty to our purpose."

"I respect the wisdom of your perceptions, sir. Yes, you do read my desire and my personal ambition in this request. I do need to rise above this shadow upon my reputation. Success in this research will better my career. Would you expect any less of me?"

"I pride myself in knowing my staff. Your actions don't surprise me. As you wish. We'll postpone this assignment on a month-to-month. But I will expect to hear glowing reports from you. And I want results to justify my confidence in your actions. Is that clear?"

"Crystal clear."

"So what have you brought me so far?" he demanded.

"From what I've gathered thus far," she said, recalling details from previous research, "earlier data studies suggest these native peoples are fixated upon this imminent, mystical planetary change. They have prophecies and old legends that suggest this Changeover is gathering in strength. Especially interesting to me is their belief in one mythical account of an invading plague of warriors who would appear in the last days before this apocalyptic change. The appearance of these warriors, written about and foretold hundreds of years ago, seems to equate with our Arian conquest. They're waiting for those events to force our departure.

"They believe our conquest has triggered the signal for this planet's rebirth into a form of a newer and higher life. And the beginning of this change began with this rebirth event.

"They believe their leaders and the remainder of the population were waiting for our invasion to appear to begin this cycle and that's why most of their population can vanish into that unknown dimension. Their prophecies say, 'although they seem not there, they are… they still live…they still wait.'

"It seems their myths suggest the largest portion of their population lives and waits in a parallel energy dimension which we can't see or perceive. The good news is it does confirm we are in no imminent danger of attack. They won't be coming back."

"I've reviewed all those historical myths. In my opinion, it's all a desperate hope of a conquered species trying to rationalize the inevitable progress of change. If no one will be looking to enforce this mystical Changeover time with any violent actions, my question to you, Cest 21, is then more timely and to the point.

"In your readings of them, do you truly feel there will be no reappearance of any unseen members of this society? Do they possess any real exploitable technologies or skills? Must I sterilize and reconstruct this whole world to make it of some value to the empire?"

"I can't answer that from just one visit with the natives."

"Well, then find me some answers." He waved her away.

Cest 21 drew a sigh of relief as she exited his office and returned to her quarters. She had much to think about. She did find it most curious how convincing Moria had been with the Prime Director.

She felt strangely excited and comfortable with these natives; more than she had ever felt upon any other planet. She looked forward with gathering anticipation to her next meeting Orlycia and Yeto.

# MORIA PLANTS THE SEEDS OF HER QUEST

Moria woke and rolled over to face the window. Morning light from the twin suns peered through the shades of the Prime Director's bed chambers. She reached over to brush the ear of the planetary ruler.

"Do you have to be anywhere early in this day, Prime Director 32?" She spoke softly.

"No, and I wish you'd go back to slumber." He'd consumed more than his fair share of his favorite brandy the evening before. "Don't you remember? I'm the Prime Director of this whole planet. At the very least, I should get to decide my work schedule!"

"Oh dear, how could I possibly have forgotten that?" She snuggled closer to him so she could stroke his back and his enormous ego.

"Fraternization with me will get you nowhere, woman. I'm ordering you to let me rest."

"Prime Director, I'm not a woman, at least not of your species. And I'm not one of your militaries."

"Moria, if you're not to be considered a woman, then what were we doing last night? You're a very convincing actress, my dear, skilled, and compliant companion."

"Prime Director, I have had considerable training in the ways of...a courtesan, I believe your species would call it.

Have I been accommodating your interests with convincing performances?" She puffed out her chest slightly and alluringly exposed one of her artificially implanted breasts.

Now he was fully awake. "Yes, you've been a very convincing girl."

"I'd rather you called me a woman. A girl sounds a little too innocent for me. I've already given birth, and that experience should have removed me from any of your ingénue categories."

"I have to admit it. I didn't pick up on that bit about you giving birth. Why haven't you told me these facts before? We've been spending a lot of time together. Moria, I AM your planetary Prime Director. I should have been informed of these things. Now are there any other pertinent facts I should know about you?"

"Why? Just for security? I was caused to deliver one son prematurely during my wing cropping, and recently my daughter was taken from me by your soldiers before I had time to sing her birthing songs. I can only assume she's healthy and in one of your state facilities. I don't know how to trace her. I don't dwell upon these events much, so I'm only left with those memory experiences as ones of loss."

"You've never been informed where this daughter of yours is? I could have my staff make some inquiries. There should be official records."

"Oh, Prime Director, I would be ever so grateful. I don't know how I could ever repay you."

"Well, I'm sure we can think of something. In fact, if you roll over I think I'm getting an idea about how you could stimulate more research right about now."

"Whatever you say, Prime Director."

Moria didn't let her voice betray the small victory she felt. *Whatever it takes, my daughter, my Ethra. Whatever it takes, I'll find you. I'll never give up trying. I WILL see you again.*

# TERI 38, HIS NEW AGRI-CAMP, AND ETHRA

The shuttle rattled and thumped to a dusty stop in the cleared area beside two lonely, dusty buildings that bordered the edges of acres of grain fields. The facility sat adjacent to a large primeval Zolag forest. In true military fashion, Teri 38, the former incubator inspector, was unceremoniously dumped into his new command assignment. Three new workers exited behind him.

Part of his early training had been in the areas of plant tending and maintenance; he recognized the grain cycle was already well under way.

As he approached the buildings, he recognized the veteran who nearly bowled him over. "First Centurion Dratus 86." the soldier shouted. "The door's open. Here are the keys for the worker's lockdown." He tossed them at Teri 38, and they landed in the dust at his feet. Teri 38 saw the marks of combat laser burns on his arms and the brown teeth of Orlac misuse

"It's about time our glorious empire got my tail out of here. I abandon it all to you." The old soldier never looked back as he strode toward the door of the waiting shuttle, threw in his bag, and slid into the seat. As he buckled in and reached to slam the cargo door behind him, he shouted back to Teri 38.

"Learn to carry two Volt whips." He spoke with a leer. "That way you don't have to wait for them to recharge! The woggies out here work better if you persuade them!" And with that, the shuttle door slammed shut; the craft lifted off, up and flew away blowing dust over all four of them standing on the dusty designated landing ground. Within moments it was out of sight over the horizon, and Teri 38 stood alone with his new arrivals.

Teri 38 gave a short command to the group. "Follow me." The dusty group moved toward the compound. He found the correct keys and let them enter their building. Then he entered his own.

Inside, racks of equipment spilled their plugs, wires, and contents over everything. Leftover cape material draped and hung like filthy shrouds over dusty boxes.

Finally, some of the indistinguishable shapes were becoming recognizable. The communications console dripped with stains of some unknown origin, and the blankets of the sleeping couch barely covered its surface in contorted patterns. The smell of burned field rations and traces of many half-consumed meals clung to the food prep counters. Teri 38 sighed in deep resignation, found one of the few relatively bare spots of the floor, kicked the dried, squashed body of a dead tuft mouse out of the way, and set down his bags.

After directing the newest workers where to lodge themselves, they'd set down their meager bags of clothes and possessions. *What are you called?* Mental questions filled their compound.

The two males thought spoke first. *I'm called Weston.*

*And I am Artus.* They seemed hesitant and uncertain how to continue in this new world.

The female of the group was not so shy. *My name is Ethra.* She mentally beamed out strongly; *I'm pleased to be free of the leering eyes of too many Arians, and I'm eager and ready to learn. I'll find my place within the ways of this motley tribeflock.*

The others registered Ethra's boldness and sent back their mental welcomes. Then she slipped into verbal speech. "Is there anything to feed on? They haven't offered us any nourishment."

# MEETING WITH PRIME DIRECTOR 32

Prime Director 32 spoke with his staff. "This follow-up meeting is for me to probe the current extent of your research. Does anyone have anything brilliant to report so far? Admit it. Your daily reports are lackluster. How do we solve these problems? Firstly, where are the other natives?

"Secondly, can the remaining population successfully breed enough new offspring to turn this world productive? All their eggs have now hatched. Are any new ones appearing?

"Thirdly, must I initiate an appeal for migrant labor from other worlds? Have any of you suggested that alternative?"

The medical staff member, Serzi 66, turned to the screen. "These scenes represent the remaining native population at work in a variety of activities: agricultural, work crews, domestic market workers, cleaners, refuse haulers, bar staffers, and the state incubator staffers. This group represents all adult and younger native survivors remaining after our conquest. This membership also includes some of the latest batches of new birth orphans."

Turning off the project view screen, Serzi 66 continued. "The packet in front of you is our report regarding the forty native cities, over the three continents. Our Intel suggested their numbers be in the hundreds of thousands of natives, maybe several million before the invasion.

"We experienced no native response to our attack. Their only retaliation seems to have been in their ability to instantly vanish en masse, and in their continued ability to elude capture. The population did not fight back. At this point, Conquest historian Wento 49 will continue about other historical events."

Wento 49 was a small man, bent slightly from year spans of view screen monitoring. "After our assault, the remaining natives appeared bewildered and seemed to be suffering from mass shock, almost like an amnesia condition. Our most rigorous questioning brought out little usable Intel. No research has yet solved this mysterious disappearance event."

Serzi 66 added, "As you see, Prime Director 32, this is more than a complex medical problem. To encourage breeding and reproduction, we still have yet to discover how their termination cycle works."

Prime Director 32 asked, "Med-Inquisitors could get no answers from the remaining population?"

Serzi 66 responded. "We could get nothing more than some mumblings about ancient councils, old legends, prophecies of a mythical change. If these natives are to be believed, they were expecting us. The rest of their population members somehow stepped out of this world to wait."

Cest 21, listening intently to all this, thought of her questions. She had yet to grasp its full meaning, but feelings in her stomach flip-flopped at its contemplation. She blurted out, "I represent that group."

Her abruptness stopped the meeting cold for a moment. All eyes turned to her. Cest 21 now had to stand and say something. "I've already spoken to our Prime Director 32 about this, but from what my initial research has pieced together,

146

they believe all those other population members are waiting for us to go away.

"As much as that makes little rational sense to us, they believe they were waiting for us to appear and they are still waiting for what they call the Changeover time. According to them, the rest of their population is in a higher energy state or higher life. We can't see or register them, and they won't return."

There were mutterings and whispers around the room as the Prime Director 32 stood. "The Arian Empire offers them a higher life, Cest 21. It should be an honor for any species to be part of this growing body of the state's' will."

"This notion of a better life is not unusual, Prime Director, even on the many conquered worlds throughout the galaxy that have already joined us. There are many people and creatures that will wait, feeling that our conquest is only temporary."

Cest 21 felt the heat of mental disagreement rising from those in the room. *I must walk a razor's edge and find a safe way to say this.* "Within our history, there has always been a need to learn, to grow, and to expand. The state's policy has always been one of leniency if the conquered world remains in compliance."

Serzi 66 spoke. "I'd like to move back to the immediate matters. Until recently only about thirty-three percent of eggs which had been gathered survived their births, but now we have recently witnessed the most curious, spontaneous birthing of ALL the eggs in our possession."

Their Prime Director stroked his chin in thought. "The state has been very active with its incubator program. And yet those were the sad results? Are you suggesting this low rate of reproduction survival was attributed to ineffectiveness in your care? Or is the blame to rest on the chemicals Gene 10 or in AR-15?

"Even more importantly, how do you explain this sudden and spontaneous birth explosion? Why have you wasted so much time avoiding this crucial issue?" The Prime Director stomped and strutted around the room.

Serzi 66 gave a meek response. "I find it difficult to point to our genetic-modifying vaccinations as a cause, sir. I regret my choice of not revealing it sooner, but the startling event of all the eggs birthing at once is still difficult for me to explain. Until now, we've had such success with our chemical genetic engineering programs. This new eruption of births can only mean something more is involved; not directly caused by our genetic engineering."

"Well that seems pretty obvious, now doesn't it?" The red-faced Prime Director asked. "Would more eggs have survived if we hadn't interfered? Why didn't we just let them grow wings and have cropped them later?"

"That decision was mandated directly by the wishes of Prime Director One, ordered, and executed in concert with the first director here." Serzi 66 was quick to add. "Wings of all survivors of Aryll 8 were clipped to eliminate escaping, and in our scientific favor, the continuation of our rigorous genetic modification research has indeed produced a wingless species."

"At what costs in reproduction? And have these costs been too high?"

"All natives are banded with wrist-homers of the latest design. They can't wander far from their assigned stations or their other duties. Those devices require a ferrotorch to remove them."

"Those initial decisions will remain final for now. No wings and no flight. More young need to survive. More eggs need to be born. Again. If you have no more eggs approaching their birth time, must I need to request the Empire's assistance; to import labor from off this world?"

Doctor Rotz 27 spoke. "We did run a study to encourage some of our young soldiers to make advances upon their females. They have the reputation of trying to mate with almost everything, any time, any way, but unfortunately, even these unions have proven to produce only sterile results."

The director caught the humor in his remark. "I'm certain my feelings are correct when you tell me these prime young men have certainly risen in every effort to maintain their reputation." Laughter broke out at his humor. "I've seen those reports. Unfortunately, your findings indicate reproduction appears impossible between our species. I'm also aware and very confident that experimentation into these matters will continue as an ongoing research."

There were stifled bursts of laughter throughout the room.

Cest 21 said, "I feel assured that is correct fact, sir."

"I believe this will be enough for now."

# SOUNDS FROM THE GROUND

Once again, outside the Arian Central Administration buildings, the ground began to emit strange sounds and shook with an unusual trembling. All felt it. The sounds varied. At times, somewhat like a loco-train; at times somewhat like a giant fan; at times, somewhat like grinding beneath their feet.

Cest 21 felt the trembling ground on her way to her quarters. She stopped and put her ear to the floor once she'd arrived there. She was moved to ponder the sounds welling up from below. *Is this the planet speaking? What's she saying? And what DOES the planet have in store for us?* She became even more lost in thought when the sound and motions unexpectedly ceased.

# TERI 38 HEARS THE HOWLING
# OF THE PLANET

Teri 38 lay in his cot and, through the dusty window, reviewed the fields and forest he was now responsible for. His mind became aware of a cacophony of sounds rising from beneath the floor. The hair on the back of his neck stirred and tickled up in fear. As in the Capacity, the noises started out as a grinding sound, then transmuted to a mechanical-like scream like the metal-on-metal sounds of a lathe. The floors of the compound buildings trembled in rhythm like being close to the passing of a loco-train, softened to rush like a giant fan, then as quickly as the sounds came, they faded away.

Teri 38 found himself standing rigidly in a posture of full military attention. *What was that all about? I didn't know what to do. What else does this world have to do to get me to focus my attention? How far will she go to make her point?*

# A NEW AGRI-DIRECTOR FOR ARYLL 8

Prime Director 32 stewed over recent events. Politically, it was bound to happen. Prime Director One chose a new Agri-Director for Aryll 8.

Harcos 86 was called back to Ariana to report to Prime Director One for training and orientation in his new agri-responsibilities. Now, freshly arrived on Aryll after his sojourn, brimming with latest theories from their home world, freshly inspired with positive attitudes, and new mandates, he sat silently with Prime Director 32 and waited to be addressed.

Prime Director 32 laboring under his covert agreements with Prime Director One, only appeared as if he was trying to get success in the agri-fields. He had secured his director-ship position on a convincing promise to deliver this world for stericyclation. He banked his success on claims that only he had new ideas enough to get that result.

Harcos 86 contended to him the failure of producing successful grain and fruit crops must have been caused by the natives themselves.

"But the natives are the only labor force available to handle the crops. None of the chemical checks and weather surveys registered any problems. All readings are well within plants' tolerances. Can I prove this an argument for a native worker's quiet rebellion against the empire? Perhaps production values will never succeed unless we sterilize the planet and start over? Harcos 86, do you detect a potential uprising?"

"Volt whips traditionally do have a way of sparking submission. The state can tolerate no disobedience, and this is how it has usually been done."

Prime Director 32 spoke candidly. "With our mutual backgrounds, long-time friendship, and training, I trust you will help to justify their confidence in me for complete success."

"You have my complete support. I will fully acknowledge your authority if you wish me to implement these new discipline policies."

The new Agri-Director added. "I assure you, Prime Director 32, I gave you excellent ratings in my reports, and I would like to go on record as having contributed to your successful planetary term here."

"We've both learned to be ruthless enforcing the will of the state. We've both given aid and officiated on planets all over remote fringes of the galaxy. This planet must be the gem of my career and yours. All my other command records were good, but I've gambled with this assignment.

"We can solve these production mysteries, but additionally, Aryll 8 MUST be considered the first candidate for the new stericyclation techniques. I must find a way to request it through official petition. I need strong arguments to succeed. If we are successful with this technology, it will gain Prime Director One, even more political advantage."

Harcos 86 agreed. "Yes, I've been brought up to speed on the works of Doctor Niertz 48. He's the top ranking environmental technician for this radical procedure. He has the official benefits of a new laboratory set up on Ariana's Moon

7 where Prime Director One is known to be quite a frequent visitor."

Prime Director 32 smiled knowingly. "You are well informed, Harcos 86. I do believe you may be just the man I need."

"May the state prosper from the confidence you shown in me, sir. I feel my first OFFICIAL duty will be to personally tour all our agricultural fields."

"Don't get overzealous and kill any of the native workers. They are too close to being considered an endangered species. We need them to breed. Just confirm their impossibly low levels of production."

Harcos 86 set his jaw. "Oh, I'll not kill any of them, but if it's true they can never be convinced to be more productive, then I'll know why."

They both laughed.

# DRING LEAVES FOR THE AGRI-FIELDS

"It's time." Orlycia gave Dring one last embrace. Yeto gently squeezed Dring's shoulder and gave him one last look.

Cloaked in his cape, he also held a small bag that contained all the other possessions that were allowed on his duty assignment.

"I hate waiting."

Orlycia addressed him as Yeto stepped back. "Dring, you have received the best training we could give you. You're filled with our love. This assignment won't last forever, but you must stay alert. The other workers will accept you, but remain definite in your range of thoughts. Don't dwell on the coming future Changeover. It may let them read your deeper secrets. They don't need to know you have wings."

"Yes, Mother." Dring heard the thumping sound of the shuttle landing. "I've got to go now. They'll send an inspecting official inside to gather me for this duty. I know you are both mentally prepared to assist me to pass this inspection."

Orlycia responded to noise from the hand plate at the door. Outside, a short, stocky woman wearing an inspector's uniform announced herself. "My name is Phaethon 16, official duty inspector. I've been sent here to confirm the readiness of one native male, Dring. Is he prepared for my final inspection and departure?"

Yeto engaged her eyes in a soft-focused gaze. He blinked his eyes in a slow and deliberate response, from the bottom upward, as he read her natural brain wave pattern. His mind prepared to insert new, more dominating frequency images, into her mind. "Yes, of course, Inspector."

Yeto escorted her into the great hall and nodded to Orlycia and Dring as they waited. Orlycia read Yeto's thoughts. *Have you gotten control of her internal thought frequencies?*

*Yes, her thinking is very linear, and her mind is very sympathetic to accepting disciplines and new imagery. I have begun her mental conditioning. As she proceeds, she will become more open. We will easily be able to mind control her approvals.*

"This is Phaethon 16, Orlycia. She's here for the final inspection." Yeto deliberately remained close within her energy field.

Orlycia voiced a greeting. "Welcome. This is my son, Dring. He is ready. I have all the forms in order."

Phaethon 16 blinked slowly as their combined minds slowed her perceptions. "I need to have a quick physical inspection confirming the effectiveness of the wing suppressing chemicals upon his body. This will only be a brief, official observation his wings have been successfully mutated. Dring, you need to remove your cape so I can confirm the medicines have worked."

"Of course." Dring set down his bag and nodded to Yeto and Orlycia. Dring had para-folded his wings as tightly as he could. Now he needed to depend upon their skilled techniques to cloud this inspector's mind.

"You know it's been so long ago since I thought of those chemical treatments. Why, whenever I think of his lack of wings, I get an image of blue roses in my mind. The blue roses of forgetfulness fill my mind." Phaethon 16 felt hypnotized and very relaxed. Dring removed his cape and revealed his back. Yeto and Orlycia focused upon blue roses filling her conscious mind.

All Phaethon 16 saw were the images of mutated lumps of skin where his wing nodes should have been. The clarity of two native minds projected images and overshadowed her limited mental and visual programming.

"You see? That wasn't so bad, was it now, Dring?" Phaethon 16 sighed and blinked slowly. "The state thanks you for your cooperation. Get your cape back on. I'll wait in the shuttle."

When the inspector left, Dring spoke. "I'll think of you both. Often."

"Be true to yourself, son. Everything will happen in its own time."

# THE AGRI-FIELDS

Teri 38 faced a difficult daily work life. Each night he and his two-member security staff returned to quarters exhausted. His was the responsible position. It required he stayed on site but offered nothing remotely comparable to the near-luxury conditions of the Capacity.

He received some advanced reports from the other stations that Harcos 86, the new Agri-Director, was inspecting all the fields. Warnings were clear. It would eventually be Teri 38's turn to receive this group of official prying eyes. He had no concern about inspections. His plants responded with higher than average yields.

While Teri 38 was tough and demanding, he wasn't cruel. Food rations had been doubled, and two females were pregnant.

Obviously, Teri 38 didn't recognize his newest worker, but certainly, the same wasn't true of Dring, who knew of Teri 38's role in his birth.

In the fields, Ethra had easily moved into an unofficial supervisory position in the pecking order of the natives. Her spunky authority came from growing up and surviving in one of the older, more backwater state homes. She'd learned long ago to fend for herself and demand her respect.

"Time to cease work for a rest?" Ethra voiced her question

verbally. "You find a lot of moments to fall into contempla-tion, Dring. Why don't the rest of us hear your thoughts in those quiet times?"

"How should I know? Maybe I was drugged too much as a young fledgling."

This unusual young female generated a particular interest in him. Clearly, her body had nearly defeated Arian attempts to poison her birth genetics. She sported traces of stubby wing growth. Her tiny wings seemed large enough that Dring was surprised the Arians hadn't ordered surgical removal. Ethra wasn't afraid to let her cape slip enough to remind the other workers of this fact, either. She inspired the others to be proud of themselves and their heritage.

Despite his curiosity, Dring maintained his composure. He also maintained vigilance to hide the tight bulges of his real wings.

He re-engaged in clearing thistle-weeds from around the grain stalks and observed the other crew members. Most of them were near his age. These stolen males and females were a mixed population, survivors of a dozen cities. State incuba-tor born, they'd all been assigned and shoved together here forced to serve the empire.

The long days of field work tested his concentration, and soon cramping fatigue built up in his wings. Even with the long hours of practicing the para-fold arts, he could barely conceal his fully maturing wings. It was difficult to find a private space to stretch them.

Some of the workers mentally discussed insurrection by killing the plants or a work slowdown. Dring responded, *No, if we take part in that sabotage, Teri 38 will be made to suffer, as well.*

There was a stunned silence, then a question. *We all know who you are, Dring. So what? He's just another Arian.*

Dring held firm. *Yes, but he hasn't the same disposition. The Volt whips are left in his quarters. He's ordered his two-day span assistants to treat us fairly, and the Volt fence around our quarters is not turned on at night. During the night, couples can find quiet places to be alone together under the Zolag trees.*

*These behaviors aren't allowed in other camps. Count these things well before you spoil this Arian's record. Any of the others who would replace him could be far worse. We cannot change what has happened in the aftermath of their conquest, but we must make the most of this situation. Keep strong, for the time is near when all will be restored.*

Ethra interrupted. *None of us have wings!*

The electricity of the silence, the mental probing, and the breaking through of his mental screens was deafening within Dring's mind.

Questions buzzed through the air like bees as Zena and Mata shared their observations.

*Ethra is from Dring's Raptor tribeflock. And now we have Dring. Before the conquest, he might have been considered a prince. Rumor has it that he was a product of the last of the private incubators. If my readings are true, Dring has gone through the birth song ceremonies. Ethra's correct. She's started to put those pieces of her perceptions together.*

One of the other young males voiced a mental challenge. *Why haven't we noticed how special this Dring is before?*

Zena displayed her enigmatic smile. *This bird is clever, my dear ones, and he's been carefully trained. I was formerly in regular attendance to his father's court. I suspect now young Dring has been using the feeling mask of ignorance. Dring's simply reflecting back our painful memories to shield the fact that those lumps on his shoulders are not scar tissue, but they are a full set of wings. As I think about it, he's also probably been trained in Prana-Bindu to keep them folded. How simple a ruse; how effective for one skillfully trained in the starlight arts.*

Mata, the other eldest member of the workforce, added. *If that is true, and he is trained in special arts taught only to the worthy, he must not be disturbed. To be able to conceal his wings this long, and I now sense he is here for a special purpose.*

*You are all too young to remember the conquest. I watched the first phase of the Changeover happen when our tribeflocks translated their energies into the starlight dimension under Dring's father's noble leadership. I know they are all safe. They assured us. We must wait. The Changeover will be the way for us to return with them to safely.*

Mata sighed and added, *I had all but blanked those days from my mind. It seems like only a moment ago; now it's returned with even more clarity. The predicted Changeover may be now upon us. The runes foretold he would be born of a royal tribe. Dring is Ospra's son. His father led the initial mass exodus.*

Other workers flooded more questions toward Dring.

*I was young when I witnessed it in a vision. Is now our time? Is this all true? How have you escaped the inspectors, the surgeon's knife, and the chemical mutations?*

The tone of these thoughts was flavored with personal sorrows, but as more and more they were given expression, a new frequency of hope flowed. Many felt these truths as deep, personal realizations.

Dring lowered his thought bound and let them probe his mind more deeply.

*Please, all of you be at peace. Whatever has allowed me to remain intact until this time is not yet finished. I do know this. Unconsciously, Teri 38 has had much to do with allowing my development escape Arian detection. For now, you must all promise me you'll keep my secret at all costs, and only within this group.*

Ethra's thoughts rang through all others. *On one condition, Dring.*

*And what condition is that, Ethra?*

Her response welled up like a joyous expectation. It came rolling into his silent mind like a mighty, single thought wave joined like a symphony from all the others.

*Show us your wings, and let us feel what it's like to fly.*

Dring had no choice but to agree. *Alright, late tonight meet in the large clearing in the Zolag forest. There I'll show you.*

# NIGHT IN THE ZOLAG FOREST

Under cover of darkness, groups of native workers left their quarters. Whatever slight airs of sadness rose through recounting old histories faded as it mixed within this night's air of excitement filled with future hopes.

Their captors had kept them separate, scared, disciplined, and dominated. The group never considered meeting this way before. To defy curfew and hold a clandestine meeting was a major awakening for their psyches. Excited about their awakening, their minds embraced this freedom.

Frule, a young male, spoke. He removed his cape and revealed mutated wings as he sat on the cool forest floor. "I'm Frule. Here's how it's been for me. I feel things. Even the horrific history of pain and the drugs we've all endured can't take away the haunting feeling something big is about to happen."

One by one, others joined him. "I'm Hesse. I've felt premonitions. I couldn't get focused to understand what they meant. But I do know this. Workers in other camps are experiencing changes too."

"What did you think back to them?" Dring asked.

"I instructed them to focus their minds on our collective pasts, and all will be well."

Zena, the elder, added, "We've all had dreams of the old

times and returning to our homes. We've all had dreams of flying the clouds with our families."

Without capes, the natives realized how unique they were from different tribeflocks. Some with darker feather tips were from Peeptweet, some from the Dovereal. Zena and Mata were Owlaface; Dring and Ethra were Raptor, and there were slight coloration differences in those who'd been sent there from the tropical regions. All assembled felt the collective joy of being together, being part of something natural to this world. They wore their scars of butchery, enslavement, and genetic poisons, but those pains faded now. They were soothed by sharing these feelings of trust with each other.

Ethra stood tall and striking in her white plumage and stunted wings. "I somehow resisted their programming poisons and kept my mind clear. Larger than any individual story is what's happening here, this night, at this gathering. Something vital moves in the life of our planet. Please gather close so we might feel its experience together."

They all held that moment of silence together until the ground moaned with sounds and vibrations of a soft, lullaby-like song. It rose from the heart of their Mother Planet to these, her children of Aryll, and it cradled them all in her love.

# TERI 38 AWAKENED BY HARCOS 86

Teri 38 slept so deeply that he didn't hear the arrival of the shuttle or the accompanying gravity sleds. He had long since stopped the constant bother of the security alarm's drone. The relentless buzzing during the night kept him awake and it reminded him of the faulty audio sound system he'd grown up with in his former state home.

All the lights in the command building blazed to full illumination. Groups of uniformed figures burst into his quarters and startled him from his sleep. He recognized his immediate supervisor, Mikius 9.

"On your feet, soldier."

The door opened, and another official entered, they were joined by Harcos 86.

"At Attention!" Guards stiffened beneath the blazing overhead lights.

Teri 38's years of repetitious discipline yanked him to attention for this new officer, Harcos 86, who said, "At ease. Agri-Unit Keeper. If you had been properly monitoring your beam set, our little visit would not have been such a surprise to you. But then, I like surprises, don't you, Teri 38?"

"Yes, sir. There have never been calls this late. In the interest of conservation, I shut it down during the nights. Messages received are always held until the following morning."

Harcos 86 moved forward for a closer examination. He spoke, demanding more from Teri 38. "Where are your two security guards, soldier? The equipment readings say your Volt fence is not activated. How can you be sure your entire agri-force is safely tucked away?"

Teri 38 struggled to answer. "The guards have no proper quarters here, so they return to the Capacity each night for rest and recreation." That remark only got him a look of disdain.

"Besides," Teri was trying his best, "wrist readouts can always provide the exact whereabouts of all workers. As for their safety, they never wander far. In their defense, they have an excellent production record, and they seem happier if they have some time to themselves."

"Quiet." Harcos 86 moved to overreact and act dramatic to emphasize the power of his rank and demonstrate a rampage of his increasing command for the others. "This man needs a firmer grip here. The methods by which you are running this crew are a travesty! No discipline! No regulations! No compliance with the uniform and behavior codes!

"Inspector General Mikius 9, why was I brought to this place? Tell this simpleton."

"Our new Agri-Director is heading up an official review study mandated from Prime Director 32 himself to obtain an immediate, up to date review of all facilities. This crucial first-hand knowledge will be the research and intelligence for..."

Harcos 86 normally never wearied of his praises, but the night's inspections unnerved him. "I'm here because while your production remains quite high, I can't possibly under-stand how you do it."

Teri 38 didn't immediately respond when Harcos 86

snapped, "Where are all my Agri-crew members at this very moment?"

"The wrist displays can tell us. They never wander far. There are no other facilities within 50 milli-lengths of this one."

He surveyed this man, "Are you always so lax in your supervision?"

Not usually fast on the uptake, Teri 38 desperately tried to think on his feet. "No sir, but with the state mandate to encourage reproduction, it seemed a looser tether might be worth a try."

Teri 38 hated to dialogue with supervisors, but it usually worked to cover his backside. "Encouraging native activity of the male-female nature under our usual tight security methods was not working. I've had nothing but negative results in that area. It occurred to me since these are sensitive creatures, perhaps a little breathing space might encourage things along. This method has encouraged two females to be in preparation for births."

"I see. You have an experimental mind, have you? Did you decide this all on your own? No reports or requests back to your supervisors? This will be considered only if you are successful. Otherwise, as well you should know, the penalties for breach of disciplines are severe!" Looking at the screen, Harcos 86 reacted to the obvious. "They do not appear to be nesting in their coops!"

"Let me check the readings." Teri 38 moved nervously toward the equipment but stopped as Harcos 86 took command, and motioned to the soldier next to him. "Guard, man this equipment." The soldier pushed Teri 38 aside to review the readouts.

"They'd better not be missing! You, sit down."

Tensions grew in the small room until the operator finally spoke. "The entire population is gathered in a forest clearing about 500 lengths east of their quarters."

Mikius 9 asked, "Shall we send a detail out and return them to their compound?"

Harcos 86 looked scornfully at Teri 38 and replied, "Yes, General, have your troops muster them back here to the inspection grounds. Since the entire population under this delinquent's supervision appears to be up and awake, I'll inspect them NOW." He leveled a vocal volley at Mikius 9. "Inform me when this detail has them assembled. I'll be in the shuttle. Soldiers, do you have your Volt whips handy?

"A firm hand never loses its grip. This entire affair will be taken before a review board immediately. Consider yourself under arrest." Then Harcos 86 exited.

A speechless Teri 38 collapsed on his cot. Clad only in his sleepsuit, he found a strange chill overcame him as he felt the shiver of impending Arian discipline.

# THE CLEARING IN THE ZOLAG FOREST

The workers admired Dring's fully outstretched wings when suddenly, utter silence cut through the air like a dense fog. They all sensed the danger Ethra spoke aloud.

"Arian soldiers are coming this way! Fast! Dring. Cover your shoulders."

Dring struggled to tighten the last buckles on his wrap-cape when the forest flooded with overhead lights from the approaching gravity sleds. An amplified voice bellowed commands at them from above.

"What's going on down there? All of you move to the center of the clearing. Immediately! Don't try to disperse, or you'll taste our lasers. Assemble yourselves! Now!"

As they landed, a guard grabbed Hesse by her arm. "Out here for a little pleasure time? Everybody forget we can always find you with those little beepers?"

He laughed and jolted Hesse with his whip. Hesse's chosen life mate, Frule, moved toward him to save Hesse and to draw attention away from Dring whose wing tip remained slightly exposed. The guard caught Frule's actions and waved to the other soldiers to approach with their stun guns.

The guard released Hesse and grabbed the young Frule. "Why are you moving around? Don't you have respect for the discipline we give you? You've been allowed too much freedom."

The bully pushed Frule away and grabbed at Mata who was thrown off balance and fell to the ground. Electrified tensions surged around the group as the soldier stung her with his whip. In sympathetic response, all could feel its sting as Mata's body received the first of its lashes. This crew had not felt that searing lash for the last year while under Teri 38's supervision.

He struck her again. "How do you like a taste of that, you old crone?"

As Mata moaned in excruciating pain, the native's emotions boiled over with emotion. They attacked the guards with flying stones, tree limbs, anything they could find and tried to avoid the crack of whips and laser blasts. Some members of the group struggled to stop the fighting. Two of them fell to the ground, stung by the lasers.

When Dring struggled to free old Mata, the guard grabbed at his shoulder causing the buckles and fabric to give way. Illumined in the spotlights of the gravity sleds, the Arians saw his wings unfurl and flap widely behind him. For an instant, everything stopped.

A guard shouted, "Well, look at what we have here! A native birdie! Forget all of them. Get this one!"

The troops moved in to capture Dring when Ethra rushed forward. They shoved her aside. An angry Dring snapped to attention, shed his disciplined training, tensed his wings and crouched to attack.

Dring stood alone. All his life he had hidden in training; coached to fold and hide his true self. Now spotlights blazed out his secret. He always feared this day would come, but he had been well-prepared. Without warning, he launched himself forward at full speed like a great bird, tucked his feet in flight, dodged the shots from the stun guns, shifted to a roundhouse side-kick, and snapped the neck of the nearest guard.

That soldier died as another one moved in to use Mata as a shield. Dring deftly spun around in mid-air over the Arian. He avoided the thrust of the Volt whip and gave his jaw a swift kick knocking him away from Mata. His helmet went flying into the woods.

In unison, the others joined in defense. A Zolag branch crashed down upon another guard's head, and he dropped to the forest floor where he tried to resist and remain standing, but the group's combined wrath overpowered him. The guard collapsed, beaten unconscious to the ground by the other natives.

The farthest gravity sled drew attention. Even without a helmet, the last guard had retreated, jumped aboard, and began its lift-off. Apris, a young native, jumped on a nearby sled to chase after him despite his lack of experience with the machine. As Apris was catching up, the fleeing guard put his sled into a fast turn, fired his laser, and escaped as the native rider, and his sled burst into a ball of flames.

But Apris never even heard the explosion or felt the flames. Before the sled destructed, a dense, pink fog enveloped and saved him. His life entered the unseen starlight dimension with outside help.

As the wreckage plummeted to the ground, the only trace of Apris was his wristband. Supposedly only removed with a ferro torch, it made a strange ringing noise as it struck the rocks below.

# DRING FLIES FOR HIS LIFE

In the forest, workers nursed their wounds with a quiet, exhilarating sense of victory in this brief yet intense scrimmage.

*Dring, you must fly. Flee for an old city, or you will be taken. We will endure and wait for your return. Now go!* The two elder females mentally urged him.

Dring, still feeling the shock and transition of what had happened, stood dazed for a moment. Ethra rushed to his side, to shake him, to awaken him to his eminent danger. *You must go, my love. You must survive for me and all of us.*

Dring had been so busy concealing his true nature that he never allowed his personal feelings to evolve. Now he realized Ethra had always been the one waiting for him. He looked into her eyes. She was the one!

And although she had hidden her feelings until now, she loved him. There was no question; their deeper selves resonated, unlike anything he could have known or experienced before.

Dring mumbled to Ethra, "I know I need to go now. I'm a freak in this world. It won't take long for more forces to return. I'm going to be the best aerial target they've had in a long time. Where can I go?"

Ethra held his face in her hands. "Dring, you must fly now. Be strong for all of us! I love you. I'll wait for your return. We shall all wait for your return."

Dring looked deeply into her eyes. "Ethra, I will return for you and the rest of our tribeflocks. Whatever happens; stay alive. I will find you. I will find a way."

Suddenly, one unified voice rose from the minds of all the natives present, and it resonated from across the veil between them and from the starlight dimension. Dring's head filled with thoughts of hundreds of other voices.

*Fly, Dring. Fly. Escape. You must live. You must escape.*

A dazed Dring gave Ethra one loving embrace; wrapping and enfolding her completely with his wings. He kissed her with a passion he'd never felt before. Her taste was electric and inviting. Her touch drew him into her mind. *We will always be together my life mate* rang between them as a single thought.

Ethra struggled reluctantly to escape his embrace. *Dring, you must only come back for us when it is safe.* She stepped away from his embrace.

Dring unfurled his wings, sighed, and drew his deepest breath. He flapped his wings with all his strength and launched his leap. From the forest floor below, all those of his kind felt and experienced the wonder of his flight as he soared away. They connected mentally and felt the freedom of his wings as he soared into the air above the trees. They looked after him sharing a united sense of joy, excitement, and sadness.

Ethra, too, stared at him until he faded from view. Her heart overflowed with love for Dring and the new future just begun.

# ARYLL TREMBLES AT DRING'S ESCAPE

Clearly resonant in support of their actions, the ground beneath the Zolag forest floor trembled once more. Its steady, staccato rhythm began softly and grew in a beat unerring and continuous. Its low moan frequency grew loud enough to be annoying for the ears of the natives. Its sounds triggered a shaking that, in places, rippled the soil.

The one remaining Arian guard still alive awoke to these strange vibrations, limped, stumbled onto his sled, and then sputtered off in an erratic retreat.

These children of Aryll nursed their wounds as they felt the beginning rhythmic glow of new hope for changes in their world.

# HARCOS 86 GETS THE NEWS

An outraged Harcos 86 received the flustered appearance of the single pilot with surprise. "What is this about, soldier? Where is your helmet? Where are the others? And where are the agri-workers?"

Out of breath, the flustered soldier stammered. "They attacked us, sir. And one of them has wings! They massed together. They resisted us. I barely managed to escape. I shot down one of the natives. He tried to attack me with one of our sleds. The one with wings flew off. I don't think the other soldiers survived."

Harcos 86 shouted furiously to the rest of his staff. "Action Alert! Order more shuttles. Get out there and round up those rebels. Carry all of them back to confinement." He turned to his com. staff.

"Get me Scanner Alpha. I want two of our best long range pilots scrambled and in pursuit of that winged bird immediately."

Harcos 86 added, "Tell them to use whatever deadly force is necessary to blow this creature out of the skies. Shoot him down. Then drag the body back to the Capacity. I'll impale it on a pole myself if I must to display as an example. The empire shall not be mocked."

"Two of our best pursuit-flyers have taken off to target

him and accommodate all your orders just as you wish, sir. Your orders shall be obeyed; I'll make certain of it." Mikius 9 returned his attention to the transmitter.

Harcos 86 said, "That whole worthless bunch of natives will pay dearly for their affront to Arian rule. I will know every detail surrounding this affair. We have ways to squeeze truth fact answers out of every one of them."

He pointed to Teri 38. "Drag this worthless Agri-Keeper out into the assembly area with them. This happened on his watch. I'll find out how much of a role he played, and how any of this could have happened in the first place."

# DRING'S FLYING ESCAPE

Dring couldn't waste any flying time. He pushed rapidly as land and forests raced below him in the darkness. Driven as he was, his body trembled in response to the repercussions of the recent attack.

He'd been discovered, not only by the mental perceptions of his other companions but by their strength of retaliation shown in their native assault upon the Arians. Dring never thought of himself as leader of a revolution.

His mind sought retreat. The only possibility it saw was back with Yeto and Orlycia in the Capacity. As he flew, his thoughts were of the others and especially of Ethra.

He soon discovered the long-range rhythms of his flight; the emotions and panic settled within him. For fear of being detected, he'd never been able to practice long distant flights like this, but as for his body, Yeto's intense training worked.

*My previous life is over. I recognize the foolishness of times when I wished I didn't have these wings. Mother and Yeto worked hard to train me. I now understand what drove them so be steadfast in my education? This is my Destiny. I'm not just a freak of birth.*

*Mother and Yeto must be warned. The Arians will retaliate against the ones I love.*

# IN THE PRIME DIRECTOR'S
## LIVING QUARTERS

"No, the Prime Director is not available right now, he's resting," Moria responded to the videophone's signal.

An incredulous voice and face glared at her. "This is Harcos 86. I don't know who you think you are, or what you think you're doing, but if you do not rouse Prime Director 32 and get him on this call immediately when I get back to the Capacity, I will personally come over there and tear your throat out."

"My name is Moria, sir. We've met before, but we were not expecting any communications this late in the night."

"I don't care what you were expecting. Listen to me Moria, or whatever you call yourself in the bedroom; this is official business. Get me Prime Director 32 on this call NOW."

The director had been roused by the tone and volume of the communication. "Harcos 86, what seems so urgent you need to scream out of this call connection at this hour?"

"I've had to scramble the forces. We have a native revolt on our hands."

"Report fact. They've never retaliated before."

"A group of the natives fought back. We flushed out a native male with a full set of wings. One of my guards was killed. I've ordered fighters scrambled to shoot him down and bring in the dead body. We must eliminate the leader of this rebellious behavior. He's flying back your way. They'll get him."

Harcos 86 betrayed his emotions by his run-on speech. "I've also ordered the supervisor and all natives to be rounded up and thrown into lockup for interrogation."

"Slow down. You've acted well. You and I are in complete accord. Where are you now?"

"I'm returning to the Capacity."

"Report to my office immediately upon arrival for debriefing. You've acted very well. Proceed with the full protocols you've already set in motion. I wish to hear all of this debriefing from you in person. Out."

Moria poised very attentively at this information. Her mind soared to think members of her race had now retaliated against these barbarians. And a fully winged male? How curious. She carefully probed the mind of the director for his thinking concerning all this.

"It appears members of your species have decided to fight back, as you no doubt could hear. How do you feel about of this?"

Moria sensed the lethal entanglement programming behind his questions, and his feeble mental attempts to probe her mind. She proceeded to navigate his mental-mine fields very slowly and to speak very carefully.

"Sir, you've allowed me into your daily personal life to some extent. Surely I've shared my body's pleasures with you enough that you would never doubt my allegiance to you. Please be assured I've long since abandoned any traces of my former self in body, mind, and in spirit. I am a happy, loyal citizen of the Arian Empire.

"Prime Director, whatever this small group of dissidents has done, whoever this mysterious winged leader is, they will be no match for the empire's glory you orchestrate for the future of this planet."

With the practiced strength of her mental training, Moria radiated those correct belief frequencies into his mind. She skillfully looped her electromagnetic responses to him in frequencies and brain wave patterns that had programmed into him since birth.

He had no clue as to the scope of her abilities to read his thoughts or that her subtle control his mind far overshadowed his meager programmed, perceptual abilities. With his domestic fears and concerns allayed, he rummaged a closet for his best uniform.

He broke from his official tone for a moment to look at her. "You must rest here. Stay out of the public eye for right now."

"Yes, Prime Director 32. I shall discreetly await you here."

The Prime Director relished this attention. "I'll see to this alone. I'm fully trained for any such emergencies. Harcos 86 has my every confidence. He's perfectly capable of instigating alert procedures."

Lost in his self-importance, he rushed to his office for a rendezvous with his future.

Moria dwelled upon the recent events. *All the eggs in the State incubator birthed at once. A winged native arousing the workers? Noises from beneath our feet? Could these signs be anything except the immediate precursors to the Changeover?*

# DRING PURSUED

While Dring experienced flying memories trained into him, two experienced fighter pilots aimed in an intercept course for his flight.

Afterburners pushed to maximum, dispatched in their deadly mandated pursuit; accelerated, heavily armed destroyers moved to the fastest attack speeds their sleds could muster. Smelling opportunity for easy victory, commendation, and pay raises, these instructions came to attack and destroy -- not capture.

Dring's wrist signal appeared as a single, clear green, screen blip on their scanners.

"I've got him, Alpha, and confirm the visual sighting." Rider One reported.

"This is Rider Two. Affirmative."

"Proceed with caution. Don't panic him. Make it a fast high dive and kill maneuver. Don't get in his way as he goes down."

"Copy Alpha. Banking vector 134 for the first pass."

They maneuvered into a coordinated high arc formation; staging as twin birds of prey would pounce down upon an unsuspecting dove. They were practiced executing this deadly, coordinated air ballet. "Affirmative. Rider Two copies. Locked and loaded. Laser guns set. Max kill. One bird destined to be prime target objective."

# DRING ATTACKED

Dring's acute senses screamed in his mind as this he registered their approach, despite their stealth mode.

Keenly aware of the enemy's company, Dring easily computed they flew faster, maneuvered better in the air, and they were most certainly in deadliest attack mode, coming at him from above.

He suffered brief muscle cramping, but there was no time to stop. He'd never flown such a distance at his maximum speed before. Even with Yeto's training, and keeping his breathing paced, he'd stretched his body stamina to its limit. Rest would be needed soon.

Instinctively, his ancient predatory senses screamed to drop his flight into a sharp left turn. It was a little late. The Arians were too close. The slashing stab of a laser beam scorched and cut him under the wing on his right side. He momentarily fluttered in flight.

The edge of the old city he knew well lay ahead. He had often practiced outside flying when the patrols were asleep. Now, he needed to reach one of its old towers.

Despite losing altitude, he wobbled back up to flying speed. While some feathers had been singed from the lasers, he skidded to a stop on the top perch surrounding the tower's pinnacle and slumped to avoid detection. He pressed his back tight against the cool, emerald green wall.

Above him, the aggressors circled in frustration over who had the kill position and who had broken formation.

"That was not a standard formation firing. You'll be on report for this. Did you copy that, Rider Two?"

"I copy. I was a bit over-reactive. It didn't kill him. The shot only singed his feathers."

"Come on, Rider One. By the book. Let's take another pass around that tower. He was wounded in the first shot. He's not going to get away. You take the first shots. We've got all the firepower we need to finish him off, Rider One."

"What's going on there? This is Alpha Scanner, copy."

"This is Rider One. Initial burst has knocked down the target. He's holed up atop a structure in the old green tower. We're proceeding with the next run now."

"Copy that. Alpha Scanner standing by."

Dring sensed the approaching attacks would end his life, and his mind began to scream for an answer. At that moment, the tower switched on, came alive. The wall behind his back trembled, warmed to his touch, and the dome top of the tower began to glow. It wasn't uncomfortable or frightening, and it surprisingly filled him with hope and almost a feeling of maternal support. He'd never experienced that from any building or machine or in any of his training.

The pilots chose to dismiss the glowing of the dome as reflections from their headlights, and they dove together as a single unit when suddenly, twin bolts in two blinding flashes of energy, fired out from the tower. The discharges precisely targeted the rapidly approaching enemies. A brilliant corona of crimson red light bathed each sled, and the shriek of their high-pitched screams echoed into the quiet night.

Before the two enemy flyers could activate their lasers, the energy fields blazed with clouds of red light and the sleds exploded. Vaporized pilots and debris rained to the ground in a shower of sequin-sparks. Dring froze with astonishment.

"Thank you tower, for your protection. Since you worked so well to protect me, can you release me from this as well?" Dring held his arm out and looked at the wristband he'd worn nearly all his life. The tower sparked again, and a small narrow beam hit upon it. A moment passed, and it heated, parted, and fell in a molten cinder near him.

Desperate to warn his mother and Yeto, he flexed his wings, pushed off from the tower and flew in the direction of the palace.

As the wreckage fell to the ground, the airwaves were alive with urgent messages. There would be no response. The only sound was the wind carrying the future forward on soft wings of new promise.

Everywhere on Aryll and in the sky filled with sounds of low trumpeting and shrilling. Everyone heard the sounds. Deep beneath the ground asperses of strata moaned as some rock was being compressed while other sections were pulled apart.

Many battle-hardened veterans plugged their ears and shivered as the ground moaned.

# DRING'S FORMER HOME

Sore and exhausted, Dring entered through the back terrace and burst in upon an excited conversation between Yeto, Orlycia, and Cest 21.

Cest 21 was hushed to silence when she saw the appearance of his wings. Orlycia and Yeto rushed to help him. He didn't notice Cest 21 at first.

He gasped with exhaustion. "Our lives are in danger. My wings have been revealed."

Orlycia spoke as she touched his tired shoulders and moved to apply healing ointment to his burns. "Yes, my son. We have heard of your exposure and the events. We have a guest here who is not of our family."

Cest 21 knew the amazing Pictart, but to see Dring in full wingspread left her stunned. "Probe my thoughts as deeply as you wish, Orlycia. I would never think of hurting Dring. Please be totally clear with me, I am not weak. Just help me understand what this all means."

Yeto addressed the situation for them all. "Eventually, this was bound to happen. Orlycia and I would have wished these revelations to happen later, but destiny, it appears, happens in its own time. You have been drawn here to learn these things for a reason."

"Dring has reached a pivotal point in our collective, larger destiny; for him, for all of us, and most certainly, for our planet. He can no longer conceal his true planetary nature and genetic design. Even his growing mental maturity, personal development, and his clarity in the transmission of thought were bound to reveal him. His radiation alone would contagiously trigger those same faculties in his friends and other workers. Dring's birth and growth have always been guided from beyond this physical realm."

Yeto then turned to specifically address their Arian pupil. "Cest 21, look upon Dring as representative of the last missing link from the evolution of our ancient past. After this day, view him as the one to embody Aryll's imminent future. He alone has the necessary facilitating development and ability to be the catalytic agent of this Changeover."

"He is the living agent of the Changeover?" Cest 21 asked with curiosity.

Dring was finally catching his breath; he held his comments verbally as thoughts reached out. *Orlycia, Mother, Yeto, can we trust this Arian in our midst in these times?*

Cest 21 heard his thoughts and responded. *I have grown in my sensitivities, Dring. I am no longer a confused Arian woman. These two have accepted me and act now as my instructors, assisting me to unlock the benefits of my own deeply moving experiences. It appears this potential within brought me here to Aryll. In discovering the importance and awareness of my feelings, my life can finally experience value as an individual. My higher self ached to be discovered on your planet. I can only ask you to understand and allow me to prove my value.*

Yeto spoke. "We must give Dring his final instructions before this night ends."

"You are correct," Orlycia agreed.

"Dring, this will be the first place the Arians will look for you," Yeto said. "These events signal the reality of end-times which now, even more quickly, will manifest upon us. Recognize it! Now respond to your purpose. We've all waited for such a sign."

"Our Mother Planet is already starting her Changeover songs. Your path is now clear, Dring," Orlycia said. "And so is mine. My time to remain with all of you in this physical form is complete. I have honored my service obligations. I will shortly elevate where I may join Ospra, my life mate. At long last, I may translate my energy to sanctuary in the starlight dimension. There need be no worries from any of you when I pass. All life is eternal. We shall all meet again soon. Dring, you have my every confidence. You are ready and trained to play your role bringing these events to their fruition." Orlycia took Dring's face in her hands. "You must go now, my loving son. Your future calls to you."

"But Mother, what if I'm not ready for all this?"

"Ospra, your father, and I have dreamed together of your success every moment of your life. You do not have it in you to fail this great task."

Yeto agreed. "Dring, you've been exposed to and absorbed all the knowledge you need to assist this Changeover. Just as you discovered ease in flying, allow that innate training and preparedness to unfold naturally within you. Your inner being will show you the way. Now gather your wings and fly. You know the other old city location for our next steps together. I will meet you there."

Dring stood tall and flexed his wings. "Thank you both for all your love and support. I will honor your faith in me.

I will rise to this challenge." Before he moved to the exit, he spoke. "Cest 21, you have certainly traveled a long journey to be here, and I do accept you. I hope to meet you again."

He leaped from the terrace into the darkness. It filled his wings and carried him away to fulfill his destiny.

# INVITED TO JOIN THE CHANGEOVER TIMES

Orlycia and Yeto drew her close in an embrace. Orlycia let her thoughts be known. "Cest 21, you came to us as a representative of the empire, but you are no longer that person. Because you have developed great sympathy for all that we are, I, as the last remaining queen of this realm, formally invite you to join us in the great Changeover that so rapidly approaches us. I will leave this world soon, but you are invited to join us there, with my tribeflock, in its continuing journey.

"Yeto and I have deeply probed your motives, and we both agree. Whatever you have done with your life, we acknowledge the sincerity of your quest. If you choose to accept this invitation, we will meet again.

"I sense your Arian world will rigorously test you. Your superior officers will want to know what you have to reveal. Stay firm in our promise. You were always more in touch with this Changeover than you realize."

As they released her from their embrace, Yeto spoke. "All major forces have been activated to pursue and capture Dring. It would be best for all of us if you now return to your base.

"Cest 21, this is the last you will see either of us for a time. You are free to reveal the facts of Dring's return. Neither Orlycia nor I will be remaining in this Capacity after tonight. All our tasks here are complete. You will be questioned about all this. Just keep yourself safe and be ready for events which will unfold. Have no fears; the other Arians can do nothing to prevent the course of these approaching events. You must leave now, Cest 21, but if you choose, we will meet again."

Cest 21 had to speak. "I have attended to royalty before, but never have I found the peace and nobility which you both have shown me. I will help you and this beloved planet in any way I can. Just as you have so generously assisted me and extended to me your trust, I'll not disappoint you. By way of respect, I offer you both this bow in love and honor and respect to whatever you must have done to be whoever you are now. Both of you may be assured I will see you again. Travel with light, my dear friends."

*Cest 21, no words are necessary between any of our friends. Your mind and heart are true. Know with certainty; you are now loved as an adopted member of our tribeflock.*

Yeto kissed her gently on the forehead and sent her out toward her gravity sled. Outside, the soil moaned beneath her feet, and she felt the acceptance of Aryll's planetary love for her newly adopted child.

# REPORT FROM HARCOS 86

"Harcos 86, report to me," Prime Director 32 demanded. "As I understand it, your late-night inspection tour presented you with surprises more than it allowed you to inflict disciplinary fears into the natives. You sought to bring me info regarding increasing production numbers, but my dear Harcos 86, you have returned with news of much greater importance than that."

"What I found was an agri-site in total disarray. The natives were grouped in the woods; I had to send guards to find them, and ..."

"I'm well-informed of that incident."

PD 32 smiled as Harcos 86 continued with vibrant and animated descriptions of what transpired up to and including losing the troops over the tower.

"Lost, shot out of the skies or destroyed in some unknown way. Yes, yes I've been briefed. This mysterious, unknown winged native is still missing. Delicious!" The director smiled again.

"Sir, I'm dumbfounded. I fail to see how any of these disasters could make you happy."

"Don't you realize what you've done? This is a moment so brilliant even I couldn't have thought it up. We were looking for a REASON. Trying to prove a little agricultural administrative upgrading would never help this planet succeed. You have given me a war."

"I still don't understand, sir."

"This false flag incident will play out so very effectively colored in my reports. The title in bold script: 'Native Workers Rebellion Stages Armed and Aggressive Revolt Against Arian Troops.' Don't you see? Remind me to grant all of them posthumous decorations as martyrs of the revolution."

"What revolution?"

"You, as newly appointed Assistant Director, have uncovered this conspiracy. Well done. You drove their winged rebellion leader out of hiding with your brilliant unscheduled inspection. Because of your diligence, a major revolutionary plot against Arian occupation has been revealed. This can all be wonderfully turned to our advantage. You sought to tighten up discipline. You've given me a WAR. We can now win acclaim for securing this entire planet.

"Politically, war is so much more noticeable than increasing agricultural production any day. You must continue to oversee this for me of course if you think you can manage a field commendation for Assistant Prime Director."

"I'm here at your command, Prime Director 32. How do you suggest I proceed?"

"You must be ready to enact my orders exactly as I command. Firstly, do you have a small squad of specially-trained soldiers that can remain totally discrete and loyal?"

"Yes, sir. As you well know, any officer wishing to rise within the empire keeps their staff close. My trusted guards have covertly served with me through many campaigns."

"And you're certain they're all discreet, classified-cleared and commando trained?"

"Yes, Prime Director 32."

"Excellent. I'll need to orchestrate some very carefully planned and executed examples of how violent all these terrorist acts are unfolding. That requires several operations for your staff to perform. Their actions will guarantee this revolution succeeds."

"You have my undivided attention."

"Now, concerning this present situation, what are the specific circumstances of this affair? My reports indicate the revolutionary leader is a direct descendant of an old royal family."

"His name is Dring, and you are accurate as usual, sir."

"And who was in charge there?"

"Teri 38, a former incubator inspector, sir."

"Was this Teri 38 also the same inspector responsible for signing off on the final inspection for the private incubator in residence at the palace?"

"Yes, he was."

"He inspected and approved the unborn egg and issued a certificate of preliminary birth, but I found him to be lacking in motivation, and I shipped him off somewhere. I'd forget where until now."

"Yes, sir. That's the same man."

He clapped his hands. "This is too perfect. Does that not sound like a set of perfect conspiracy coincidences? You have handed me a script for success far better than if I'd written it myself."

"Elaborate, Prime Director."

"I sent you to research native reproduction, and you've brought back a plot for a revolution."

"And, sir. Teri 38 is currently under arrest for dereliction of duty. He will be thoroughly interrogated."

"Marvelous. I'll weave the scenario around this 'weak link' in his Arian discipline. And what of the winged leader?"

"I regret to inform you; the creature escaped and is still at-large."

"No. Wonderful! He must stay at-large for some time. He must be seen to be extremely effective at alluding capture. Staying free allows him to continue to further inspire his reign of fear and terror upon our empire."

"I might point out you also assigned your Philomystic First Class to continue surveillance on that same former royal residence."

"Ah, my enigmatic, but vocal Cest 21." The Prime Director took a second to turn that thought over in his mind. "Keep an eye on her. First, I should select a target for an attack. Find a vital facility here in the Capacity, and plant a noisy but ineffective bomb. I want a lot of easily repaired destruction about the place. It must make a noisy splash. We need to raise a public outcry. Start to blame the natives for the strange planetary trembles, noises, and phenomena we've been experiencing. Cast those suspicions. It can be seen to be part of their plot against us."

"I see the wisdom of your ways, sir."

"I was sure you would. Harcos 86, we must handle these clandestine affairs with the utmost secrecy. If these events are planned properly, they can be orchestrated as a great stepping stone for both our careers. Well, Assistant Director, are you prepared for this operation?"

"I serve at the pleasure of the Empire, Prime Director 32, and of you in particular."

"Now go and quietly get a little demolition party planned.

I think your team should attack a photogenic section of something big like piping in our central water supply. Blow up conspicuous plumbing that profusely leaks and sprays water. If you do it right, our technicians should be able to turn the leaks off immediately with a master valve but only after the visual filming and damage reports are completed by my staff."

"I hear and obey, sir."

"Now leave me to my plotting and planning. I know just how I'll spin this story to catch the attention of Prime Director One. After the initial bombing, we'll need a highly published assault upon one of my close staff members.

He wrote a name and instruction on an order, "This name came to me immediately," and handed it to Harcos 86 as he exited. His raucous laughter ensued.

# FAREWELL INSTRUCTIONS

Seeking a private farewell with his mother, Dring re-appeared on the balcony outside Orlycia's private quarters after Cest 21 left. Orlycia had opened that portal to the outside. She and Yeto were waiting.

"We knew you would return to us. Cest 21 could never grasp all we've prepared you for. It is better not to stretch her mind with too much at one time."

"I feel lost and confused how to act, despite your training. It's proving I'm part of a larger something I don't understand. One issue I cannot resolve is how is it the tower's defenses responded so effectively in my protection? Its intelligence saved my life. Why didn't our native population use those structures in every city to fight back; to defend us all when we were invaded? I wished those two aggressors wouldn't hurt me, and I was saved."

Yeto gave Dring an understanding look. "There was no need to burden you with this in your training up to now. Your intent became the eyes and focus of those energy beams which protected you."

Dring was aghast. "Yeto, do you mean to say I directed that tower to defend me?"

"Your emotional plea for help switched it on. They attracted that same outward force back upon themselves. Stand down the hall. I'm going to throw this vase at you. It's heavy enough that it could break one of your bones. Watch it with your eyes and stop it with your mind."

Before Dring could ask any questions, Yeto hurled the vase directly at his face. Dring let his instincts react. Energy flashed from his eyes. The vase slowed to hover in the air right in front of him. When he stopped thinking about it, it started to drop to the floor, and he caught it before it shattered. "Yeto, what if that had been an object that was life threatening?"

Yeto picked up a knife from a sideboard. "This is a sharp blade. If you do not prevent it, this blade will hurt you." Without another word, Yeto threw it as hard as he could. Dring didn't panic. His eyes switched on, and a pink cloud of force surrounded the knife, and then dissolved it in mid-air.

"You have no idea how thoroughly you have been trained, Dring. You are ready to face the Changeover. You need only believe it."

"What about the other workers? You've always had the answers for me. I can't fly off over the forest and abandon them to Arian questioning and torture. How can this be made right? Ethra and the others fought as bravely to save me as I fought to save them. Now my Ethra is imprisoned within that group. I'm certain of our feelings for each other. Surprisingly, it took the intensity of that conflict to reveal my life mate. I'd do anything to save her. However, I don't know how to save any of them."

Yeto smiled. "Now you have a personal motive to save them all. This is the first step."

Orlycia touched his cheek. "Your perceptions mature. You will find the answers to all this. Trust me. Ask, it will be given. Now you must depart this place.

"The Changeover is upon us now, Dring. Our training was meant to keep your sensitivities focused so you'd perceive the rising urgency of its signals. We approach the climax of the most sacred time in our planet's life. You have every ability to respond with inspired action from your knowings."

Dring smiled. "I respect you both. I increasingly grow in appreciation for the preparation training you and Yeto have given me. Knowing wells up in me like the waters of a warm spring. From my deepest heart, I do feel the Changeover, and more than ever, I need your higher counsel."

Yeto was definite. "Only your conscious choice can save Aryll now. The Changeover will not carry you along like some Zolag leaf in a flood. Only evil men use the threat of force to control others. Is it not better when you, as an intelligent life, exercise your free will and CHOOSE to help this planet align with a universal purpose? As our planet elevates her frequencies, she aches to carry all her children with her."

Yeto clapped him on the shoulder. "She invites your help; she does not impel. Aryll will move into her future. It will be in a different octave and of a different harmonic pitch. Help the others join her."

"Aryll will be a very new and different ascended world, Dring," Orlycia added. "The conquest has served its purpose. With a few exceptions, these invaders were attracted here unconsciously. Our planet holds the tuning fork seeds of their genetics, and the technologies to accelerate their race's higher development. You must not be distracted by their history. Suffice it to say; they'll never consciously realize the role they've played here until they elevate their minds to evolve on their own."

"All born after the conquest have developed strengths

from their experiences. The torture they endured triggered the choice-making ability of all members. Their desires, too, have played a vital part in triggering the Changeover. Aryll can now manifest permanent elevation into her next dimension and take all her planetary children with her."

The atmosphere in the room shifted. Orlycia moved close to her offspring. "I will now bid you a final physical farewell, Dring." Orlycia kissed his forehead and embraced him. "Your father King and I shall both await you."

Yeto added, "Dring, I shall remain in this physical world a little longer and guide you to your one final interview with the council elders."

Dring agreed. "As you've pointed out, I must flee this vile Capacity. I'll dwell upon all you've revealed, and I will see you both again very soon."

He embraced his mother one last time, exited by the back window, and vanished into the shadows of the night.

# ORLYCIA DEPARTS

"It's begun." Orlycia felt her legs go a little weak as Dring flew off. She looked to Yeto.

"Yes, it has." He took her hands to address her officially. "Orlycia, at long last you've finished your dedicated service. You've successfully completed your part of this great mission. Feel the love of the old ones and your planet as it showers over you. It is expressing their profound and loving gratitude. Join Ospra, your life mate, and companion. He awaits your return to the Starlight."

Orlycia gave his hands a soft squeeze. "Yeto, I thank you for your dedicated support. I shall await your presence there. Make it soon as well. I will join my Ospra this very night."

Yeto witnessed her exit, returned to the window, levitated himself out, and flew off into the night on a course to accompany Dring.

She quieted her mind and reflected upon the glowing Pictart of her life mate, her king. In her private quarters, she chose the finest of her royal ceremonial gowns. Once properly attired, she set the tiara on her head, took position upon her throne, and looked out lovingly over the dark quietness blanketing the old city.

She started the ancient chant; softly at first and then increased its volume. She sang the harmonies that would release her to its freedom. The ancient melody began to resound more and more in harmony with her conscious ceremony of will.

She felt her consciousness began to expand as the entire room resonated. Her vision softened as all the room and its hard edges began to blur. Orlycia observed the experience of lightness filling her being as she levitated off the floor. Her energized body drifted through the physical matter of the walls and into the great hall.

Within the great hall, a cloud of pink energy began to condense and anchor. It drew her toward the Pictart. It took on a new vibrancy of color and sound as his image animated and reached out to her. She felt his love extending out to embrace her.

"I've finished all my tasks, Ospra. My time in this world is finally complete. I could never have survived these years apart had I not felt your constant love and support. Dring has all your noble qualities; I feel them inside him. Our son is imbued with all the strength he'll need to face the adult challenges before him.

The joyous sound of her mate's voice filled her mind. *You have done well, Orlycia my queen. I've come to escort you now and forever into the safety and sanctuary of our starlight. Take my hand so that we might ever be reunited.*

Orlycia reached out as his hand materialized and drew her forward through this energy portal. Orlycia passed through his Pictart and out of the physical dimension. Her life mate received her open-armed and wrapped his arms and wings around her in his most tender embrace.

Ospra touched her face. "I've missed you so much, Orlycia. I've watched over you every moment, my love, my life mate." He kissed her softly and held her tight.

The atmosphere in the great hall slowly ended its resonate hum. Images of the king and his queen faded.

No trace of Orlycia remained in the palace. The soft evening breezes tugged at the curtains to wave their farewell.

# TERI 38 IS ARRESTED

Harcos 86 lost no time having Teri 38 moved to a maximum-security cell deep within the bowels of the Capacity.

Teri 38 sat alone tightly trussed up in the inquisitor room. Cool walls of the building foundations surrounded him; featureless walls permeated with dank smells of basement moisture, surgical chemicals, and fear. Nothing broke the flatness within the stark, white holding cell, except for a single built-in two-way mirrored surface.

The padded and soundproofed door faced him. Teri 38 had not been allowed to change from the clothes he was wearing when arrested.

*Is it still night? I wonder. You can't tell when you can't see the sky in a windowless room. It's always cold in a place like this, and it reeks like a jail.*

A frustrated Teri 38 shouted aloud. "What am I doing in a place like this?" He shivered. Neither the thin fabric of his clothes nor his fears helped to warm him.

"Teri 38, here. Waiting," he shouted aloud, again.

*The concealed built-in med-inquisitor equipment, with its meters and dials, graphs and buttons, and restraints are hidden from my view; I know it's secreted here somewhere.*

# CEST 21 BEFORE THE PRIME DIRECTOR

"Come in, Cest 21." PD 32 waited in his private quarters. Moria sat quietly nearby

"As ordered, sir."

"Ah, good. Cest 21, my Philomystic in charge. You must proceed immediately to visit the former royal figurehead you communicate with so much. There's been a disturbance at one of the stations. I want you to probe their minds as deeply as you can to see if they know anything of this.

"I'd be interested to know if they may be connected to this incident. Especially since it might be the beginnings of a serious native revolt against authority. Her offspring appears to be deeply involved."

Cest 21 acted surprised. "That's terrible, sir. Were any members of our staff or forces injured?"

"There were several casualties, but the supervisor and the entire crew have been brought here to the Capacity for interrogation."

"Might I ask the name of the supervisor in question, sir?"

The director manipulated his speech. "The supervisor, one Teri 38, is now with the inquisitors. The workers are sequestered in the old wing cropping compound near the shuttle launch bays."

"Proceeding as ordered, I shall visit the old palace, sir.

Then, I'll attempt to get further readings by questioning some of the other natives in custody."

"Excellent, Cest 21, but hold for a moment. I'll send you with an official request form. Get them to sign a new loyalty oath. As leading citizens of the Arian Empire. It can help me in public statements."

He exited, and Cest 21 connected with Moria's mind. *What else do you know of this?*

Moria responded quickly with an overview of the plot between the director and Harcos 86. And she asked if Cest had seen Dring.

*I saw him last night for a short time at the palace. One of the names he mentioned on his crew was Ethra. I don't know if it's your daughter, but it might be a lead.*

Moira's audible gasp was cut short when the director burst through the door. "Moria, why didn't you offer Cest 21 some tea while I was away?"

"I must apologize for my rudeness. I'm clearly in error."

"You should be on your way now. Here's your official packet, Cest 21. Dismissed."

She directed a thought. *Moria, get his permission to visit the natives under lock-down. Your daughter may be among them.*

Moria sent thoughts back. *I see why Orlycia and Yeto trust you. Go with great care.*

# THE QUESTIONING OF TERI 38

The cell door clanged against the wall, and a small group of doctors entered.

A short round man with glasses stepped closer to him. "I'm Doctor Rotz 27. We've reviewed your case. We think you've been working too closely with your native agri-crews. This would not usually concern me, but only from your agri-crew have two reproductions occurred.

"This may have occurred because of your rather unorthodox methods of supervision. The most extraordinary part is that your crew also contained one fully winged male of the species. The same revolutionary leader that escaped and continues to elude capture.

"You will be questioned concerning all periods leading up to this discovery. This planet is being considered for complete stericyclation. Do you know what that is?"

"No, I don't."

"It would mean sterilization and eradication of this ecosystem. All forms of native life now upon Aryll 8 would be sterilized. It would mean the purging and loss of all but a few of the native species that would be saved for study.

"Scientists will be engaged in producing a completely different, productive, and compatible flora and fauna species. It is a radically new and revolutionary proposition for our empire's growth and expansion. Now do you understand?"

"Yes, sir, but that proposition is horrific. How could anyone even think this way?"

Doctor Rotz 27 ignored him. "Prime Director 32 must assess whether this outbreak of violence is a threat to the success of the project. Our position as first candidate for this bold new terraforming process is at stake.

"Don't you see the honor providing scientifically proving the value of this technology? We need to know what you know of these natives."

Doctor Rotz 27 failed to get the programmed response he expected, so he addressed the business at hand. "Where you are concerned, you must also be made aware the inquisitor's office will conduct the questioning from here on in. Have you ever witnessed one of their interrogations before?"

"Only once in training, sir."

An official twice the height of Doctor Rotz 27 stepped forward. He didn't give his name or rank, but Teri 38 recognized the steely glint in his eyes: this was an inquisitor. "I'll take it from here, doctor. You and your team are requested to retire to the observation room. You will be able to speak by audio-link if any consultation is needed during these procedures."

"As you wish." Doctor Rotz 27 and his team vanished behind the mirrored walls. The assistant placed a headdress of electro-leads upon Teri 38's head. Once the equipment was secured, baseline-establishing questions began.

"Teri 38. You have been confined in this place for interrogation. At this time, no formal charges have been placed upon you. All admissions occurring as a result of this interrogation will be recorded. This session is intended to disclose or bring to light matters which could lead to formal charges being brought against you. Is that clear?"

"Yes, sir."

"You are ordered, under your sworn military training to reveal only facts. This is required of you at all times. Do you understand all these requirements?"

He responded. "Yes, sir."

The man changed his tone slightly. "This will not hurt yet. This is a test. Can you feel this?"

Teri 38 felt a warm vibrational hum flush throughout his body from every terminal connection. Then the slight warming sensation began to increase. It flowed through his entirety. In a moment those sensations passed. It left a slight metallic taste in his mouth and with a hint of a tickle in his throat like when he might need to vomit.

Teri 38 knew this was only a test.

# CEST 21 MEETS WITH FOUL PLAY

Cest 21's anticipation grew as she landed near the palace. She had to play this out, even not being certain how to handle the whirlwind of experiences that immersed her. She'd returned here for so many other evenings of extraordinary conversation with Orlycia and Yeto in the past. This visit was a ruse. She was aware Orlycia and Yeto would not be there.

Her personal communicator vibrated. She was surprised when the director's face appeared on the screen. "Cest 21?"

"Yes, sir?"

"Urgent matters have forced me to call you back to my private office immediately. Please attend me at once." The signal faded.

Intent upon her final checklist and distracted with details for re-starting her sled, Cest 21 never saw the attack coming. Distracted, lingering in her sensitive state, a fast blow to the back of her head knocked her from the seat and sent her helmet flying.

She tried to block another blow with her arm. It stressed the bone too much. She screamed out in pain at the cracking sound. She fell to the ground and huddled next to the sled hoping for its protection. She tried to compose her mind; to defend herself somehow, and to keep her body from fading into unconsciousness. A searing pain throbbed in her head.

Heavy boots kicked at her soft flesh. She tried to curl into a fetal position, to roll away from the pain, to fold her body into the dirt, and to cover her face. But the impact of the boots struck her again and again. Their savage kicks sent all parts of her body into crescendos of agony.

Cest 21 squinted out a view from under her good arm to catch a glimpse of her attackers. They continued to pummel her with no mercy, and she took a kick to the jaw, and before she lost consciousness from the pain of the violence, she heard a heavy male voice say to the others, "Remember, don't hit her in the face too much."

She lost consciousness, and her body settled limply onto the ground as a loud explosion echoed in the distance near the vicinity of the municipal water plant.

# TERI 38 GETS THE WORKS

The inquisitor began with easy questions: name, rank, and current duty assignment. That allowed the assistant to establish base readings.

"How long have you held this duty post?"

"For a little over nine months."

"And to what duty were you previously assigned?"

"I was an inspector for the Capacity's old green section."

"What was the extent of your duties?"

"In addition to maintaining high profile security patrols, one incubator remained in that sector. It fell upon me to inspect and report any possible new birth."

"Did you have occasion to inspect that incubator?"

"Yes, sir. I did."

"And you submitted this report concerning that one incubator, did you not?"

"Yes." Teri 38 felt a tightening in the pit of his stomach and a growing ache in the back of his neck. His hands were moist and a deepening apprehension flooded over him.

"Your report states when the inspection took place, the birth was proceeding under state standards, and it fit all requirements of incubation control?"

"Yes, sir."

"You reported that specific egg sac, containing that young

native male was characteristically dull in appearance because it was on a continuing regiment; receiving the appropriate dosages of Gene 10 and AR15?"

"Yes, I did report that."

"You also reported the egg containing this male of the species had no observable wing formation, did you not?"

An uncomfortable chill ran up Teri 38's back. He swallowed hard. "Yes, sir."

"How is it upon confirmation of his wristband number that this same WINGED male has led a violent revolt against his Arian guards?

"Then, that same native, after causing the revolt, assault, and the termination of one security guard, in his flight for escape, also somehow triggered the unusual destruction of government property and killed two pilots. How could this all happen?"

"I don't know, sir. I was transferred to the agri-fields right after that pre-birth inspection. I didn't approve any final inspections. An officer named Phaethon performed that."

A flush of red hot pain few up Teri 38's spine. He would have convulsed, but the straps held him down.

"Quiet. How is it possible, as a trained observer, his wings escaped your birth inspection? Haven't you been part of this conspiracy from the beginning? Haven't you been assisting him most of his life?"

"No, No. It's all been a strange set of coincidences, sir. Please believe me."

"You have ALWAYS been there to shelter him. It's on your record. You have a long history as a native sympathizer. On this planet, it began with your embarrassing involvement with his mother at the first wing cropping ceremony."

Teri 38 was silenced by a massive jolt of electrical force painfully flooding his body. His body convulsed and struggled against the constriction of the electro-straps. Skin burned under the restraints. He smelled his scorched skin while his brain burned from the high voltage sting of electricity probing every cell.

There was knife edge sharpness to the inquisitor's voice. "Weren't full skin inspections part of your assignments?"

"They were embarrassed by those inspections, sir; I could feel it. They kept in good health; they kept clean; they loved having new capes; they worked hard, and they met and surpassed all their production quotas. They were already conquered and captured."

"Quiet."

His mouth and jaw clamped shut tight with the sting of another electrical shock to his head. Teri cried. He had bitten his tongue and tasted the warm, salty flow of blood.

"Did you know this male with wings was among your crew?"

"No, sir, I did not."

"Does all this not stem from your lifelong record of disobedience to the state? Your misdirection of purpose? Your lack of discipline? Even as a youth, in your destruction of state property?"

"I didn't destroy anything. I was given broken equipment."

"Now we see the culmination of all this. Your pathetic, deviant behavior has finally revealed itself. It started when you were assigned to witness the wing ceremony. You broke ranks to the embarrassment of your leaders. You were busted in rank and duty then. Your actions have continued including now in another deliberate conspiracy to disrupt and embarrass our leaders. Is this not how it is, Teri 38?"

"No. It's not true." He gasped, trying to stay conscious as he fought the consecutive surges of searing white heat up and down his spine and around his head.

"What a hero you would be if you had been the one who discovered this winged flyer? Or perhaps you planned to sell him on the black market as an exotic, endangered species? Which was it, Teri 38?"

"No. It was nothing like that. You have to believe me."

Doctor Rotz 27's voice boomed in over the microphone "Please, don't knock him out. My commission still needs information from him."

"The state needs answers. My inquisitor office has been granted priority to question. You will be catered to later.

"I submit for the record, as presiding inquisitor, and after direct examination, I have become resolved. By state-approved methods of inquiry, this subject, Teri 38, is at this moment confirmed and registered as having a deep-seated guilt and sympathy for this revolt; and for holding a profound and integral hostility for this Arian Empire and all his state duties."

Teri 38 whispered, "No, I knew nothing of these things." An intense surge of pain rendered him immobile.

The Med-Inquisitor moved the questioning to its final phases.

"You are demonstrating an absence of these truths. Therefore, you, Teri 38, are pronounced mentally damaged. You are not fit to live within this empire as a free member of its society."

Doctor Rotz 27 yelled again, "Wait; we still need to ask him some questions."

"Teri 38 will not be terminated, Doctor Rotz 27, at least

not now. This last testing sequence will allow his systems one final opportunity to align with the universal entanglement patterns of Arian learning. If he should reject this realignment, he will be yours to experiment with at your leisure."

The inquisitor nodded to his assistant to release the highest testing energy bolts.

Teri 38 experienced PAIN as if a thousand strobe lights were turned on in his brain. He couldn't focus on any one image; the pain too was intense to allow that. A kaleidoscope of a thousand agonizing memories glared up all at once. Images and orientation lectures, night drones, textures, tastes, smells and sounds all crashed in upon him. He slumped and passed out in the chair.

The inquisitor studied the readouts. He would have expected, from the education programs that Teri 38 received by saturation, a fairly stock set of readings. What came upon the printouts startled even him. The parameters clearly showed differences from the most basic of programming.

"This subject's brain, confirmed by our readouts, has never been receptive to any of the frequencies of a state education. He should be reclassified as a functional illiterate and should be removed from any position of authority. I recommend he be held on charges and sentenced to the most severe punishment."

Doctor Rotz 27 kept asking. "But what of the prisoner? Is he dead? Will he survive?"

"He's not been terminated, but he's entered into a coma. His detention is now out of our jurisdiction. These results release my staff and me from any further action or responsibility. Protocols suggest he should be held pending further executive orders. Any additional investigation upon this subject you wish to pursue must continue later."

# LATE NIGHT IN THE
# PRIME DIRECTOR'S OFFICE

"I commend your covert team for their quick and efficient results in these matters."

"I live to serve, my Prime Director." Harcos 86 accepted the glass of brandy. "My new appointment as Assistant Director encourages me to expedite this campaign forward with no delays."

"Your team has been extremely effective generating the outward theater of convincing revolution. Your propaganda mill has fueled every rumor. I could not have hoped for more. They may be even more efficient than my personal guards."

"I've embodied your every excellent suggestion as a model, Prime Director."

"All right, all right, stop the verbal groveling. There's still more to do. I'm pleased. Cest 21 is recovering nicely in the infirmary. The images concerning this native terrorist attack upon an Arian official mesh well with my voice-over commentary. Remind me to pay her an official visit and ask the media to join me."

"And the bombing damage at the water plant was repaired within an hour, and the documenting commentary continues to get extensive media traffic replay across the empire."

"I dearly love the way you've presented their ancient myth

of a rising savior woven into the *Irrational Cause* show."

Harcos 86 raised his glass. "My staff and I await directions for the next terrorist demonstration activities, Prime Director. What will you have us do next?"

"I need to figure out a way to strengthen the images of this false flag; maybe have our domestic terrorists convincingly knock another couple of gravity sleds out of the sky. That mixed couple murder event was very good, but increasing casualty deaths within the ranks of a few higher profile military personnel should be next on the agenda. Events of that nature offer for me much greater political leverage. Be certain to image the crashes to maximize our media coverage.

"Oh, and get some visual footage of some disciplined actions, like Volt-whipping some workers refusing to tend to their duties. Create some damaging headlines like: 'Rebels Threatening Food Production' or 'Grain Production Lowest in Planet's History,' 'Threatening Food Shortages Face Our Planet.'

"Create documentation using images of the crew from that Agri-camp where the winged terrorist leader was hiding. Include a special exposé on their conspiracy corroboration with this traitorous leader, Teri 38.

"Lead everyone to believe he's been the mastermind. Make him the scapegoat for planning all these recent events."

"Prime Director 32, you build a very convincing case for stronger military intervention and for your request that this is the very first stericyclation planet."

"Well said Harcos 86, now finish your brandy. As requested, I've laid out your next campaigns."

# MORIA MEETS HER DAUGHTER

"Moria, is that you?" Old Mata was looking out from the confines of their cages. Have you altered your body that much just to survive?"

"Yes, Mata, I needed to disguise my true nature to satisfy my purposes and further my agenda of finding my daughter."

Mata, in thought, asked *what purpose could call for such a sacrifice, my friend?*

Moria was direct. *Long ago I came here to conceal the birth of a son, but he was lost to me. More recently, I concealed the egg of a daughter, and I was discovered. The Arians pried her egg from my grasp before I could sing her birth songs. I have not seen her since. My heart aches to be reunited with her. I swore an oath to find her, to teach her the truth of her heritage, and to seek vengeance upon these barbarians who separated us.*

*Clearly, I have sacrificed all pride from my former life to fulfill this promise. I've been frantic to find my daughter. Assuming this disguise has allowed me to mix into the highest ranks of Arian leadership. I felt it worth every price to obtain records of where she might be and to see her again. I received a report this crew held a young female with the name I'd chosen for her. I had to find out if this could be my daughter.*

Mata was reading her mind as she formed these thoughts.

*And her name was to be Ethra?*

*You read my memories clearly, old woman.*

*I have read your thoughts, and I've read hers. She IS your lost daughter.*

*Where is she then? I must meet her. How will this Ethra, a daughter I've never known, accept the truth?*

*I will find her for you.* Mata read her concerns. *Be patient Moria. She is strong and willful, not unlike her mother. Stay here.*

Mata vanished into the rude shelter behind them and returned with Ethra. Moria and Mata shared their thoughts again. *This is the daughter you bore and tried to prepare for birth. I can do no more than bring you together. Approach her with truth and love. You can do no more than offer her this.*

*My heart leaps at this opportunity. You've assisted me well, old friend. My thanks and love to you, Mata.*

Ethra held back a few steps. She smoothed her field worker clothes and brushed her hand over her short cropped hair feathers as she cautiously approached and scanned this female she did not know.

*You two think in your old speech? Did you believe I could not read these thoughts as well?* There was silence between them all before Ethra spoke.

"You've had to be clever to survive, as well." Moria anticipated the questions about her body work as Ethra scanned her. "It's not what it looks like, or what you may think. I am pleased they gave you your proper name."

"Proper name? They found this name on a scrap of rag you wrapped my egg with. I read that story from the minds of a staff member in the state incubator. My name is all I had. All I have. How could you have given me up?" *I needed you so desperately when I was small. I had no one. And no one knew anything about you. I was just another orphan.*

Moria wept. *They caught me. I wasn't clever enough to hide you. They had to pry you out of my arms when they stole you from me. I've never given up looking for you.*

"Yes, I've changed my body. I've done these things and more to follow any hint or any trace of you. Finally, I've found you, but I don't know what to do now. That decision is up to you. May I get to know you as a daughter? May I share with you your genetic history and that of your tribeflock? Might you ever forgive me for my absence from your life?"

Ethra's thoughts probed as deeply as she could into Moria's mind. She was flooded with the love she felt. She ached with her mother's pain of separation and loss. "It's all a little overwhelming right now. Let me ponder it."

Moria wished she could reach through the cage and embrace her. "Take the time you need, Ethra. So much has inundated your mind. I must tell you; it was knowledge of this Dring that brought me to you."

"How can this be so? I've only recently decided he was the one I wished for my life mate. I, too, have done things to survive. I've entertained a few of the young Arians. All that is in the past. Loving Dring has finally inspired a future in me."

"We have no life history together until this moment, but I can read the goodness in you. I read your feelings of love and your desperate search for me. All I can do is to give you this little bow of respect, my Mother-Bearer, and acknowledge who you are, and thank you for your every effort to finally find me."

Moria broke down and released the sorrows she'd carried for so long. She felt the weight of a lifetime melt away. "I now have your frequency. I will never be far away from you again. I promise you, Ethra, I will work in every way I can to free you and all your agri-crew so we may be together."

She pressed her hand to the cage. The energy of her love flowed through the mesh.

Ethra raised her hand and touched the metal mesh from the inside to overlay her mother's palm. Their energy flowed together. *I willingly accept your love. We will never lose each other, again.* Moria reveled in this frequency-mind-link touch with Ethra at this moment. Then, she reluctantly drew her hand back.

*Now I must go. I will be missed if I tarry. Keep strong, my daughter. The Changeover will soon begin.*

With that, Moria turned and disappeared into the shadows of the Arian world.

# THE PRIME DIRECTOR VISITS

Prime Director 32 staged his public visit to Cest 21's bedside. He made certain its coverage would feature his stern looks and voice coverage for any Arian watching the video screens.

"I'm here with my injured Philomystic First Class, Cest 21. She's only one of many brave Arian forces injured or killed by the growing native rebellion. Cest 21 has very active leading attempts to win further support for the empire's presence here. Her most recent assignment has called for her to act as my personal liaison, and to meet with former native rulership."

The camera then added her to the screen.

"Cest 21, your Prime Director is here to wish you a speedy recovery and to inform you the officials you've dealt with have abandoned their old palace."

"How are you feeling, Cest 21? You've been wounded in service to your empire." Prime Director moved himself to a better camera angle. "Now that you've regained consciousness, all that remains is for you to report your incident and to fully recover your health. I'll take care of the rest."

He produced her letter of commendation. "I am here to thank you for your bravery and your valiant efforts to avert this rebellion. This letter will be placed in your personnel file for future considerations."

Cest 21 played the part for his public relations image. "I

don't know what to say, sir. I can only hope these attacks will end soon."

*What else could I possibly say to the whole Empire-wide audience, Prime Director? I wish for this Changeover with all my heart and it will certainly not be chalked up as one of your petty victories?*

"Thank you Cest 21. Citizens around the Arian Empire most certainly support you in that desire." He moved to sign off this fiasco by striking a serious posture into the cameras. "This is Prime Director 32 leaving this injured member of my staff to recover, and asking all empire citizens to rally in support of victory here on Aryll 8."

*What a trite pile of statements.* Cest 21 thought as she spoke with insincere humility. "Thank you for your visit, sir."

He smiled. "Take as long as you need to heal. In time, I'll find you another assignment reflective of your brave service."

As the crew gathered their equipment to leave, Cest 21 asked if she could have a private moment with the director. "While I've heard the rumors of terrorists, bombings, assassinations of personnel, and violent uprisings, and the media continues to exploit those stories, I've come to know these natives. Let's be honest. I believe this whole scenario is being built on a false premise. I can only believe this is all being played out for some other reason.

"I realize these statements may threaten my safety, but I believe this to be only a false flag operation, perpetrated only to benefit the rank and status of its Prime Director."

He raised his hand. "I think you should stop right there Cest 21." He took a deep, commanding breath. "I'm sorry you feel this way. It seems the rest of the empire is more willing to listen to reason. Prime Director One is now convinced this world needs to be used as an example. There have been enough confrontations with the natives that he's approved us for total stericyclation."

"No. You can't let that happen."

"Oh, don't worry. We'll save enough of the natives to eventually get them to reproduce. They're a fascinating species, don't you think?"

"These beings have a remarkable ancient heritage and extraordinary personal sensitivity. I can't believe you'd let them destroy this planet to simply play out some role as a planetary leader. I'll find a way to inform the entire empire of this charade."

He gave her a chilling look. "You are hardly in a position to threaten me, my little Philomystic First Class. Your credibility rating remains extremely low. The empire stands ready to assist in your rehabilitation. They remain very adept in special techniques for attitude re-adjustment, as you may wish to recall. Not all that long ago, their office was very reluctant to allow your approval for this assignment in the first place.

"If you insist on making trouble, I have only to order a total review of your reports. Your rehabilitation would then include total re-assessment of your mental stability. They have assured me they would undoubtedly call for your total mental stabilization. I don't think you'd pass those tests with your present mentality intact, do you, Cest 21?"

"That appears to be a very thinly disguised threat, Prime Director."

"I'm just stating the facts. The empire's course for Aryll 8 is clear. Will you be part of the future? Or be locked away being measured for your sanity?"

He pouted toward the door like a spoiled child and then

glanced back. "I have a planet to run. Let me know what you decide."

Moria entered earlier and concealed herself behind a curtain until everyone had left. "I must commend you on your ability to stomach that dazzling display of verbal dung." She flashed a wry smile.

Cest radiated a smile back. "Moria, it's so good to see you."

Then Moria switched to thought-speak. *I will ever be in your debt. My daughter, Ethra, was among the crew they've sequestered. I have finally communicated with her. I can't thank you enough.*

*I'm so very pleased, Moria. What of Orlycia and Yeto? Is Dring still managing to elude capture?*

*Yes, Dring remains at-large, much to the political advantage of the director's agenda. Yeto has slipped into the starlight until his rendezvous with Dring. Orlycia is no longer in this physical dimension and has joined her life mate, King Ospra.*

*On another very joyous note, Ethra tells me she and Dring feel the vibrations of bonding between them. They wish to become life mates. I'm so pleased with her choice.*

*Moria, that's wonderful.* Cest 21 beamed. *I'm truly happy to hear that. It won't be a surprise to you why I'm here. You know as well as I do my injuries were orchestrated from his treachery. I'm not sure why he didn't have me killed and make a martyr out of me, but maybe I haven't outlived my usefulness. What future will I have here now? Can this planet take care of all of you, and proceed with her Changeover if they instigate this stericyclation process?*

Moria touched her arm. *Our planet knows of you, Cest*

*21. You've won a place in her heart as an adopted tribeflock member. We will all experience this Changeover together. Don't worry. She fully understands how to deal with these barbarians.*

A female tech was startled as she popped into the room. "Oh. It was so quiet in here after the Prime Director's visit. I thought you must be asleep."

They both smiled back. Cest 21 spoke. "No, my friend here was checking on me after all the excitement."

*We're not just friends; we're now of the same tribeflock.* Moria's thoughts were clear.

"Well, buzz me if you need anything."

Cest 21 assured her as the young girl was leaving. "Thanks, but my needs are being resolved." *Thank you, Aryll. I feel your planetary love for me.*

Both women shared a knowing nod as Moria exited.

# LATE IN THE NIGHT

Dring had been flying at a steady pace. Even with all his training, his wings ached from the long, protracted flights to and from the Capacity. He needed to clear his mind; leave the history and sanctuary of that life behind.

As he set his pace into the future, a storm was brewing over the Zolag forests ahead. As he flew, his eyes added some of his moisture to the landscape. He blinked his middle eyelids to clear the tears. The first gusts of the approaching storm struck his wings. He struggled to stay his course.

A sharp gust of wind shear abruptly lifted him up and pushed him down in his flight. Dring fought to stay true to course, but heavy gusts and pouring rains buffeted his efforts.

I can't keep flying in this weather. I've got to find some shelter from this storm. "What do you want of me?" Dring screamed into the wind, into the rain, and down to the planet far beneath his wings. I'm only one of your children. What can you expect me to do here by myself?"

The rain washed away his tears, but the wind and storm delivered no answers. His sodden and water-soaked wrap cape pressed heavy on his back. He flew on, not from the certainty of destination, but the action distracted his mind.

Through the storm, the abandoned structures of an old city below him revealed themselves. Dring glided down and landed next to a large fountain. This walled garden behind its villa gave him some protection from the wind. Fatigued after his long flight, he fluffed up the soft down of his wings, folded them tightly around himself to protect his thermal energies, and slept.

# TWO GRAVITY SLEDS IN THE COURTYARD

Dring snapped awake. The storm calmed. An inordinate feeling of danger caused him to cautiously send out his expanded senses and probe what it was he could detect in the perimeter.

The sky erupted with searchlights that scanned the garden and villa. Two patrolmen cruised silently overhead then landed and dismounted.

The taller of the two walked the area and stretched. "I wish we flew those Model 380s for these extended, long-range flights. My backside is bent into the shape of that seat."

The other pilot stretched his arms. "Yeah, you're right, but the Model 245 seats are still the most luxurious if you ask me. And I've been at this longer than you."

"Yeah, yeah... the campaign on Ovus 8 and all that... at least this storm is starting to let up. How important is this bird-man we're chasing, anyway?"

"Important enough to get us called on a night like this for the first all-world search I've ever been involved with. I thought that procedure was only used for drills."

"I agree. I'd only read of the maneuver in the training manuals. Torius 29 over in Flightcom told me all forty of the old cities are on red alert. There are multiple patrols flying over every area between here, the Capacity, and as far out as the closest ocean shore."

"Because that winged terrorist has ditched his wristband, almost all our machines are now equipped with heat and motion detectors like the one on your sled."

The younger pilot moved back next to his gravity sled. "That's one of the reasons I was so eager to check the readings in this place. Even with the storm settling down, the seeker read a strong signal here. Look at this fountain."

"The sensors were delicate enough to measure the water flow despite the storm." He stuck his hand in to feel the water. "And, it's one of those warm fountains. The splashing and temperature readings must be high enough to set off the sensors."

He let out a sigh. "I hate it that the reward might go to someone else. Maybe he can't be found. Maybe he's dead somewhere."

"Command center must not think so or we wouldn't be flying in this lousy weather just on rumor."

"Speaking of patrols, we'd better check in."

"Scanner Alpha. Follow up from the heat sensor turned out to be a functioning warm spring's fountain. This team will now proceed along assigned grid vector SW6734. Out."

Traces of the old city below faded beneath them as they lifted off, circled the site for a final check, and then flew off over the lush forest lands to continue their search vector.

Only the fountain splashing its song to the courtyard remained.

With peace restored, Dring felt free to breathe after his near discovery. He noticed a Pictart's soft glow on one of the villa's walls.

In his near slumber state, he could just make out the image of the unusual Pictart. It appeared to be a young girl, probably about his same age. He noticed her loveliness. He slipped off to sleep with the warm welcome of that strange girl's smile wondering who she was.

# A VISIT FROM MORIA

Inside that villa dwelling, time passed slowly. The rooms had gathered a thick layer of dust since the conquest. A warm glow of light coming from the Pictart softened the shadows, but then the glow increased as it became activated. First, the background clouds lightened. The girl's image fogged over with a pale blue mist. The figure then became more solid as the mists cleared, and her body's image floated out of the frame and into the room.

She smiled. Her body matched the Pictart perfectly. She wore the tight-fitting bodice of her tribeflock. Light boots covered her feet. Her wrapcape was sleekly thrown back between her light-shimmering wings. Even in this dim light, their iridescence was clear.

Her image leaped and dove through the dwelling's walls and out into the courtyard. It floated down gracefully beside Dring. He stirred slightly but slept.

She looked down at him with a soft, knowing smile. She registered his pain, felt his loneliness, confusions, and fears. Her etheric hand brushed lightly over his arm.

She thought herself into his dreams. *Your name is Dring. I speak to you now through my connections from the starlight worlds. I still have a body in your world, but my mind has used this Pictart-link from my old life to locate you. You recognized my appearance. It resembles Ethra's because I am her mother. My name is Moria; my mind has been searching for your frequency since Ethra and I were finally able to meet. I've learned of your desire to become her life mate. I am graced and honored you were drawn to the love of my Ethra, and to the safety of this, my ancestral home.* She paused and checked to see if Dring had stirred to consciousness; he hadn't.

*Our tribeflock myths have known and expected your coming for a long time. Sleep now, rest, and let all be at peace in you. This period of uncertainty and confusion will soon come to an end. You begin now to experience your great future.*

*Remember my name is Moria. You will meet me again soon, my tribeflock son. Sleep now.*

Moria's projected image floated back inside the villa. She sighed as she dissolved into the hazy mists of the Pictart.

Dring stirred for a moment and smiled in his sleep. "Moria," he mumbled.

Physically, Moria was already back in the Capacity quarters beside Prime Director 32. Weary from expending the energy of her searching, but pleased with the results of her mental journey, there was much to tell Ethra now.

# PRIME DIRECTOR ONE

"Can you get that?" Prime Director 32 pulled the covers over his head to hide from a call.

Moria was quick to respond. "The director is not available at this time."

"He will want to take this call, my dear." Moria's mind instantly recognized the beady-eyed face on the screen at that of Prime Director One.

"Yes, sir. I'll rouse him immediately." Moria rushed to him, but he quickly brushed by her and positioning himself to face the screen and smiled.

"My greetings, Prime Director One. To what do I owe this great honor?"

"Oh, cut through the babble, 32. You must already be aware I've been watching your little domain with scrutiny these days."

"I've made certain to send your office my full progress reports."

"Look. 32, we had several long talks before you managed to convince me you could be my Arian-for-the-job there. You seem to be mounting a very useful program there on Aryll 8."

"Thank you, sir."

"Stop groveling. You were ambitious enough to have gotten my attention and this appointment. And now you seem to have found an effective methodology for furthering my agenda for the empire's success."

"The empire grows by the success of its branches."

"Oh shut up. I get enough of that political crap from my people here. I wanted to commend you and your staff. You've moved that backwater disaster into the spotlight. Moreover, you've presented me with the opportunity you promised."

"We both know your appointment wasn't to increase agri-production...well, not in a traditional sense, of course. You convinced me you could set up this world for my first planet-wide stericyclation experiment. And now you're doing it."

"My Assistant Director Harcos 86 has been extremely useful in this success."

"Yes, yes, he'll get his rewards. It's you who's gotten me the leverage I need to activate this project. This will be my swan's song of success."

"I'm honored to assist you."

"Keep things on the course you've already set. The Senate harbored a few members who could still have opposed my stericyclation program, but by blowing up this rebellion, you've given me enough fuel to override their objections. Besides, they'll make enough kickback revenue from manufacturing the chemicals to satiate their every greed.

"After the stericyclation is completed, the agricultural cartel is most anxious to see grain production increased, and they believe your planet may be prime for their facilities."

"Excellent. In the meantime, as we both know there is no real revolution, I'm creating another diversion. I've given the military contracts to build the gas bombs and a major budget increase for the offensive to install those devices."

"Are there any groups who would oppose these plans?"

"The environmentalists have objected, but I can easily buy them off. No, you need to keep doing what you're doing. Complete your request to me for the stericyclation process. When the time comes, I'll let you step in as a planetary leader and save the world." He laughed.

"Is this native female someone who can rise to become an advocate for her planet's change? Will she support you in your rise to power? It's very well proven that behind every great man is an even greater lady. Can she act out that role to support you as a great man?"

"I would trust her with my life," PD 32 said.

"You already have. Ask her to present herself before me on this call."

Moria, monitoring the communication, moved to stare into the screen. "I'm here, Prime Director One."

"I've read the Intel reports on you, Moria. It would appear you have been very successful making your transition and becoming a true Arian in body, mind, and spirit."

Prime Director One revealed some of his skills as he switched to mental communication. *Your race is of avian descent. You use your telepathy to read the truth of your companions. Do I read your communication back to me as truth? Or will I read some deception in your thoughts and actions?*

Moria felt his mental probe but easily limited its depth. *My only interest is in giving my total support for my planet's upgrade.*

"Then I look forward to meeting you in person."

"I anticipate the great pleasure that meeting shall grant me."

Moria smiled. *Think anything you want. I hold my real inner self close. Aryll's future will never be as your thinking has it planned.*

The screen went blank. Prime Director 32 said, "It seems we have become mated in this purpose, Moria."

She quietly responded. "The future of our lives has indeed become intertwined."

# TERI 38 SURVIVES HIS OWN CHANGEOVER

As night neared, Teri 38 had been ignored all day and remained strapped in the chair, his body thrown unceremoniously back against the electro-straps. Something inside him became destabilized by that final massive energy surge of the questioning. Its psychological assault upon his core triggered a strange separation of consciousness deep within him. That last jolt of searing heat-energy hadn't killed him because his consciousness re-focused itself inside; upon his true inner being.

The amperage of their shock treatments had caused new areas of perception circuitry to activate within him. He entered into a more advanced altered state. It elevated his mentality into the role of observer, not a simple prisoner.

He realized he was still imprisoned, but not terminated nor paralyzed by the electric shocks. As he lay back, his legs felt tingly and light. His arms felt like they were soaking in warm water. His spiritual body began to float away from his physical being.

*Is this what termination will be like? If they killed this body, I would still live like this?* Teri 38 could see through his transparent hands. But I'm still me. *All of me is here in this new body of light!*

The sensations of this new experience left Teri 38 puzzled

yet fascinated. His consciousness had broken through an unseen barrier within. He'd left perennial loneliness and the torturous pressure of his questioning behind. He and this body were free.

He spoke to himself in his mind, *I feel so light I could fly...* and suddenly his body rose to the ceiling in the corner of the room and he looked down at his physical body still restrained in the chair.

I can see right through this body like a ghost. *Can I go outside? Only a crack of light shown through one small window, but this body seems quite flexible. I...*

Then he found himself floating above the central precinct building. Teri 38 began examining the building as if this kind of experience happened every day.

With an enhanced vision, he digested the vibrant colors. He didn't want to waste this experience. *This is better than drinking that native brew. If I could float up here, I can fly.*

That thought turned his mind to Dring. *He can fly too. I wonder where he's gone. Is he all right?*

Teri 38 held Dring's frequency in his memory. That vibration attracted and connected him to Dring. He heard the knowing of it in his mind. "If you have a thought, you create it. If the thought already exists, you occupy it."

As if in response to a mental wish, Teri 38 felt his body begin to pick up momentum. He was flying at an astounding speed over the buildings, over the old parts of the Capacity, then out over many quiet Zolag forests.

His body flew to one of the uninhabited cities and hovered above a small palace where he slowly descended into the back garden near a fountain.

Next to the bubbling waters, snuggled into his wrapcape,

was Dring sound asleep. Teri 38 was ecstatic. He's alive, he escaped. He could see Dring as clearly as if he was standing beside him.

Then, out of nowhere appeared a blinding flash of light, and he snapped back to his physical body, strapped to a chair in his holding cell.

# DRING AWAKENS

Dring woke. *I'm still back in this old city.* He sat up from his hiding place by the fountain. He shook his groggy head to recall an image that had drifted through his mind. He seemed to have registered the brief sight of Teri 38 standing in the corner of this garden.

*He looked so real in the early morning light. I could swear I felt his presence as well. I must be overly tired and seeing things. What would Teri 38 be doing here?*

He dipped his hand into the fountain's warm water, then doffed his wrapcape, and hopped up to sit on the pool's rim. Without hesitation, he spread his wings and leaned back into the bubbling waters.

Warming ripples of its pleasure tingled every aching muscle. While Dring let his legs dangle, he raised and lowered his wings up and out of the water, then splashed them back beneath its waves like a child.

He flapped his wings again, hard this time. Droplets flew in all directions. "Now this is fun." He spoke to the waters. He switched from floating into full flying speed and water splattered everywhere. Dring found the whole exercise immensely entertaining. He laughed. Faster and faster he drove his flying wings.

*Nothing like a big bird bath,* he thought. Feeling rejuvenated, he crawled in to let all his muscles soak in the comfort of their healing embrace.

Dring looked out from the bubbling fountain. It would have made more sense if it had been Yeto I saw in that vision. I could always expect something unusual was about to happen with him around.

# YETO APPEARS

Dring crawled out and sat upon the fountain's rim. He turned his open wings to dry in a salute to the rising suns. Almost as if on cue, he looked up, and Yeto appeared.

"Greetings, Yeto. I'm relieved you're here. You've always guided me. I felt so alone. It's like I'm standing on the edge of a precipice with no wings. Part of me doesn't want anything to do with this drama. Part of me wishes you'd show me a safe place to hide until the Changeover finishes on its own. You', however, always remained steadfast. You've told me my time would come, and I'd be asked to play an important role. Am I that important to this Changeover?"

Yeto spoke. "Your thoughts are correct, my young Dring. Destiny prepares an opportunity for your coming of age. I've already been dwelling within the starlight. I return here now only to guide you for your final interviews."

"And why must I meet the old ones, Yeto?"

"It's time to confirm your decision with the elders. They represent our planet's new life. At this pivotal moment, you approach it as a new, young, immature life. Orlycia and I have given you the best training we could. You decide if you're mature of body and mind. I will escort you to meet the council. They only wish to know if you will act in total service to all our tribeflock people. If so, we must join them. It has always been a truth. 'No bird flies too high which soars on its wings.'"

Yeto broke that mood. "So I think you should get out of your bath, and prepare for your journey.

"Dring, while you've only known the two of us, the elders have always followed your growth and development. The planet knows you as well. You are not alone and never will be.

"None of us have ever been abandoned. Most of the tribe-flock members prepared for their dimensional exodus before the Arian's attacked. They await us in the starlight dimension. It is now time to rescue the rest of Aryll's children."

# HOWLING NOISES

Trembling noises from under the ground halted Dring's inquiry. Groaning sounds deep from beneath their feet showed no sense of diminishing. They noticeably increased worldwide in an unrelenting moan augmented with matching rhythmic tremors.

Yeto spoke. "These groans and tones are symptoms, Dring. Signs that signal to us. Rock plates deep beneath us are moving, compressing rock, and pulling it apart. Her body shutters to life. Our planet is going through her changes.

"Convulsions like this will continue until her final Changeover moments. Her planetary rotation will cease. Her atmosphere will compress in plasma-like heat amid fearful moanings, and the air will be filled with her planet-wide birthing songs. All that sound energy will explode into light. She will experience complete planetary sonoluminescence as she moves into her elevated birth. These will be the final signs before her Changeover is complete."

"What could my role be amid this change?"

"The council has charged me to instruct you. These are the moments to test your development. Here are your first inspired action steps. Lie down and prepare yourself for a full astral body projection."

After only a few moments of quieting his mind, an energy

cloud appeared around him. His identical astral form manifested, fluttered, and hovered in space directly above his physical body. The moment Dring realized the projection was complete, his etheric self smiled and flew to Yeto's side. *I am now ready.*

Yeto rose in the air to match his flight. *So, you are. Now is your time. The Council waits.*

# TERI 38'S BODY IS EXAMINED

The inquisitor and Doctor Rotz 27 had switched on the examination lights to look over Teri 38's body. Still connected to all their monitors and restraints, after a brief examination, the Inquisitor spoke. "This man is very far gone. By my readings, his body's as close to termination as it can get and still be alive."

"But then these readings are more peculiar than any I've ever seen before; most likely produced from some form of rejection shock." He waved for the removal of the headdress and straps.

Doctor Rotz 27 was quiet for a moment. "I've seen something like this before. I'll attempt to talk with him further if he awakens."

The two officials left the room. Teri 38distantly registered their departure. His body reacted like being hit by a lightning bolt as the click of the closing door lock signaled their exit. He sat him bolt upright in the chair like a spring had been released. A marvelous feeling of calm remained inside him.

Two med-attendants laid his body on a medical cart to wheel him to another cell. He looked into the eyes of one pushing him. "The scenes were so real. I flew in the air. I saw the winged one."

"Sure you did," they smirked as they made a joke of it.

Once alone in his cell, he vowed, I will help you, Dring, no matter what. And in whatever events are about to happen, I know you will help me. I know I can depend on you.

# THE DANGERS OF THE TASK

Yeto instructed Dring as they flew. *To save your friends, you'll have to be master one specific technique. You must be able to dwell and hold a stable frequency state. Do you remember what attaining and anchoring means?*
*You have taught me that. Yes.*

*Once the Changeover cycle begins, you must become a living portal and anchor yourself in that frequency. If you waiver for only a moment while serving in that function, it will cause you great bodily harm; perhaps even the deaths of you and all of your friends. Is this clear? You will be testing your life's limits in the ability of your body to maintain its balance and survive as a doorway between two dimensions.*

Dring quickly shared his thoughts. *I understand the gravity the situation. Will my holding in this state serve this as a portal for both male and female natives?*

*Yes.*

There was no hesitancy in his response. Then *I must save the others; I'll do it. I'll consciously offer myself for this service.*

With that confirmation, they continued to fly together in silence over wooded forests, beyond the hills, and toward a mountain range. Yeto said, "You must realize how vital this Changeover is for the life of our planet. This process will herald her complete Ascension. Sonoluminescence will be produced from the released energy similar during every birth, but this will be on a grander scale."

*Are you saying the heats of anger and passion experienced by our tribeflocks because of the Arian tyranny and could trigger such a planetary change?*

*In sympathy, and in conjunction with her cyclical timings, yes they can. Within her population, the collective emotional power from all of us will serve as the trigger.*

*But all the tribeflocks had been in harmony with our planet for centuries.* Then Dring was struck by the simplicity of his statement. *Our planet required enough emotional reactions from a portion of her members to strike this spark; to accelerate this heat as its catalyst. That's how the coming of the Arians fits into all this?*

Yeto smiled at Dring's reckoning. *Aryll defeated them soundly in their first invasion attempt. Our elders retained their energy technology devices. By using these same devices to amplify their core frequencies, our planet sent out a signal to attract them. She required this race of humans. They function unconsciously but still embody their heated properties. Aryll needed their heated behavior here considering it had been developed out of most of her tribeflock members.*

*Yeto, explain why my generation needed to remain after the conquest.* Dring felt his emotional heats rising as that realization manifested within. *This planet used all of us? How dare she manipulate us in this way?*

Yeto registered his emotional temperatures.

*Remain calm, Dring. Observe how this reaction can benefit you. Regain your flying rhythms. Remember, I have lived through this reign of tyrants longer than you have. All this was orchestrated for a higher purpose, and for the greater good of our planet. These events have all been carefully monitored and sanctioned by the Council.*

*These are the same members you and I are flying to meet? Have they the power to make such decisions?*

*Yes, Dring.* As they flew, the mountains loomed closer.

*I understand.*

*Yes, Dring, it was necessary for a few of her children to remain, and to be subjected to the violent, non-harmonious ways of the Arians. The collective energy of all these life experiences has now reached a critical level. The emotional fires discharged within this energy will facilitate this cycle. When you meet the council, and you've accepted this opportunity to serve, they will instruct you further. There's one more thing I can reveal to you now.*

*To bring this into realization, the Changeover requires one member to save our planet. The chosen representative is you.*

# MORIA AND ANOTHER VISIT TO ETHRA

"Mata, can you tell Ethra we're here?" Moria brought Cest 21 to meet the daughter she'd helped to locate.

"Ethra sensed you were coming. She's right behind me." Mata looked over Cest 21 and gave her a scan. "So, this is the Arian who helped you?"

"I'm Cest 21. I'm glad I was able to assist." She switched to mental. *My friendship with Orlycia and Yeto allowed me to meet Dring as well. I was with them the night you were all brought here when Dring's wings were revealed.*

Mata smiled. *Your destiny has brought you to us. Welcome, adopted daughter.*

*My gratitude for your greeting cannot be expressed in words, Mata.*

*I know, dear. I also know you'll help in any way you can to get us freed. Here is Ethra. Communicate to her all you know of Dring.*

Ethra approached them as they stood outside the cage wall. *Greetings, Mother. I see you've brought your source of information as a companion.*

Moria was very pleased to see Ethra again. *Yes, my daughter. Cest 21 has worked with Orlycia and Yeto. She met and talked with Dring many times before he was assigned to the fields. And she was present when Dring made his last call to his mother and Yeto before he flew from the Capacity.*

Ethra's eyes betrayed her interest in that information. *My greetings to you, Cest 21. How did you become so close to our tribeflock members?*

*My history includes travel to many worlds. I was brought here to get close to Orlycia and Yeto so that I might learn of your race. The Prime Director didn't realize I'd had experiences which caused me a personal interest in growing my development. They read my sincerity and began to teach me. I was most fortunate they accepted me.*

*And what of Dring? Did they reveal facts of the upcoming changes? Did they tell you of his destiny?*

*I first met Dring before he left on his assignment. Even though he was young and immature, I felt the greatness in him. Until the night he arrived home to warn Yeto and his mother, the fact that he had wings had been withheld from me. But now, Ethra, I know my first impressions were correct. Dring has the heart to succeed.*

*I am grateful for your presence here with us,* Ethra thought, *but can she get us released from here?*

Moria responded. *We're both working to achieve that goal, my daughter. As soon as we know something more, you will feel my thoughts. Keep strong. Right now, we can only manage short visits. We'll find a solution for this. I promise that for all of you, but we dare not stay here longer.*

Moria and Cest 21 faded into the shadows of the shuttle bay. And all the time of their visit, security cameras had been recording both women for Prime Director 32's private viewing.

# CEST 21 QUESTIONS TERI 38

Prime Director 32 re-assigned Cest 21 to divert her from observing his activities too closely. Teams of doctors had already questioned Teri 38.

After most studies of Teri 38 had been completed, Cest 21 was permitted to speak with him alone. He seemed puzzled about her inordinate interest in him.

"I stopped speaking to anyone on the medical staff about this," he confided. "They think I'm mad and as burned out in the head as the marks on my skin." He held up his arm to reveal pink traces of scar tissue.

"Are you certain these experiences were real?"

"Yes, I am. I've even managed to question some of the guards and building maintainers. Details I told them about this building's exterior could only be confirmed by a staff member. I was even able to accurately describe graffiti writings on walls at the top of the watchtower.

"None of the supervisors climb there. One of the guards almost turned white when I told him what I saw. I think he's the one who wrote that disrespectful graffiti and was afraid of being charged with speaking out against the state."

"All right. I agree that you may have seen something. What about now? Experiences of leaving the physical body for travel, communication, or to gather information is spoken of on a dozen worlds I've studied.

"In our history, training forbids such studies. Only in the Philomystic Corps are such things reported. To Arian-controlled minds, such behavior breaks from uniformity and opens the door for individual incentives.

"Teri 38, I speak to you of these things in the strictest confidence because everyone on this planet has been convinced to disregard your credibility."

"Cest 21. I've grown to have little concern for my credibility. At least everyone seems to have lost interest in torturing me for information, so that's something. Their sole obligation is to feed me. The remainder of the time, they leave me alone. If they're given orders to terminate this body, I'll have little to say about that. I'm left here alone; somewhere in between. I don't fit any of their programs, especially with all the interest in rebuilding this planet by stericyclation and starting over. ...It won't work, you know."

"What do you mean it won't work? This planet's preparation rapidly nears completion. It's being mined and wired with bombs. The evacuation process began three days ago. One of the largest spacecraft is loaded with its flora and fauna. Preparations are being made to load a few couples for continuing attempts at breeding."

"It won't work. Look at the conquest. More than three-quarters of the native population disappeared in an instant. Where did they go?"

"Officially, they were terminated."

Teri 38 gave her a sly look. "No, Cest. They're still here."

"Why would you say that?"

"I'm not mad. This planet is alive, and not just in growing plant life or having humans on her soil. Aryll is alive. Every worker knew it. They knew when the winds would blow. They knew to seek shelter before it rained. They knew when they needed to wrap up warmly. They listen. Not only that, they carry on with conversations in their heads with no audible sounds around them. They're so quiet because talking in their heads is faster, safer, and travels farther."

She tested him. "How do you know all this?"

"I used to watch them and let them relax. I never used my whip, and I stopped the other guards from doing it too. I watched them. I listened inside my head. They got so they didn't mind me around. They went about their business since I wasn't disturbing them. It got to be that I knew who was talking to whom. They'd smile at me like kids getting away with something, but they knew that I knew. That's why they don't write things down."

Cest 21 tuned to Teri 38 with scrutiny. "I understand what you're saying. I've studied the archives of their ancient cultures. It is true. They rarely recorded their history. We only possess a few scrolls that appear to be religious texts."

"Don't you see? They live their lives in complete harmony with this planet. She silently communicates with them. If you must, call it their religion. They elevate their minds to connect and study higher things. They don't need to speak to pass on their knowledge. She stores every event, every memory, and every thought that's ever happened here. Like how to prepare for the Changeover, which is approaching."

"How do you know of this Changeover?"

He smiled his wry smile again. "I used to talk with Mata, one of the older females who'd been alive at the time of the conquest. She showed me the scars where they'd cut off her wings, and she had inquisitor marks like I recently received."

There was no bitterness in his voice, only a deep sadness. "That old bird knows a few things; I'll tell you. And you couldn't lie to her, either. She knew what I was thinking. I got to like her a lot."

"Teri 38, I understand what you're saying, but no other Arian has a clue about these things."

"Our culture has advanced by not wanting to know." His anger flared. "If they can't prove it by conquering it, cutting it up, killing it, or diagnosing its symptoms, then it doesn't exist."

"What are you saying?"

"It has never been clearer to me that the empire doesn't belong here anymore."

"Please explain."

"Something big and wonderful is about to happen. I can't tell you exactly what that is, but this planet is not going to let herself be stericyclated."

"How can that be? Most of the stage is set. The charges are already in place."

"Yes, but something happened to me when I survived their ordeal. The medical staff thinks they drove me mad, but I've never been saner. I love this planet, Cest 21. And I love her tribeflock people. They are sensitive and caring and have a fierceness and honesty and live with dignity. They are not just going to roll over and die. There is so much more going on here than our sciences know about."

"You seriously believe the rest of their population is still here somewhere?"

"They are. And they are not the terrorists or freedom fighters. They're all waiting in that same unseen dimension I traveled into. I saw some of them there, and lately, they've been coming to me. Even my old friend, Yeto, who supposedly vanished during Dring's escape, he's come to me here. We've been communicating mentally."

"Now I've heard everything."

"It's true. How do you think I know so much? Yeto tells me that when our Arian forces leave Aryll, they will never return."

"But the planet will be sterile for eons."

"The Changeover will not let that happen. Besides, all the people hidden in their dimension are waiting and expecting to be joined by the rest of their tribeflock survivors from here."

"The fleet is preparing to evacuate most of the remaining natives."

"Only those who might erroneously choose to follow Arian ways will want to leave. None wishing to stay true will be lost. That's what Yeto told me. What's important to me is the fact the council will allow me to stay with them on their newly elevated world."

"You requested the council to let you stay?" Cest 21 was shocked.

"Yes. They give voice to the planet's decisions concerning what happens here. They've been functioning in that capacity forever."

"Where are they?"

"They exist in that same unseen dimension. They're holding on to the artifacts lost in the first Arian invasion attempt. That's what caused this attack. The Cave of the Arians and all their treasures are here. They're holding them shielded away in their starlight dimension they call it."

A stunned Cest 21 needed to wind down the session from the video cameras. "Well, that's quite a story, Teri 38. I see you believe it, but it's a bit farfetched for me. I need to go for now, but I'll be back to talk again before the evacuation. You're scheduled for the last shuttle like me and with all the couples."

"Perhaps I'll see you again, perhaps not." He smiled his small but enigmatic smile as she left.

She walked away deep in thought. She was amazed he knew all this because she knew it was all true.

# CEST 21 CONTEMPLATES

*High command claims not much will change after stericyclation except to increase the agri-production. Already the area buildings have been reconstructed. The only things to be lost will be a few trees and some other insignificant flora and fauna and, of course, any remaining survivors.*

*Not much is supposed to change, they say? They're in for some very large surprises.*

Most of the other specimens were loaded onto the orbiting craft. Last minute preparations included twenty mated tribe-flock pairs, chosen as specimens, to stock their zoos.

She was thinking to herself as she hurried to talk with Moria. *I've got to find out if Ethra is scheduled to be taken. Moria and I must prevent that at all costs.*

Struck with a knowing, she stopped and asked herself. Do they seriously plan to take Teri 38? A revelation flooded her mind and then burst into her consciousness. *No. They plan to leave him behind. To command, it will be a simple termination. If Teri 38 is left behind, it saves them the trouble of a trial.*

# PRIME DIRECTOR AND MORIA

"I know you and Cest 21 have been visiting your daughter because I reviewed the video footage at the shuttle bay."

Not surprised, Moria pressed him. "Have you come to any decision about my daughter, sir?"

"Moria, why didn't you come to me about this? I'm the director of this planet. I would have helped, if only out of affection for you."

"I didn't know how to ask." Moria sensed that whatever else this man was, he might be telling the truth. "You gave Cest 21 the assignment to keep following up on native investigations. I mentioned I had lost a daughter. She thought she'd heard a name. This did turn out to be the one."

"So, it is this Ethra?"

"Yes, you're correct."

"You've been approved by Prime Director One. He's made us a team. I can't have you losing this daughter again. I've issued orders. She is being selected for inclusion with the couples to be lifted off the planet with us. I can't save them all, but at least she'll be safely evacuating with us."

*Oh, mother Aryll, he thinks he's helping me.* Moria's response was interrupted by a call.

"Cest 21 would like to speak with you, Prime Director. She says it's urgent."

"Send her through. I'll see her now."

Cest 21 approached the duo.

"Whatever it is, can it wait? I've been telling Moria I discovered that you helped her find her daughter. I'm issuing an order to make sure her daughter goes with us at lift-off. I wanted to thank you for your help."

*Oh, goodness no. Moria, he can't take you and Ethra off the planet. The Changeover is about to happen. Teri 38 has been communicating with Yeto.*

"You're welcome, Prime Director. It turned up in my investigation that she was among the agri-field workers."

Cest 21 smiled, but she frantically sent her thoughts to Moria. *How can we save her? He has no qualms about sacrificing everyone to this mad stericyclation scheme.*

Moria's thoughts soothed her mind. *Be at peace, Cest 21. I have a plan to work this all out despite him and his feeble games. You must let me play this out for its greatest success.*

"Then, I'm sorry if I interrupted you both." She headed for the door.

"Cest 21, what was so important you needed to tell me?"

"I'll write it up in a report and give it to you tomorrow. It can wait."

"Thank you, again for all your help, Cest 21." Moria was very formal in speech. *We will all fare very well through this Changeover. You'll see. This parting is only temporary.*

Cest left the room with the warm glow of Moria's temporary farewell filling her heart.

# APPROACHING THE STONE CIRCLE

Dring and Yeto arrived outside the center of the temple city for their meeting with the old ones. Before them, the cone of a dormant volcano rose high into the sky. Terraced plots of ordered gardens, waterways, and parks surrounded its base. They descended to land closer to its base.

Despite forested Zolag trees that towered hundreds of feet above Dring and Yeto, they landed safely. Only the oldest ones developed rainbow-colored spiraling up their bark, and these all were resplendent with those hues.

Despite earlier apprehensions, Dring felt a warm welcome. Before them, a weathered stone path with vibrant, soft green moss bulged up to accent its stone shapes. The path invited their journey into the trees, and up the mound of the forest. A low fog held to the ground in shaded areas catching the dappled rays of dual sunlights peeking through the leaves.

The path directed them toward an arched, cave-like opening cut deep into the mountain. Dring could dimly discern structures far inside a hollowed-out sunlit chamber. The extinct volcanic cone was open at its top and shafts of the sun's rays lit up sparkling patterns upon the structures from the open crater above.

Switching on his long-range vision, there appeared to be a circular formation of standing gray stones on the cone's floor.

Dring could barely make out the top of the outermost ring through the mists and ground fog.

Yeto sent out his thoughts. *Dring, within that circle, the old ones await you. They send you their greetings, and they bid me bring you closer.*

Dring's heart and mind were buoyed up, and he felt more vibrant and alive than ever before as he embraced their loving welcome.

*Yeto, what shall I say?*

*There is nothing to fear. This is a place of peace.*

Moving closer, Dring saw the outer stones clearly. *Yeto, how long does it take to get to this council? Is there an anomaly in space and time here? It appeared as if we traveled a long way yet the stone circle seems so distant. Is this like a mirage? It seemed so close at first.*

Yeto didn't respond.

Through clearing mists, a second, innermost ring of stones, slightly smaller in size, appeared. He saw its dark blue stones with veins of color running through them, and as he drew near, the inner stones' energy throbbed and pulsed inside him.

His mind flooded with knowing from a voice.

*We have always finely tuned any decision to harmonize with our world. We move not as a government forcing its will by conquest, but as a fully conscious entity. By this living science, the life of Aryll is allowed an overriding vote in every mutual decision made here.*

Dring tried to synchronize his vibrations to the great peace and feelings of coming home that filled him. His mind churned from needing to know what to do and what to say next.

Yeto led Dring into the transparent blue metal, innermost ring set, of upright stones. *The Arians are so foolish never to have understood how this metal is formed. All they had to do was to duplicate the chemical compounds found in the blood stream of any native.*

Yeto touched the warm humming surface of a tall stone as they passed and approached the innermost center.

# HOWLING GROUND AGAIN

Howling sounds reverberated from under their feet. The firm soils began to shake and moan in harmonic, song-like rhythms. They widened their stances to maintain their balance when the noise abated.

Yeto spoke out first. "Dring, you were trying to ask me questions before we were interrupted by Aryll's song and trembling dance. You gave voice to your most profound query. Why me? I can't answer that. For now, be assured. You are in the right place, at the right time, and you alone have the potential to forge this destiny. The council must know if you consciously choose to accept this challenge. As I've made you aware, nothing and no one in all of creation could force you. It needs you to surrender and serve in this higher good."

"I'm ready. Our planet stands poised with her pulses and surges to begin her Changeover. If she is not allowed to complete her cycle of rebirth, bombs will be used to poison her forever. If she fails in her transition, all her surviving native children will be terminated, including my Ethra?"

Yeto responded. "You are correct. All her children need to be alerted. There is only one way available for them to enter the dimension.

"This exodus can only be opened for them if the one living example of our race is present for them to catalyze their perceptions. It demands a living person usher them through the gateway so they may reunite with their tribeflock families.

Dring was crystal clear on this picture. "And I'm that one living example?"

"And it is you, Dring." Yeto turned from Dring and bowed slightly to the seated figures around them who had been their witnesses.

# DRING BEFORE THE COUNCIL

The council sat motionless, fixed in stoic postures on identical rainbow-colored material seats of composed stone. Their faces were almost impossible to focus upon. An illumination of silvery light radiated like a luminous egg around their heads. Their faces were like kept transforming images inside haloed globes. One moment they appeared old and wise; the next moment would be a young face; the next moment the head would appear as a dried, shriveled skull. Somehow, this collective glow of energy from these ancients comforted Dring.

The sense of peace, life, and existence within their circle ran infinitely slow. Dring was fixated from a sense of timelessness.

The voice of their collective council sounded within Dring, and it penetrated his every atom.

*This voice you experience may seem frightening and to you, because its frequency is a great unknown; have no fear. Know you are loved unconditionally in our collective mind; loved since the first moment of your birth appearance. Yeto and your mother, Orlycia, have been witness in your preparation for the Changeover for our beloved planet. She beckons you, Dring. Confirm your choice to assist her by your free will.*

Dring focused his feelings and knowings to register Aryll's life deep within him.

*Only you can save all her children. Only you can lead those remaining in physical bodies into sanctuary here. You must go to them.*

*I sense their trouble. Is Ethra all right?*

*As we communicate here, a select number of native couples have been chosen as specimens to be stolen from our world. Your Ethra is among those chosen.*

*No! Have they boarded yet?*

*No, all are gathered in the shuttle bay areas.*

*Are they heavily guarded?*

*Our combined awareness can perceive only a small security watch force attends them. Most of the guards are flight crew members. Some of them meant to be guarding those departing are sleeping at this moment.*

*What more is there to know of the Changeover?*

*That depends on what you already know now, doesn't it, Dring?*

*Yes. I'll try to be specific. I have no powers to do anything. What can I accomplish? How will I save those who wait?*

*Oh, but you will have powers. You will not be alone to perform this deed. Your planet is well-aware of your unique electromagnetic frequency. She will lend you her strength at the proper time. Stay receptive. We, too, will extend our powers and knowings to you. In the final moments leading up to the Changeover, you must be in place.*

*Can't Pictart technology translate only one single individual's body from the physical world into this dimension?*

*You must attain and hold the state of becoming a universal, living Pictart. Your image will embody their lens and their portal. You'll be their catalyst; their exodus to safety. Any life can rise to accept this. It is within each of them to personally respond and join us. Dring, destiny is settled in small, quiet moments, not large, noisy ones. Yeto has taught you well in the natural aptitudes of your bloodline. You already have vast knowledge and experience in the starlight arts. Look, even now you meet us in your Starlight body.*

*I respect the assistance and training all of you have provided. I trust when the right time comes, I will know what to do. I now sense a deep urge to leave this gathering. I must fly to save those I've come to love. I can never express the appreciation for what you've given me. I believe it's time to face my destiny.*

*Dring, you ARE aligned. We register your urgency. Yes, your sense of timing is correct. The future calls you. Go and open the portal to our destiny!*

A sonic note echoed its humming around the lintels of the great circles.

# DRING FLIES TO THE RESCUE

A howl rose under beneath his feet, and with a blinding flash of brilliant light, Dring was propelled like a shot up through the open volcanic cone high into the air above them all.

Filled to overflowing with an extraordinary confidence and knowing, Dring faced his journey. He traveled at the speed of thought. In an instant; teleported back to the fountain by the villa, Dring took a deep breath and let it out slowly. His body awakened.

Calm and determined, mind vibrantly filled with the urgency of purpose, Dring leaped up and flew. With unadulterated focus, he was committed to his journey. He drew power in every breath. It surged through him with every flap of his wings.

As he increased his pace toward the Capacity, pushing flight speed to its maximum, sounds of rushing air weren't the only noises filling his head. Aryll's escalating Changeover cycle actively manifested herself with birthing sounds and songs. Dring became increasingly aware of them rising from the forest floor and the lands rushing beneath him.

With each pulse of the planet, his wings filled and charged onward. When Dring pushed down for his lift, the downdraft of energy from his flight created rippled depressions into the soil of Aryll's planetary flesh. This Changeover shift was being activated and responded to the rhythmic beat of his wings. Matching energy convulsions began to surge through Aryll's entire surface. She pressed back in response to his wing's undulating force. Dring could intimately feel the planet's body as it surged up and down with his flight rhythms.

The flatlands beneath him rose and sank like ocean waves; becoming more and more pliable. Growing urgency pulsated from deep within.

Aryll's rhythmic convulsive surges simultaneously fueled her deep tectonic plates; they opened chasms in the upper crust then slammed them closed in pulses, shooting geysers of soil and dust high into the skies.

Energy tensions, unrelenting in their demands beneath the movements of Dring's flight, were universally sympathetic everywhere across the planet. Internal trembling was overtaking Aryll throughout all the flexible skeleton of her tectonic plates. Her outer crust was becoming the fascia theater of intense physical strata movement.

Her urgency provided Dring new energy reserves to hasten his flight. The trembling vibrations of rock layers under tremendous tension released piezoelectric energy stored in her crystalline structures. Aryll's planetary rotation was slowing to a stop.

Plasmic heat filled the atmosphere. Increasing howling and groans from deep within her land masses continued to grow in intensity. Dring sensed her release would occur when the planet's rotational movement stopped. When the shift and halt of her magnetic and rotational poles produced the completion of her birth, Aryll would enter her elevated life.

Dring felt pendulous, in a dream state; moving, yet suspended within the sequences of each moment.

Thankfully, no Arian patrols flew to impede his flight. He continued to fly, driven by undistracted purpose and pure concentration. All Arians proceeded uneasily in their evacuations, but could not ignore what they heard and felt in the rumblings beneath their feet. *Thankfully, they will be harried in their attempts to finish loading personnel and materials for their departure,* he thought.

Dring was certain in his knowing. The natives would be the last to be loaded. *I must reach Ethra and the others immediately. She mustn't be allowed to leave me.* It was the only thought that occupied his mind.

# PRIME DIRECTOR ONE ON ARIANA

Prime Director One stepped back from his chair. This roundtable gathering represented his platform to orchestrate planets separate from Ariana.

The conference room held only a handful of planetary directors with short travel distances from their planets. Members of this august ruling body not able to attend, due to their planet's distance, were connected by view screens set around the conference tables.

Prime Director One addressed the group. "You've all heard the general announcements sent out across the empire. With this confidential meeting, you may be certain it's not simply for more political rhetoric. It concerns the pending stericyclation operation on Aryll 8.

"You should be aware of one unusual member here in attendance for this highly-classified meeting. Let me remind you of his position. As head of Internal Thought Monitoring, Okadimus 66 reviewed and cleared each of you."

Okadimus 66 nodded to them all. "If I may say a few words, Prime Director?"

"Of course. They need to hear what you've told me."

The pithy man stood to walk around inside the table's open arena. He addressed seated members and waiting faces upon the screens. He wore the formal toga uniform befitting his rank. A purple sash securely wrapped the slight bulge of his middle. He also wore the skullcap with laurel leaf design designating his high position in the Office of Internal Thought Monitoring (OITM). He gave each of the faces present his most serious gaze.

"I come before you to report the gravest situation. The OITM has been reviewing the overall strength and consistency of the empire's mind and thought programs. Sadly, the dream of conquest across this part of the universe is losing its conviction. Citizens from a variety of planets are mentally failing to respond and to take up the banner of its essential nature.

"These observational readings from members of my office you, as planetary leaders, should already have sensed in the masses you govern. There is an eroding of beliefs in our old gods, distraction among some of our leading representatives, growing reluctance to follow in the ways of the ancestors, and a lackluster dedication to our ancient motives.

"This is not unprecedented in recorded histories. Our ancestors left their original planet, Earth when Rome and its traditions fell. From our most sacred legends, you know they also carried artifacts given to them by the gods. These treasures were placed into the Cave of the Arians. These gifts of the gods were placed in that sanctuary to serve ever more as energy beacons; to radiate outward into the universe, and to inspire the minds of all future generations of empire citizens."

Okadimus 66 returned from pacing to stand next to and point at Prime Director One. "This man has held our motives strong. He has incorporated the best of mind control and entangled a core spirit within our citizens for centuries now.

"This classified meeting is being held to tell you why this victory on Aryll 8 holds such grave importance. My office was made aware of research archives unearthed upon Opus 4 a little over three years ago.

"As legend portrays, Opus 4 is acknowledged as the very first planet Arians conquered in this sector. It served as the launching base for all other advances until our central command conquered and established itself here on Ariana.

"Gentlemen, from the ancient accounts we have uncovered, we can confirm the Cave of the Arians does indeed exist. And we can now pinpoint clues as to its location."

Questions and comments swept through those assembled. Audible roars filled the room from the view screens. The Prime Director stood and raised his hand. With that action, he silenced the group.

"When Okadimus 66 brought me this information some time ago, I made certain to silence anyone involved in this discovery. The dead will not speak nor reveal my plans. Sharing this knowledge before this leadership body carries with it the same mortal weight. Any leaks of this knowledge will result in your termination. There is no corner of this space you could hide. I'm certain this warning does not warrant repeating.

"The first planet chosen for conquest, as the original Arian fleets moved out into space, became the home for the gods' gifts: the Cave of the Arians.

"However, as much as they underscore the credibility of the cave's existence, they, unfortunately, record an Arian battle retreat. The native population of Aryll 8 rose with greater, unexpected technologies and defeated our ancestors. That defeat caused them to abandon those precious artifacts only to our legends, and now it appears even our distant access to their powers is rapidly waning.

"Fortunately, through the fortitude and bravery shown by our ancestors after that initial defeat, they did go on to conquer other worlds. Thus, we live here rich and prosperous.

"These archives assure me rediscovery of the Cave of the Arians shall renew inspiration and recharge this lagging of spirit across the stars. All reasons for this victorious conquest should now be abundantly clear. In the depths of that cave, we shall once again have the gifts of the gods in our hands and secure our place in history."

# THE GIFTS

"I will remind you now of the articles we seek." Okadimus 66 rose to support this revelation. "We seek to recover use of the gods' scrying bowl. When filled with pure water, it was said to enable one to gaze through time as if it were a divine window. Plans and strategies could be studied along with various timelines to the empire's greatest advantage.

"We also seek Jupiter's scepter. Once held, this rod was said to be able to direct the power of lightning upon any opponent. This could greatly benefit the weaponry of our military advances.

"We need Aeneas' invisibility cloak, which was said to be able to hide, from sight and detection, anything it surrounds. It goes without saying this artifact would guarantee our rule in a myriad of unseen ways.

"My office has sincere hope one more relic may be stored there, the original Book of the Arian Word. That document would prove invaluable in strengthening morale and resolve within our citizens.

"Once in possession of all these original treasures, they will provide undeniable proof of our superior genetic, and confirm the charge placed upon us by our most high gods."

Prime Director One moved to end the meeting. "Gentlemen, you occupy the planetary director seats for all our planets. Hold this plan and these revelations privy only to yourselves. Be ready to manifest total support for any and all of my action decisions. The time rapidly approaches when the first complete stericyclation experiment will be completed.

"I am certain that once all life radiation is removed from that world after stericyclation, our detection teams will be able to read the energy signature of exactly where the Cave of the Arians is located. These treasures will strengthen and guarantee all our futures. There shall be no more defeats. Our Arian victories and the richness of our spirit shall grow hand-in-hand with the abundant riches of new tribute. Your patience and loyal support will bring us all great rewards.

"Be of good cheer. As these events unfold, share in witnessing by live-feed broadcasts. We shall all reap the profits from this new renaissance of spirit throughout our glorious empire."

With that, Prime Director One signaled with a final wave of his hand, and the meeting closed.

# THE ARIAN COMMAND SPACECRAFT

As the Arian command flagship orbited high above the surface of Aryll 8, within its command conference room, surface maps of the planet's topography displayed the pinpoints of Arcon bomb locations. Expansive portholes afforded live panoramic views of the world below. Prime Director 32 addressed final briefings as he dramatically paced, making sure his persona was large enough to fit this function. "Take the opportunity to speak with Doctor Niertz 48. He is the principal scientist in charge of the stericyclation.

"We anxiously await the opportunity to witness live reports of this experiment's success. Our world is fortunate to have been chosen ground zero for this radical new technology. All of you will prosper from the fruits of this success. Please welcome Doctor Niertz 48."

The doctor stood. He waited until the light applause subsided. "Thank you, sir. Fellow Arians, as your Prime Director 32 has so eloquently stated, this grand opportunity will confirm the viability of complete reformation of any ecosystem. All eyes will bear witness to our great success.

"This project nears completion of its first stage. This is a historic moment for Arian history. I'll refer to the outlines set out before you."

# PHASE ONE: BOMBING

"First stage has to do with the strategic planting of nine hundred eleven neutron-style bombs. Their locations are displayed across all major land masses and within the oceans. Once detonated, these bombs will effectively shroud the entire planet with clouds of Arcon gas.

"Expected fumigation results? We project termination of approximately 98% or more of all native organic life from these devices. Residual radiation should eliminate the rest.

"It's believed the only life forms able to escape this primary detonation treatment may be those that can reach or live on mountain tops higher than 3000 yards.

"Some irregularities in prevailing wind patterns may temporarily hold pockets of the original native atmosphere, but the saturation of all planetary fresh water sources will occur through natural precipitation cycles as the entire ocean's waters will be seeded with these concentrates."

# PHASE TWO: STERICYCLATION

"Phase Two will be a major cleanup operation. Within one day, levels of the gas will be stable. Drone patrols can safely recon the surface of this newly sterilized planet to seek out and laser-cleanse any surviving life that may have survived on high mountain peaks or freak weather islands."

# PHASE THREE: RESULTS

"Life readings will be monitored for five more days. And as soon as all gas readings are clear, your orders will be given to return to quarters on a new Aryll 8."

Doctor Niertz 48 was interrupted by applause. "During your concentrated stay here, a tremendous, coordinated amount of work must be done.

"Phase Three begins the re-population of new ecology species. This will involve the newly planned ecosystem specimens of flora and fauna contained, and nurtured, that reside here. These are the pieces of the ecology puzzle to re-plant and re-stock our fresh new world.

"Years of careful research have gone into their design and selection. To re-establish productive life here, all life forms aboard have been carefully blended. All specimens are hardy and resistant even if minute amounts of gas residue are not completely broken down in the planet's new atmosphere.

"When these three phases are complete, the real experimentation begins. We'll witness and document how quickly our new ecology transforms this planet into a productive, geoengineered world."

Generous applause once again filled the gathering.

PD 32 was excited. "This calls for attention, coordination, and teamwork with complete discipline."

"Prime Director One will be monitoring the progress of this event by live feed. It will be simultaneously cast to every empire planet. All eyes are upon us. The names and careers of all those involved will not be forgotten."

The group reacted with greater applause.

"For now, you are dismissed. Please return to your stations. Study and review the integral parts each of you need to play. Rest at ease until this countdown is initiated." The director asked a few members to remain as the meeting room emptied. Doctor Rotz 27, Doctor Niertz 48, and Harcos 86, as Assistant Prime Director, huddled close.

"Doctor Niertz 48, how is the countdown progressing? Need to consult with any members of my staff as we approach phase one?"

"The last report gives us about a three-hour time frame. The bombs are in position, active, and ready. All relay circuitry, including the satellites, are checked and ready to go."

Doctor Rotz 27 added, "There is still the matter of the last shuttle."

"Cheer up, Doctor. We all know you tried to save this ecology as it was. But you'll still be able to research with the native pairs. You may yet crack their breeding patterns. Too bad that winged one was lost. He would have made a prime exhibit."

Doctor Rotz 27 could only add, "Yes, director."

Harcos 86 moved close to Prime Director 32 as the two doctors began a quiet conversation.

"Sir, I've received confirmation from the network. Scheduling times are confirmed for Prime Director One to address the empire moments before detonation. He'll laud this new beginning. The broadcasting networks confirm this will be the most observed event in the empire's history."

"Excellent." He spoke in a whispered aside to Harcos 86. "We're certain of two staff members who'll prosper by the fruit in its branches, eh?" He smiled knowingly. "All our hard work setting this in motion shall soon start to pay off handsomely."

Doctor Niertz 48 reminded them, "And this is only the historical beginning."

Doctor Rotz 27 interrupted the conversation. "I'd like to know if the native couples are aboard. Has this been confirmed yet?"

Harcos 86 jumped on that. "I checked on them myself. They are assembled and confined on the shuttle bay. Others have been released from confinement. It appears they wish to voluntarily remain together for their last few hours before the bombs go off. All other biological materials and specimens Doctor Rotz 27 asked about are already aboard, sir."

# CALL FROM CEST 21

One of the large screens connected with an urgent call. Philomystic Cest 21 appeared. "I'm calling from the last shuttle pad, Prime Director. What about Teri 38? There seems to be some confusion here. I was under the assumption he's scheduled to be brought up, too. Isn't he?"

Harcos 86 intercepted her. "Based upon the inquisitor's report, the director has ruled to leave him behind with the natives."

"Is that true, your Directorship?"

"Yes, it is. His final request was to remain behind rather than facing charges. He's of no use to the state."

Doctor Rotz 27 spoke up. "Is there any chance I may request him for continued research?"

"No, doctor, my decisions regarding this matter are final."

Cest 21 interrupted. "But sir, he may hold the keys to unlocking the mysteries of this ancient species."

"That may be true, but in this, the state must look to its future, not to the past. You and other members of my staff had ample time to examine this man. All reports confirm his insanity. This matter is closed. It should be very clear to anyone what the state's position is upon this matter. Cest 21, is this clear to you?"

She recognized his official tone of admonition. She also

knew her affirmation would make her legally bound to uphold his decision. It was politically sound for her to say. "Yes, Prime Director 32, the state's position in this matter is clear. I affirm."

He seized this moment to demonstrate his political control. "And you, Doctor Rotz 27, is the state's position on this matter clear to you, as well?"

"Yes, sir."

Now that some of the tension had been resolved, the room was still.

Cest 21 broke the silence. "Perhaps those natives who are left will find the answer to their waiting."

"Yes, they will have a lung full of gas in a very short time. That should be all the answer they need."

The room, again, went silent.

Doctor Rotz 27 changed the subject. "This operation will provide confirmation that all grain fruit species are resistant to the gas, won't it, Doctor Niertz?"

Doctor Niertz 48 replied, "Yes. It will confirm the superiority of Arian breeding and survivability."

# CEST 21 GOES TO SAVE TERI 38

Cest 21 disconnected her call and rushed from the shuttle pad.

*Teri 38, I'm not going to abandon you in some lousy cell. You need to join your crew. At least you can all go out together if it comes down to that.*

The power slowly rose from the ground beneath her. She silently pleaded, *Oh Aryll, find a way to save yourself and all your children.*

She recognized the urgent rhythms of the planet's approaching crescendo by the moans, howlings, and the rising and sinking of the ground beneath her feet. The aggravate sounds of cracking walkways outside the medical building validated the faint but audible building musical tones of Aryll's Changeover songs.

Jumping over uneven cracking surfaces, she ran down the hallway into the entrance of the building. The staff had already been evacuated. She ducked a ceiling board as it loosened and fell at her feet; then grabbed the keys swinging from a peg on the wall outside Teri's cell.

With a quick turn of the key, she pulled open the door. "Hurry. We haven't much time. Grab a robe and let me get you out of here. We have to get to the shuttle bay."

He didn't have to hear that twice. "I felt you coming for me, Cest 21. You feel her, too, don't you? The planet I mean."

Dodging another falling ceiling piece, she replied. "You already know that answer. They were going to leave you to be gassed in your cell."

"We have to join our friends. I'm praying Aryll can show us how to save them."

# THE ARIAN COMMAND SPACECRAFT AGAIN

Moria called Cest 21. Teri 38 and Cest had reached the shuttle, and some native workers gathered around them. Mata touched his cheek, happy to see him, and the other workers smiled their welcomes in silent greetings.

"Cest 21, Are you there?"

"Yes, Moria. I'm here, but where are you? You weren't hauled up to the command ship with the Prime Director, were you?"

There was a pause before Cest 21 heard her reply. "Yes, that's where I am. He thinks we're a fine political pair. So does Prime Director One. I'd call me a slave, but bagging me as a trophy species would probably be more his description."

"Moria, you've got to get out of there. They're about to poison your planet. You couldn't live with yourself. Ethra is still down here with me and the rest of your race. They abandoned Teri 38, but I've freed him. You've got to come back down to us."

Moria took a moment. "Cest 21, you must listen to me carefully. In a short time, the Changeover will intercede and stop all this intended destruction; I'm certain of it. But you cannot let them load the couples. Prime Director 32 thought it was the only way to let Ethra live. He put her on the breeding couple's' list. You're of my tribeflock. Save those members of your new family. Save my daughter. I'm counting on you. Find a way."

"Moria, I will. I promise. That shuttle won't leave the ground with her on it. I'll figure out a way. What about you? When can you come back to us?"

Moria was clear. "I always knew this was a one-way trip. The planet will save herself. Dring is nearly there to help you all. I swore a personal oath about this many years ago.

"First, I would find the daughter these barbarians stole from me. You have helped me succeed in that. And second, I would find a way to wreak revenge upon them for the pains and torture they've inflicted on me, on our tribeflocks, and upon our planet. This has always been my intent. This will be farewell, for now, Cest 21."

"No. No. Moria we need you. The tribeflocks need you." She panicked. "Ethra needs you. She and Dring will be life mates. You must be there to help sing the birth songs for their offspring. Moria, it's not too late. Get back down here."

"No, my dear. Have no grief at my passing. Life sparks are eternal. There is no such word as death or dying in the spoken or unspoken tongues of my tribeflock. We shall all meet again very soon in the starlight dimension. I must sign off now."

# ON THE LAUNCH PAD

Cest 21 was flooded with grief as she switched off her communicator. She'd never had any family sense, until now. Moria, and Orlycia, and Yeto, and all the others had accepted her. They adopted her. She'd been raised to be an Arian, but she couldn't let her new tribeflock down.

She moved closer to Teri 38. "You won't be the only former Arian to stay here for the love of this planet."

He squeezed her hand as they stood together and exchanged a deep look of knowing. All the workers circled them and welcomed them both.

# DRING ARRIVES AT THE SPACEPORT

Hot plasma winds buffeted Dring's face as he flew. Driven by urgency, he'd pushed his cruising speed. Despite the energies of the approaching Changeover time, he felt strangely light and buoyant. Every part of him, every molecule in the clouds, the land's song far beneath him, the air itself was charged with urgency. He was flying faster and steadier than he ever had.

A strange new calmness filled him as *Let, only the action of flight itself, fill you...* came from the voice of the council and flowed over him. Dring focused on reaching the spaceport.

The edge of the Capacity appeared over the horizon. He knew no patrols would rise to stop him because they would have been lifted off to orbit above the planet's atmosphere; watching and planning their victory.

Those that remained would soon be in for a tremendous surprise and disappointment.

He hastened flight over the buildings and approached the shuttle pads. From the air, he clearly saw the remaining tribeflock members assembled. Yes, and two more. He smiled when he saw Cest 21 and Teri 38. But where was Ethra? That thought quickened his pulse; drove him forward. He relaxed as he sensed and heard her thoughts. *I am here waiting for you, Dring, my trusted life mate.*

The atmosphere of the planet was thickening; heating

up; a cloudy fog whispered in and around the buildings. The Changeover songs grew loud enough that all could hear. Off in the distance, the ground moved and rippled with greater intensity, becoming even more like movements mirrored in her ocean waves. The volume and intensity of Aryll's songs increased and began compressing the very air Dring flew through.

Off in the distance, her ocean waters rose in larger and larger waves. The waters boiled. Huge tsunamis smashed far up upon the shores. Her rumbling sound frequencies thickened the clouds. Lightning began its occasional discharge; down to the ground and straight up to the ionosphere like tall trees with multi-colored branches.

Sound and vibrations of the Changeover reverberated all around Dring. They filled the air like the noises of trumpeting and shrilling. The steady volume of its chorus was increasing inexorably; intensifying toward a final crescendo.

Teri 38 pointed. "There in the air. Dring is returning for all of us. Dring is here."

Mental and physical voice communication swept between all those gathered. Some had been frightened and begun milling about like panicked beasts. Dring's appearance swept all fears away.

Most had never seen anything but an image of a true member of their race. All eyes glowed with wonder, and every heart filled with a new calm and enthusiastic joy. All the pains from years of Arian brutality, any suffering they might have held inside, began to wash away.

The chosen breeding couples, intended for the last departing shuttle, looked up from behind their fences. They, too, filled with hope. Ethra beamed her thoughts and her love up to Dring. *You are here now my love and my life mate. Soon we will be reunited; together forever.*

Arian inspectors and guards proceeding down the ramp from the shuttle stopped in amazement. They gasped open mouthed; stunned by this electric moment. Cest 21 seized this moment to approach and distract their attention.

"I'm Cest 21, Philomystic First Class. By order of Prime Director 32, I demand you unlock these holding cages."

As much as that confused the guards, the sight of a hovering man frightened them. One called to his flight commander. "Do you see? That's the winged guy?"

The flight commander responded, "See what? We've finished the pre-flight checklist. We only have one more hour to be loaded and into orbit."

The head guard interrupted. "Well, you'd better check your visual readings and all your scanners. Something strange is going on out here. I've got a crazy woman raving about how I need to let the breeding birds out of their cages."

The co-pilot joined in. "What's going on?"

The commander saw Dring. "Ignore that flying lunatic and get those specimens loaded at once."

The head guard jumped to comply. "Clear fact." He signaled to the other guards and called back to the pilots. "You better get those engines started now." He called out with disregard to Cest 21. "Stay out of our way."

The guards moved toward the confinement gates, lasers at ready. Dring flew effortlessly over the center of the shuttle bay area. He spoke to those assembled in his mental voice so the Arians would not hear.

*Fellow children of Aryll, for those who don't know me, I am Dring. Now is our time. Feel the Changeover time press upon us. Be at peace. It is our future destiny calling to us.*

Suddenly and unexpectedly, the Arian guards heard Dring's voice. It blared out with a clear command inside their heads.

*Put down your weapons now. Leave this planet in peace.*

Another guard, trying to cover his bewilderment, waved his weapon and responded. "Forget it. We're taking these birds with us." He moved to unlock the cage.

Dring's commands were firm and bold within them all. *You are no longer in control. You are not welcome here. Enter your craft and exit this planet immediately.*

The pilot's voice could be heard from the guard's communicator. "What's the delay? Get those specimens aboard."

"Sir, this winged guy says we can't take them."

"You stand ready where you are, soldier. I'll call Command." The pilot flashed an urgent call to the craft orbiting high above them. "This is shuttle EXHI23 calling Command. There's a situation down here. Need immediate advice. Level Red."

"Yes, shuttle EXHI23? What is your delay? What kind of a situation? Respond."

"You know that flying native everybody's been talking about? He just showed up. He says we must leave the specimens behind. Please advise."

"Use whatever deadly force is needed. Expedite effective departure. Termination of hostile approved. Expedite."

"Operation countdown proceeding with all haste to load and depart surface."

"Copy fact."

"All guards, fire upon the intruder. Collect and load those specimens."

The waiting guards responded. "All right men, you heard orders. Let's get busy, soldiers. All right, big bird, take this." They aimed their lasers, prepared to fire upon Dring.

Dring read their actions. *Your weapons are useless. Board your craft and depart. Now!*

As the guards attempted to fire their lasers, a razor-thin neon blue ray of light beamed from Dring's eyes. Nothing happened as the guards expected. Their lasers were enclosed in a dense cloud of fog and instantly dematerialized in a warm flash. Stunned and amazed, the empty-handed guards called the pilot again.

"EXHI23 flight commander. The winged one melted away our lasers. Attack him with the ship's armament."

"Copy that. We'll target attack response from here."

The co-pilot prepared to target the ship's onboard firepower. As his hands reached for the control buttons, another dense cloud of fog appeared. All weapons' technology components vaporized beneath his touch. All he could do was stare at the smoldering voids and vacant holes in his console boards.

"What the...?" A great silence settled over them.

The commander witnessed this and grabbed his communicator. "EXHI23 to operations. Efforts of retaliation against winged native have proven ineffective. All weaponry has been neutralized."

"What do you mean neutralized, EXH123?"

"Both handheld and ship's laser equipment have evaporated. We have no firepower, sir."

"Copy fact. Are engines working? What is your flight status?"

"Engines are running and ready... but all weapons systems have been eliminated."

"Has there been any aggressive threat to your personnel and craft?"

"No, sir. The only order received is for us to leave. We're left defenseless down here."

After a long pause for consultation, the orders arrived. "This is command. Prime Director 32 is aware of your situation. He's ordered your immediate departure from the planet's surface."

"You got it, sir. Attention all guards and security forces, retreat from all posts. Secure outer doors for immediate departure."

All ground forces filled the frequencies with a chorus of responses. "Copy fact."

One threw his keys back at Cest 21. None of them wasted any time. They rushed to re-enter the shuttle craft and slammed the doors behind them.

The shuttle began its rise on a silent blast, hovered for a moment high over the shuttle bay, engaged main engines and whooshed out of sight.

# AFTER THE ARIAN DEPARTURE

Shudders of joy rushed through everyone on the ground as Dring and all the others witnessed the Arian ship depart and disappear over the horizon. Teri 38 wept in relief, but old thought patterns flooded his mind. He felt once again alone, aware he was different. He might not fit here anymore. Then, in a moment, the tears stopped, and his eyes began to clear. He became filled with appreciation. The grief of his past was leaving him. His emotions welled up filled with a great and lucid clarity. Now at peace with himself and his destiny, it was time to begin anew.

*I'm not alone; I'm still alive, and now I'm adopted. All and any connection to my past Arian life flew off with that spacecraft. It's vanished, taking with it all my history.*

Smiling, Teri 38 looked around him. Someone else inspired him. Cest 21 stood beside him. *She came back for me. She remained behind.* As she moved to unlock and liberate the couples, Ethra rushed out to embrace her, and the others grouped with Teri 38 and their tribe flocks.

Teri 38 registered something consciously he'd never known before. For the first time in his life, he felt at home. All he saw around him filled with sympathetic eyes. These looked back to him with respect and kindness.

*I realize now. Finally, I'm with others of my kind. They're my chosen family.*

Cest 21 also felt her past washing away. *There's no future for me anywhere else. I longed for a home. My journey has now proven that.* She smiled and took Teri 38 by the hand. "Just call me Cest."

He smiled. "Call me Teri."

Dring hovered over the remaining crowd. They were all gathered closely now, standing quietly. Their planet sang softly beneath them. Random thoughts flitted around and within the minds of a few. Every heart felt the joy of this time. Every mind was focused upon Dring.

His voice appeared clear, yet silent within the minds of all assembled.

*I come before you a representative of the council. The ancient ones charged me to be here with you. I freely accepted this task my father performed for all the other tribeflocks before.*

*The council is consciously connected within me. The loving intelligence of our beloved planet is connected within me. All our ascended races await you in the starlight dimension. They long for us to join them.*

*This is a crucial time. Soon the invaders will attempt to ignite their bombs of death and destruction. Have no fear. As you witnessed, their weapons are now useless here. Our planet is old and wise. She has the knowledge and care for each of you. This, her Changeover event will ever confirm our destiny. You will witness and experience this transformation with her. I seek now your cooperation to prepare you for your transition.*

Dring smiled down upon the figures of Teri 38 and Cest 21. *This includes our two newest, adopted members of our tribeflock.*

A flood of joy and humor filled them all.

*The Changeover our world is about to undergo will prove most surprising for the Arian Empire as they witness it. Let the Changeover songs fill you. They will connect us all to the very living heart of this beloved planet upon which you stand.*

A feeling of great joy swept through the crowd.

*Look upon my form. I represent the image of who you are. Your bodies endured poisoning, suffering, torture, and disfigurement by the Arians. That aside, you and I are alike. You are me in your design, just like the crystal moth within its cocoon.*

*Feel the truth of what I say. You are all perfect and complete within. Picture what I say; know what I say. Allow yourselves to rise from this slumber of unknowing. Soon you will step into the starlight.*

As members of the crowd pondered this, feelings of great anticipation began to build. Small personal outbursts of sudden recognition resounded like the bursting of tiny bubbles. The feeling and frequency of the assembly changed as they registered this magic. They consciously experienced its shift and focused within themselves. Even Teri and Cest were stunned by its well-being.

A large quake shook the ground they stood on. The heat of the compressing atmosphere responded to the increasing volume of their planet's songs. The hot winds were becoming unbearable. The atmosphere, becoming almost too thick to breathe, condensed and pushed its way into every set of lungs.

Dring spoke to them again. *Be aware. As you begin to feel the realization you within, the urgency of this time presses upon us. The time has come for you to step into the higher dimension.*

The heaviness of the air about them continued to grow in

density. Bright, electric blue noctilucent clouds formed upon the surrounding horizons. Bolts of lightning flashed from the skies, then become upward bound, rebounding from the heaving, groaning soil beneath their feet.

The notable atmospheric temperature increase sent shutters through the assembly. If not for the calming effect of Dring's continued address, they may have given in to scattering away as if all this was madness.

*You need not understand this. Look upon me and trust me. I am the living Pictart. I shall serve as the portal; your gateway to your future. Feel the loving energy of the starlight drawing you. Its threshold is open for you to pass through this image of me.*

Dring, hovering effortlessly above the crowd, now ceased to move his wings and hung suspended in state, arms and legs outstretched in a posture like a five-pointed star. Around him, a circle of light began to focus and shimmer a brilliant indigo blue. Dring's body was surrounded and permeated by the light within the energy field of a dazzling luminous egg-shaped orb; his glittering form could still be discerned within.

# PASSAGE INTO THE STARLIGHT

An unfamiliar voice came from Dring. It was of a different mental texture; softer and moving. It was of their planet mother. *Come, my children. Enter through this living gate. Enter the sanctuary of my starlight. Others of your families await you.*

Dring's form glowed, a radiant, blue star of her energy. Her brilliant luminous egg engulfed him as he maintained his state of function within its center. He hovered above them waiting, enclosed in the energy bubble.

Matching energy bubbles of silky blue fog formed around each of those on the ground. Inside each bubble, the image of their old body transformed into a new energy double. A newer, more vibrant, perfect form materialized upon each of them. And as the fog dissipated, what emerged was a fully healed, fully winged body. Each member became brilliantly and vibrantly surrounded within their egg.

Mata, the most senior of the group, surrounded by her light energy, lifted from the ground. She moved rapidly through the air and zipped through the center of Dring's living image. With rapid pace, other members of the crowd were moved, elevated, and flew through the portal.

One after the other, fully winged forms zipped through Dring's center. Like bubbled clouds of light, each was merged and pulled through the vortex.

Faces of each member flowed past him and through him timelessly. To him, the motion was exquisite. He resonated his frequency to match their frequency as they passed through him.

In front of him, energy spread out in the seething hot physical world of the changeover process. Behind him, he felt a cool, stable glow. Soon, nearly all members had entered through his portal. All but Ethra and the two Arians remained, Teri and Cest. They held back in a momentary hesitation realizing that they were not of that planet. Therefore, their life signals and frequencies were different.

Dring addressed the pair. "Teri and Cest, you may also pass through. Aryll knows your blueprints. She holds great value for your lives. She holds the gate open for you to experience your starlight bodies. Set aside your doubts and cross through.

Teri remembered the projecting experiences he had in confinement. Cest smiled as she thought of the love she felt for Yeto and Orlycia. All doubts fell away from them. They manifested wings of their own and floated from the ground. One after the other, they both zipped through.

Only Ethra remained.

*Dring, I wanted to be the last life to pass through. I wish that you never forget this intimate harmony of frequency mix and blend, that, as life mates, we might ever continue to explore. Remember that with this experience, our bodies, and we may re-experience this union in our future.*

With that, Ethra raised her newly formed wings and soared to pass through him.

Dring savored the ecstasy of their mutual, joyful moment.

He allowed his personal thoughts and energies to co-mingle with Ethra's; to mix and flow love unconditionally in this mutually elevated energy state.

*We blend. You fill my mind, and my heart, Ethra. You will always be my love and my life mate.*

# ORBITING SPACESHIPS

The last Arian shuttle to leave the planet's surface approached the orbiting Arian High Command ship high above. Operational command sent a message. "Shuttle EXHI23, advise of your status."

"We've blasted off and cleared the surface. The crew is intact. Breeding specimens abandoned in the shuttle bay, as ordered. Approaching docking maneuvers approximately twenty minutes."

"Copy that, EXHI23. Priority order, report to council room 51 immediately upon docking. This order is for the entire crew."

"Clear. Copy that."

"Prime Director 32 wishes a debriefing. Don't waste time getting there."

"Copy that. Shuttle EXHI23 clear. Over and out."

# ROOM 51

Behind closed doors, the crew met with Prime Director 32 and Assistant Director Harcos 86, in attendance as the debriefing began. An officer began his presentation and named Cest 21 as the one who ordered the release of the couples.

The director cut in. "It was Cest 21 giving that order? She was supposed to be arriving here on your shuttle. What's her current location?"

"She stayed behind with the natives. She had another Arian male with her."

"Teri 38. That bitch. Well, she chose her fate. Goodbye, Cest 21. Your career was dead, anyway. She'll get what she deserves staying down there with those primitives. Finish your report."

The reporting of the failed weapons and hearing voices in their heads astonished their leaders.

The director asked, "He spoke to you in your heads and demanded you leave?"

"All the men heard it. As loud as their mic-links."

"Dismiss these men, Harcos."

"This info is classified top security. Speak of these matters to no one."

The men mumbled their acknowledgments, and shuffled out of the conference room, Prime Director 32 spoke again to Harcos 86. "Order a staff meeting. STAT."

# FAR BELOW THE SURFACE OF ARYLL 8

Dring hovered alone in the atmosphere, close to the planet's surface. The pleasure of Ethra's passing energy lingered in every cell of his body. However, the Changeover was far from complete. The air around him was becoming increasingly super-charged with heat, energy, sounds, and light.

Aryll's groans were almost deafening. The ground heaved and convulsed in quakes of increasing rhythm. Vast tracts of land buckled upward to thrust geysers of soil and dust high into the sky. Those clouds held in the sky as murky traces, and then retracted, raining down into the depth of the valleys like the tremendous crashing of ocean foam from great ocean waves.

Ethra's mind called from the coolness of the starlight dimension behind him. *Let the Changeover happen, Dring. Turn around. You're keeping the gateway open by your focus upon it. You've saved me and all the others. Now save yourself.*

A mesmerized Dring distantly listened to her pleas in his mind, but his brain wouldn't let him turn away from this panoramic spectacle of energy, sound, and movement occurring all around him. Temperatures soared and buffeted his body.

*Dring.* Ethra's pleas became even more demanding. *My*

*love.* Her mental voice frequencies begged. She screamed to his brain; *disengage your senses from this turmoil. Now!*

Ethra's tones fought to radiate her strongest love throughout his being, to break his focus. Her tone reflected the alarm in her rising concern. *Turn around, Dring. Turn back to me now. Join all of us safely here. I love you! We all love you. Your body can't take much more of these energy surges.*

Ethra's mental pleas intensified and reached him, like from over his shoulder. He registered her voice as if he was moving slowly away from her down a long tunnel. He shook himself and felt intoxicated.

He knew what he had to do; yet below him, visions of the Changeover lay before him. It froze him in place as the ground beneath him opened in a small crack that rapidly widened into a huge chasm. All the Arian portions of the Capacity were destroyed. The notes of Aryll's birthing songs blared in triumph.

Huge canyon walls formed and gleamed vibrant reds and oranges beneath him from their molten rock surfaces. Lightning bolts flashed all around him along its rim, and flaming rocks fired up out of this magma canyon. They exploded in the air around him like unstable bolide meteors.

Dring's mind finally accepted that he should wait no longer. He pulled his gaze away and released his fixation. Deep below him, from the molten rock at the bottom of this great magna canyon, a rounded shape began to emerge. It flowed toward the surface, rising on a column of the same plasmic rock.

Dring ducked and narrowly missed being struck by a phalanx of flying stones hurled in his direction. They exploded around him like fireworks.

*Dring!* Ethra screamed behind him once more. *The energy*

*attraction of your gateway is drawing this matter right at you. You must turn away now. Come back to me.*

In a flash, Dring's heart filled with awareness. This mass was the birth of a new baby moon. He now hovered directly in the trajectory path for its emergence.

# THE VOICE OF THE COUNCIL

Dring recognized the next voice as that of the council. Dring. It is time for your duty to end. You have done well for all, good and faithful servant. Now complete this vital role which you have willingly provided. You have fulfilled your destiny there. Return to all of us here.

Dring, flushed with their truth, broke the lock on his fixation and turned to join Ethra. She instantly embraced him. Her love helped him anchor himself.

"Don't you ever frighten me like that again!" Ethra was firm, yet relieved, in her demand. "You've done it, Dring." She relaxed in the embracing cover of his wings.

Dring whispered into her ear.

"I don't believe I'll ever have to leave you now."

# IN THE ORBITING ARIAN SPACECRAFT

Prime Director 32 hit the operations group conference hard after the setback return of the last shuttle. "Here's the latest. A native revolt happened before the loading of the last specimens. The results: all breeding specimens have been left upon the surface of Aryll 8."

Doctor Rotz 27 spoke. "But sir, we must continue our research. We must have those specimens."

"This was my executive decision, Rotz. All factors were considered. You, above all, should be aware."

Harcos 86 tried to ease the tensions. "The importance and significance of this first stericyclation demand complete and immediate focus from every member here."

Doctor Niertz 48 still questioned. "And why was I not informed or consulted? The entire scope and purpose of this operation may have been compromised."

"Doctors, there was no time. It called for an instant executive decision to proceed. Especially since I take overriding responsibility for completion and success of this world's operation. The success of this project has more priority than gambling crucial times on the questionable breeding possibilities of a few native couples that might have been saved."

Doctor Niertz 48 softened his tone. "I must agree. Any lack of confidence, any blemish on the values of the empire's public relations, would be a cost far too high to pay if any major timing delays were to occur."

Seeking accolades for his position, Harcos 86 added, "On that note, I must also point out, through the valiant efforts of our communications staff, the first empire-wide coverage of this operation is to begin in less than one hour."

The director took that up. "A good reminder, Harcos 86. Command? What are final plans for executive linkups with Prime Director One?"

Officer Tzang 56 responded. "That link is scheduled in thirty minutes. Critical timing checks to begin the countdown of explosives are approaching. The bombs need time to warm up."

"Yes, good reminder. You must proceed with timing checks."

The voice of Doctor Rotz 27 rose above the conversation. "There might be enough time to gather up the specimens. Couldn't another craft get them?"

Prime Director 32 moved to squelch all further discussion on this. "Fellow Arians, the situation on the planet's surface is worse than you could imagine. Without violence, the native terrorist leader repelled the security detail on the site. He also thwarted all weaponry."

"This winged one seems able to display startling new abilities in tactics which no Prime Director has ever seen or heard of before."

Harcos 86 hesitated. "I have insufficient data to confirm what it was or how it happened. I'm no expert on this experience."

"Could I speak with these soldiers?"

"That can be arranged later, doctor. Considering the crucial needs for exact timing. The coordination of the director's decision to comply with the native's demands guaranteed the safe return of the flight crew, the equipment, and the other specimens already aboard the ship. Another interesting fact is we no longer have wristhomer signals for any of them." Harcos 86 was quick to note. "Other than the loss of those specimens, the countdown for stericyclation proceeds according to plan."

# PRIME DIRECTOR WITH MORIA

When Prime Director 32 returned to his cabin, he found Moria waiting.

"My daughter was not brought aboard, was she?"

He hesitated. "No, Moria, there were complications."

"You've disappointed me. She's been left to her fate? I couldn't feel her here, so I knew. There is only you and me here, then."

"Yes, but I can only stay with you a few minutes. The stericyclation is about to begin."

"Then you'd better go and tend to your toys, Prime Director. It seems you have most certainly sealed our fates together. Now go."

"I'll return to comfort you in your loss when the operation is complete, my Moria."

Her voice betrayed nothing of her real feelings. "I shall prepare to see you then."

# BACK AT COMMAND

Prime Director 32 strutted into the control room in readiness; like a contestant prepping his attitude for a fight.

"So you see, gentlemen, as Harcos 86 has briefed you, this situation hasn't altered our time for the stericyclation to begin."

"All bombs are at the ready, sir. The final countdown must be ordered immediately if we are to meet our window of success." Tzang 56 spoke and reported for command.

Doctor Niertz 48 checked his instrument boards. "Prime Director. I'm all clear to proceed. The loss of specimens is minor compared to the successful results projected for this operation. We must proceed now."

Doctor Rotz 27 hesitated slightly. "I'd still wish to lodge an appeal for another rescue attempt of specimens, but I do recognize the overall priority value of this project's completion."

"Harcos 86, continue procedures for the countdown. Command, what is the final status?"

Tzang 56 responded. "Ready, sir. From staff and equipment view, clear to proceed."

Prime Director 32 confirmed. "Proceed. We've cut our losses about the specimens. Commencement of the countdown is ordered."

# FROM PLANET ARYLL BELOW

Aryll's newborn moon slowly rose to the surface. Just as with the birth of any of her children, Aryll continued singing the songs of its birthing time. They caused the density and temperature of her lower atmosphere to reach near plasma conditions. This process kept building; converting matter; charging huge amounts of energy for her Changeover completion.

With this rising concentration of energy produced; density directed, conductive, lifting strength gravity waves propelled her moon ever higher above the planet's surface and escalated it in speed, hurling it on a direct collision course vector toward the main Arian ship orbiting out of the atmosphere. The moon cooled as it gained elevation and accelerated in its speed rising higher in altitude.

The Arian ships noticed this foreign object on their instruments and rallied their communications, but the command center was distracted by the linked broadcasts and the countdown.

"Sir, we have Prime Director One and all networks linked."

Prime Director 32 brushed his uniform and smiled into the screen. "Greetings, Prime Director One, Arian Empire Council, the Arian Senate, and all Arians throughout are present. This is Prime Director 32."

The chiseled face filled the screen. "This is Prime Director One. Greetings to all my Arian worlds for this extraordinary broadcast. A special greeting to those at Arian command hovering above Aryll 8 for bringing us live coverage of this first, historic moment for operation stericyclation. Is my valued lead science researcher, Doctor Niertz 48, there?"

"Yes, sir."

"How is everything proceeding, Doctor?"

"We've had some minor interruptions; however, the countdown for detonation proceeds as scheduled. The linkup should provide a grand spectacle for the entire empire to witness."

Command interrupted Harcos 86 to speak an aside into his headset. His face went tense as he addressed the director whose face also paled.

"This is Prime Director 32. Sir, please forgive this interruption, but we've just received new, disturbing readings. Prime Director One, might I request we temporarily hold from the connection at this time to keep you abreast of our most accurate update on events happening here?"

"Yes, Prime Director 32, make it so. We shall honor your petition for a brief delay, and will place this network link on hold for now."

# THE APPROACHING MOON

Harcos 86 approached with great concern on his face. "Sir, command has picked up a crucial interference from the planet's surface."

Prime Director 32 moved from his focus. "I got us a delay. What is going on? Why now? This was to be our finest hour."

"Massive quakes and turmoil on the surface of Aryll 8 have materialized and resulted into a massive plasma ball the size of a small moon, and it is being hurled into space."

"That will make for great video footage during the explosions."

"Command is in a panic. That moon is cooling as it approaches our location. It is increasing in speed on a direct collision course vector with this fleet. Specifically, the course of this orbiting craft."

"Why didn't anyone discover this and let me know sooner?"

"The staff was occupied with the communication link-ups. When they finally became aware of its movement and confirmed the object's course, I called for you. You need to issue a change of orbit order for the entire fleet, immediately."

"Get us out of this position, I'll try to finesse the delay, but it won't be easy." The Prime Director wracked his brain as to how to handle this. "My finest hour. Working directly with Prime Director One. With the entire network of planets as our witnesses. Why now? I've got to tell him the truth."

New navigational positions flashed out to all ships. And all flight commanders were ordered to execute emergency scramble procedures to change course and orbit locations.

Harcos 86 returned to Prime Director 32. "Your orders have been executed, sir. But I am also tasked to inform you of something equally as serious. All circuit connections to the bombs have been lost."

"Acknowledged, Harcos 86. What will it take to reconnect that network? Can anything else go wrong? Get that network up and working. I don't care what it takes. And get our backsides out of here."

*I'm still in charge*, he spoke quietly to himself. *This is just a short setback.* He took a couple of deep breaths. *Now to deal with the empire.*

"Connect me with Prime Director One." He cleared his throat and addressed the screen. "Prime Director One and all fellow Arians. I regret that due to adverse quake and volcanic activity from the planet below us, the entire fleet, and this command; stericyclation operations center must evacuate our current orbit positions immediately. This position is being threatened by a plasma mass hurtling directly this way from Aryll 8's unstable planetary conditions.

"We need more time to recalibrate new orbit location and properly redirect the operation. Doctor Niertz 48 will oversee re-calibrating this procedure once a new position is attained.

"As Prime Director in overall charge of Aryll 8, I can only extend my deepest regrets for any inconvenience this may have caused. We shall yet turn this into a historic moment in Arian history."

"This is Prime Director One. Be at peace across all the reaches of our glorious empire. We shall all yet be witness to this miracle of Arian leading edge technology.

"I ask all communication circuits be placed in a holding position, except for Prime Director 32. I will have a private briefing with him at this juncture."

All circuits were blackened out except for that of the two directors.

"Prime Director 32, get that fleet to safety. Then contact me personally. I want facts and possibilities for turning this into the triumph it was intended to be. Make certain Doctor Niertz 48 agrees with your solution to this fiasco. Out."

The main screen went as dark as Prime Director 32's swallowing any hope of winning political favor in all this. "Harcos 86, get us blasted into safety and out of this orbit. Now!"

Command circuits throughout the orbiting fleet reacted with the wail of sirens as rocket thrusters fired to reposition them all in space. The body of the newborn moon continued to cool as it moved out of the planet's atmosphere. It bore down in a relentless fixation course upon the Arian fleet's positions.

Lightning bolts flashed up and out from the planets surface. Although they were huge, they could barely be seen once they entered the vacant darkness of atmosphere. They narrowly missed the ship, but an accompanying scout craft once struck, was destroyed, ignited in a blaze of sparks and explosions.

Harcos 86 was near panic. "Prime Director. We're being fired upon. Attacked. We need to scramble into evasive maneuvers. Stat."

"Sound the alarms, Harcos 86. Get us out of here."

The pilot screamed, "Our instruments are measuring another big discharge. There's another bolt headed our way!"

"That bolt doesn't show on the screen," Harcos 86, the Assistant Prime Director, shouted back.

"It's dark lightning, sir. Electro-magnetic discharge in space, no atmosphere to light it up, and no air to make thunder, but here it comes."

Again, another bolt of dark lightning narrowly missed the command ship, but its heavy gamma wave discharge exploded a nearby, medium class troop carrier.

# WITHIN THE STARLIGHT OF ARYLL

Aryll's starlight dimension was clear. Its energy bubble's surface allowed all members to witness the Changeover events unfolding around them like a panoramic screen. Aryll's remaining buildings glowed like the colors of stained glass. The ancients understood the application of structure, harmonic sciences, and carefully placed design. These buildings and towers resonated to the flow of energy by ley line placement, composition, design, and their correct alignments to each other.

The towers were brilliant to watch. Vibrant, lightning-like bolts climbed upward from the ground and ascended to discharge into the skies. Their freestanding arcs rose to release force outward through her growing, conductive atmosphere, toward the departing fleet.

Twin towers, like Jacob's ladder, formed an upward arc until the combined duo-arc discharged. The outer atmospheric sheath was becoming denser as it pushed into the outer orbital membranes of Aryll's radiation belts. Since there is no movement of force without carrying even the slightest amount of accompanying matter, these belts glowed with spectacular gleaming aurora colors.

Birth songs rose from the planet's surface and neared the final stages of her Changeover.

Buoyant with joy, in the starlight, Aryll's children mixed freely testing their new atmosphere for the first time with newly perfect wings.

"Look at Cest and Teri." Dring pointed them out to Ethra. "I never realized their mammalian genetics carried a DNA trace for wings in its future development."

As all could observe, Cest and Teri were indeed testing their dragon-fly-like wing patterns with waves of energy within their newly charged auras. They'd each nearly completed manifesting a full double set of wings. One set was attached and ran under the arm from armpit to wrist. The other set sprouted upward from their shoulders similar to the wings native to Aryll.

Everyone saw the newly birthed moon chasing the fleet away. The newly energized state of planet Aryll began to quiet in the afterglow of her Changeover struggles. Her birth songs softened in volume. The planet's surface ceased its gyrations. The heats in her atmosphere had converted its entire extended atmospheric gas cloud to the thickness and density of energized liquid-like plasma.

As the fleet attempted to avoid their destruction, they fired all rockets simultaneously to thrust them further out from the planet's aura.

The energized plasma of Aryll's atmosphere fought back by expanding and compressing sound waves and took on the brilliance of its sonoluminescence.

In a single final response to the combined sounds and burning thrust of their fleeing rockets, Aryll burst into flames.

The energy aura of the entire planet ignited into the leaping flames of a new emerald blue sun.

# THE END OF ALL ARIAN DOMINATION

"Prime Director, the effects of our rocket blasts have ignited the growing energy fields of Aryll 8. The dark lightning discharges continue to be a threat. We must retreat; drop into hyperspace immediately to escape the heat and radiation of this, or we will perish."

In a resigned tone, Prime Director 32 sighed as he spoke into the communicator with orders. "Make it so, Harcos 86. Set escape course coordinates for the nearest Arian system. Now leave me alone."

# THE FINAL ACT

As the image of Harcos 86 faded from the communicator screen, Moria came closer. She had two glasses of brandy in her hands. Prime Director 32 reached for one.

Moria spoke first. "To both our futures, Prime Director 32." They toasted and drained their glasses.

"I don't see much future for us, Moria. I do believe my career is now over." He was visibly despondent. "What will you do, Moria?"

She looked out the porthole at the seething, burning energy ball occurring around her home below. Aryll 8 had elevated to become a sun. She knew this wasn't something caused by the Arians or even the director, but as the culmination of the magnificent Changeover she had heard of in all her legends. As this new starburst of energy burned away its old history on her planet, Moria found she could forgive her own. She could forgive them all.

*He hadn't realized the role he and his invading armies would unconsciously play in the Changeover.* She instinctively knew what was to be done. Without her native planet, she would never find peace. Before her sat a broken man and a broken leader. As a reward for being a failure in his tasks, he would be demoted to a position far lesser than he deserved.

"Have another sip of your favorite brandy, Prime Director.

It's time we enjoy our drinks and prepare for our next adventure." Moria offered it from the decanter. She refilled his glass.

"Thank you, Moria. But I think you're wrong. Our future together is very uncertain right now." He reached for the glass. "I fear there will be no more adventures for either of us. My empire is not forgiving. I think this will be our last drink together. My life is finished."

"I could have told you that."

"You offer me no options? No encouragement?"

"After all this time, I can finally know my daughter is safe. I'm satisfied no Arian influence can harm her anymore."

"Have we all been so hateful to you, Moria?"

"Of all the Arians I met, you at least tried to show me a little respect. That is why I've chosen you to journey with me in this."

"Moria, we journey together now, but only to return to the harshness of failed purpose and humiliation."

"Enjoy your brandy. As you'll soon be aware, I've already arranged other travel plans for both of us. I want you to know that I forgive you. You and your race have played out a role most important to my world.

"We both shall journey together much farther than you have imagined. The brandy you and I drank is laced with juice from berries of the female Zolag tree. That juice is an extremely fast acting poison, and it is always fatal. It didn't even spoil the flavor of the brandy. These bodies will terminate in another few minutes. This act was to be the completion of my oath as a mark of vengeance upon the Arian Empire."

"You've made this decision for me, Moria, but it is an easier solution than falling on my sword. However, you've also made yourself part of my destiny. What satisfaction can you receive from the retreat of the Arian forces? They are repelled, but your planet is dead."

"No. My planet lives. With the Changeover, she's evolved; moved to a higher level and gathered all her children with her."

"She's changed all right. She's now a huge ball of burning gas. She represents death to all that approach her."

"You have learned nothing in all this, Prime Director. This is the Changeover we waited for. The coming of your conquest has been the catalyst for this."

"But all left below us were... are dead, destroyed in your planetary change."

"You and I are better off not looking back to things we can't change. We both will end this drama here. Neither of these bodies will live again. This poison will soon end that possibility."

Storm clouds of anger began to rise in him, and then he paused. He allowed the weight of all this to slip from his shoulders. The thoughts, the pressures, the intricate plots, all that fell away as if he had been wrapped in a thick blanket which had been strangling his life. He felt strangely relieved.

Moria continued. "Shortly, I will be reappearing into the starlight dimension of my planet. Beneath the solar flashes, that new planet awaits me. You will be free of this body, but you'll only have to be re-born upon another planet which matches your life frequency."

"What are you saying, Moria?"

"Don't be concerned. This transition will be totally pain-less for you because your life spark is eternal. I can take plea-sure in that you will be reborn upon another planet where you may receive a similar living situation to that which you, and your race, presented for my people. Painlessly, I will bid you farewell. You and I will leave these bodies here. I feel relief. I would never wish to carry this altered body image back to my home world anyway."

# PRIME DIRECTOR ONE

The video screen erupted with the glaring face of Prime Director One. "Aries 45. What in the name of Hades has happened there? Report fact to me immediately."

"I'm afraid I don't know or understand it myself, sir."

"Why not? You've ruined my triumph in your blundering of this operation. The empire is crumbling into mental chaos because of you. I will see you dead. Your career is finished."

"You have no idea how accurate your statements are."

"Don't you be casual with me. What are you implying?"

"I shall be dead long before you could even order it. You have no power left over me now."

"How dare you speak to me this way, you miserable ingrate. You were nothing but a minor political upstart before I offered you this position, and now I see abilities I thought you capable of were all staged to win my good graces. You are nothing."

"You are speaking to a ghost. Now I will die to fulfill that role."

With that last statement, Prime Director 32's body convulsed. He collapsed alone and dead on the cabin floor.

Prime Director One was forced to pause, but he rallied when he could focus upon Moria. "What's wrong with him?"

"There is not a thing wrong here except you, Prime

Director One. He is now free of you and your empire. His body is dead, just as I am about to be free of you as well."

"You will never defeat me. Whatever sabotage you have performed, I shall triumph."

"Accept this reality. I already have defeated you. My planet has defeated you. My race has defeated you. Have you so easily ignored the adage 'If you do not learn from your history, you are doomed to repeat it?' Your empire is losing its spirit because you've not grown to attract anything better for it."

"How can you accuse me of that? I have always acted for the overall good of the empire and followed the way of the gods."

"You have followed a false premise. You have ignorantly proceeded to create your matrix from a poor history with a few stolen technologies."

"These are blasphemous lies."

"Your reality is only an illusion you have created and maintained. Your gods were immature visitors to a remote, primitive planet. They sought only to serve themselves and to seek pleasure for themselves with the friendly natives. They taught you no true universal values. They taught you to follow only their misguided behavior patterns. Your Arian-inspired reign of fear and terror and domination cannot last. Aryll had long since moved the Cave of the Arians and all the toys your ancestors left there have been elevated, too. Your god's archives and treasures of technology have been accelerated to higher vibrations.

"Unless you and your race can elevate within yourselves, you could never access or benefit from the gifts anyway. You didn't even realize how the law of attraction drew you back to our planet. Don't waste these lessons."

"I will see you dead, you traitorous bitch."

Moria smiled as she began to register the poison overtaking her systems. "Yes you will, but I am neither a traitor nor a female of one of your canine species, Prime Director One. They say revenge is a dish best served cold. That's just about all you will have in your possession from me."

Moria slumped to the floor and leaned against the wall. "I leave this body for your disposal. I must now allow its termination so that I may return to the starlight. I leave you now."

As her life faded, Moria's inner being projected out of it.

Prime Director One began screaming out from the video screen. "Come back here. You can't just die on me. I order you to come back. I order you. I'm Prime Director One. You can't…"

# BACK ON ARYLL

The luminous faces of the old ones appeared as images upon the reflective inner surface of Aryll's skies. Their delivery communicated into the minds and hearts of all those assembled.

*Our planet Aryll, formerly the fourth planet in this system, has now elevated through her cycle of ascension by her Changeover. In the climax of her quickening, she has now become this system's newest star. The process is near completion.*

A wave of humor, relief, and irony swept through the tribe.

*The first ignition of her fireball set the new orbit of her moon just outside the rim of her Corona as the newest Sun. Know that we may all dwell here in peace and joy within the starlight. She, who now begins her new dance with the other two suns of this system, sings a new verse.*

*We will leave you with a curious ponder. As you look out from this newly elevated view, you see the light twinkling from a multitude of other stars against the deep indigo darkness of space. Remember this; they're all planets.*

And as the children of Aryll began their new life beneath the Aryll sun, Dring and Ethra, happy in their embrace, scarcely noticed as the image of Moria condensed beside them.

She was now perfect in her body, with a full set of wings. "Greetings, Ethra, my daughter. Am I to be introduced to

Dring, your new life mate?"

Out on Zon 14, Fractious 5 turned off the video screen to speak with his old friend, Maximus. "Did you see that? I must get back to Aryll 8. My dealings with her are not over yet."

# ACKNOWLEDGEMENTS

I especially wish to thank:

Many friends in the Henderson Writer's Group,

Jo for starting the group.

Gregory for truly broadening the scope and range of its experience.

Fred for reading the rough draft and spending his time offering his support.

Kristin Johnson for her fine eye for Sci-Fi editing.

And to sweet Virginia Clark for everything.